THE LAST RUN

OTHER WORKS BY RACHEL WEAVER

Fiction

Point of Direction

Nonfiction

Dizzy

THE LAST RUN

a novel

RACHEL WEAVER

This is a work of fiction. Names, characters, organizations, places, events, and incidents are either products of the author's imagination or are used fictitiously. Otherwise, any resemblance to actual persons, living or dead, is purely coincidental.

Published by Lake Union Publishing, Seattle

www.apub.com

EU product safety contact:
Amazon Media EU S. à r.l.
38, avenue John F. Kennedy, L-1855 Luxembourg
amazonpublishing-gpsr@amazon.com

ISBN-13: 9781662537110 (paperback)
ISBN-13: 9781662537127 (digital)

Cover design by Mumtaz Mustafa
Cover image: © Michele Cornelius / Alamy; © Dave Collins / Getty; © Krit, © hafid / Adobe Stock

Printed in the United States of America

For Nate and Wes

Chapter 1

It was his boot that caught my eye. Those stupid snakeskin cowboy boots my father would pull on for a day in town. Never mind that it rained three hundred days a year on this cold, wind-beaten coast.

I slowed a little on the narrow sidewalk, the rain a steady rhythm against the hood of my raincoat, a truck slicing by on the wet road. Drew's small hand was tucked tightly in my own. My father's boot peeked out from under a pile of trash bags in the narrow alley behind the bar. Familiar hot shame flooded my chest. A cold rivulet of rain found its way under my hood and down my neck. What was he doing back in town? And how did he manage to lose one boot at the bar? I'd been expecting the call, all these years. An unfamiliar voice explaining to me that my father had finally met some painful end.

"What are you looking at?" Drew asked, stepping in front of me to peer down the dim alley. He pushed back the hood of his rain jacket.

"Nothing," I said, sounding sharper than I intended, pulling us both forward along the sidewalk that followed the one main road of town. I pulled up Drew's hood and focused on the misty gray curtain of fog that had draped itself over the rooftops and the dark mountains on either side. Drew took my hand again, our Xtratufs, brown rubber boots that were part of the uniform of Southeast Alaska, his half the size of mine, falling back into rhythm.

"Marshall doesn't like to be late either." Drew's backpack bounced against the backs of his legs as we walked. I ran my thumb over the pruning of his small fingers, both our hands wet and cold, despite the fact that it was the last day of June. "Chase said the other day that . . ."

I let his voice fade into the background. I checked up the street and back around behind us, looking for my father. But it was early. He'd be way too hungover to be out and about already. I refocused on Drew.

"Chase is always right, and Marshall is usually wrong." He was flopping his other hand around as he explained.

"Drew." I stopped us, bent down so that our faces were even. "Can you draw today instead of watching TV? Maybe with Maggie?" Jessica, the woman who ran the day care, sat Drew down in front of the TV for enough hours every day that he thought of the characters as his friends. She meant well, but filled her house with too many kids.

Drew screwed up his face, which crinkled the freckles across his nose and cheeks. He was so thin, birdlike. His bangs stuck to his wet forehead. It was time for another haircut. I had no idea how to cut hair and no money to pay anyone, so we did the best we could. Which was not very good. I reached over and gently tucked his bangs back up under his hood.

"Maggie hides and jumps out at me. To scare me. She likes to see my eyes do that thing. They make her laugh." He looked down, and my heart crushed to the size of a penny.

"Oh, baby." I grabbed both his hands in mine. His small body was a vessel of anxiety that built pressure under stress. The only relief was a rapid blinking of his eyes, usually followed by a nose twitch and a tight squeeze of his eyes followed by more blinking. In the last few months, the whole horrible situation had progressed into an accompanying shoulder shrug repeated ten, twenty, thirty times in a row. "I'm sorry. I didn't know she was doing that. I'll talk to Ms. Jessica." As if she was even in the room with them half the time, now that she'd just taken on twin infants. In a town of less than a thousand people, there was only one other day-care option. It was so far outside my salary with the City that the soft lighting and quiet artwork of three children versus the chaos of eight in Jessica's slightly crusty living room was nothing more than a dream. I touched my forehead to Drew's. "I love you, buddy. Just one more year, and then you'll go to kindergarten instead," I said for the thousandth time. He would turn five in October, a week short of the deadline to start kindergarten this fall. "You'll sit in a circle and read books together, and then you'll go to after-school care, where you'll play kickball and drink juice boxes with the other kids until I get off work." He blinked rapidly, twenty or thirty times, a slight release of the heated anxiety, his eyelashes brushing my face. "Can I just watch TV? I don't want to draw."

The thighs of my pants were now soaked as the rain ran off my jacket and spread out across the fabric. Drew leaned back, his shoulder now pulling in a steady rhythm. "It's not just Maggie. Jared says I'm weird and no one wants to be friends with me." His eyes were full of hurt. "I just want to watch TV," he whispered. "Please? Everyone just leaves me alone when I watch TV."

"Okay." I kissed his forehead. "That's fine." I needed to get him out of that day care. Maybe if I took out a loan against my most recent credit card? But it was already almost maxed out. I could pick up a second job, but then I'd have to leave him home alone or hire a babysitter, which would eat up whatever I made. What he needed was more time with me. If we had more time together, perhaps he would come to see himself as I saw him. Perhaps if I had a little room to breathe instead of spending all day locked in between cubicle walls with a boss who fancied himself some sort of small-town dictator, I wouldn't be so irritable in the time Drew and I had together.

I took his hand in mine, and we continued on in the direction of the day care. A man crossed the road ahead. I hadn't seen my father in years, but I knew it wasn't him. This man was too slight, his gait a little too staccato, to be my father.

My mind turned over all the possibilities of what sort of trouble he might be in now. Disgust erupted in my stomach and climbed up my throat. It was self-indulgent to fall apart. I had taken to considering myself an orphan in the almost five years since Drew was born. And then there it was, my mother's voice loud and full in my head: *Take care of each other.* The round words, the hollow sound of their leaving. I froze.

"Mom?" Drew tugged on my hand as the tires of another passing truck hissed against the wet pavement. A quick wind blew down the channel, funneling in between the mountains on either side, pulling at the corrugated roofs of town, the collar of my raincoat, and the branches of the spruce and hemlock that marched up the mountains. My mind would not let go of the scene in the alley. That boot was too upright. Not slack.

Not empty.

I turned sharply around. "Come on, Drew. We've got to go back."

"No," he whined. "I want to see Marshall."

I scooped him up. His rain-geared, backpacked knees-and-elbows shape took both arms to contain as I raced to the alley and ducked in between the buildings. Now I could see that the boot was attached to a leg that disappeared under the pile of black garbage bags. "Pete!" I screamed, setting Drew down on his feet. Could he breathe under there? Was he dead?

I pulled at the wet garbage bag at the top of the pile. Empty bottles clanked against each other as it slid to the uneven asphalt at my feet. The stench of stale beer swirled around me.

"Is that a person?" Drew crowded the back of my legs. I shoved my hood off in one quick motion, the rain immediately sharp and clarifying against my face. More bottles from the bar's trash cans rattled and broke as I pushed another bag off the pile. "Drew, back up!" I was now certain that it wasn't possible to breathe under there. "Pete!" I yelled, clawing the last garbage bag off his upper body.

His face was lumpy and blood-caked, both eyes puffed up tight. For all those times I'd thought of myself as an orphan, I realized now that I didn't want to be one.

"Dad!" I screamed, the word awkward on my lips. His shirt was ripped, and he was cold when I touched him. I lay my head on his chest, and there, under his ribs, was the faint push of his heart still working.

"Mama?" Drew asked from where he stood off to my side, his voice small and scared. "You have a dad?"

I spun back around to face him, hair loosed from my ponytail, sticking to my face.

"Why is he under there?" Drew asked as I barreled past him to beat on the back door of the sandwich shop next to the bar.

"Help!" I screamed, hoping someone inside would hear me, then flung myself back to Pete.

My hands shook as I pulled the last bag off his lower body. His left leg was misshapen below the knee, and his right arm took a sharp, unnatural turn where it should've been straight.

I was back on my feet, reaching for Drew, as my mother's final words rang through my head, this time so loud I knew I could no longer ignore them: *Promise me*, each of her hands in mine and Pete's, as the three of us huddled together on the bed on her final day.

A large man shoved the back door of the sandwich shop open as I wrapped Drew in my arms. The man fumbled his phone from his pocket, a rush of words and then the ambulance at the top of the hill flipping on its siren, and I knew whatever this was, it was going to drag me back into what I'd fought so hard to escape.

Chapter 2

Drew and I sat in two of the three chairs that made up the ER waiting room in the small building that served as clinic, hospital, ER, and doctor's office for Kings Creek. Drew kept running his hand over his wrist, his shoulder pulling up once, twice, building momentum. He sat in my lap, burrowed into my chest.

I dug around in his backpack for the Tupperware of smoked salmon. Maybe it would take his mind off the last time we were here. Maybe it would ease the thick, oozing knowledge that I was doing a terrible job.

Two weeks ago, Drew had tried to open the huge block of government cheese with a fillet knife and sliced his wrist open. I'd forgotten to put the knife away, out of reach. I'd been outside. He'd been alone. I'd raced in at his shrieking to find Drew, the floor, and all the food in the fridge covered in the spurting fountain of blood coming from his wrist.

We'd rushed to the ER, where they'd glued it, asked me a few piercing questions, and said they'd bill us in a few weeks. The fear had unraveled Drew. He'd slept in my bed every night since, tossing and turning, crying out in his sleep, waking me up every few hours throughout the night. I worried every hour of every day that he was too soft for the world.

I reached over now to cover the wide Band-Aid still on Drew's wrist. "It's okay, buddy. You're okay." His eyes slid from mine down to the Tupperware. I edged it into his hands.

I was already an hour late for work after I'd promised it would never happen again. I kept thinking we should leave, but I couldn't make myself go. The walls of the small room where Drew and I sat seemed to slant in toward me.

"I don't want smoked salmon." Drew slumped in his chair. "I'm sick of salmon. I want crackers and that cheese that sprays out of the can. That's what kids eat on the commercials." He crossed his arms.

I slammed the Tupperware back into his pack. "Fine. You can starve." We ate what I could catch. Chicken and beef were way too expensive by the time those enticing plastic-wrapped packages made the journey to the forgotten corners of Alaska.

"Can we get the spray cheese?" Drew's face was a crumpled mess.

The anger always rose from deep in my belly, as if there was always more being made. "No. We don't eat things like that, Drew." Partly because cheese shouldn't spray out of a can and partly because it wasn't on the WIC list.

I closed my eyes and leaned my head back against the wall. Why did I let my anger at our situation slide so easily into anger at him? Why couldn't I untangle the two? Why couldn't I just say I got it? I didn't dream of spray cheese, but I would've given almost anything for a four-dollar latte and a cell phone, both indulgences I'd had to give up long ago.

Every dollar I made was spent on day care, rent, rubber boots that didn't leak, and secondhand sweatshirts. It seemed as soon as Drew had what he needed, he outgrew it. I'd been using credit cards to bridge the final $100, $300, $500 gap between paychecks until I'd maxed out three and, now, almost a fourth. I'd had to go on government assistance to supplement our diet of salmon, halibut, and crab with milk and bread. Rent was due at the end of the week, and I didn't have enough in my account to cover it. And once the bill for the ER deductible showed up, we'd be sunk. Drew's dad wasn't an option for financial help because he didn't know Drew existed and never would.

I twisted my neck in one direction and then gently the other, the dull ache of responsibility my constant companion. The feeling of barely keeping my head above water was exhausting, no matter how much sleep I got. This town life wasn't working. And it was Pete's fault. If he could control his gambling and drinking and fighting, we could fish our family boat together, and I'd make at least twice what I did at my low-level accounting job with the City. A job I should be grateful for, my soft-bellied boss loved to remind me. I felt queasy at the thought of the lecture I'd gotten on numerous other occasions about all the applicants he had lined up to take my job in this town, where there were only a handful of jobs with health insurance and regular hours.

I settled my eyes on the wall behind the check-in desk, full of fishing gear that had been extracted from various body parts belonging to the folks of Kings Creek. Eventually, I found the bright-pink lure I'd lodged in my eyebrow with an errant cast at age six. My hand came up to the raised sickle-shaped scar it had left behind as I remembered how proud my parents had been at how calm I had remained for the long trip back to town on the *Sarah Louise*, our forty-two-foot power troller, and throughout the time Dr. Stone spent removing it.

I dropped an arm over Drew in the seat next to me. He was still pouting. To distract him, I said, "See everyone down on the docks getting ready for the season?" I pointed out the window at the rush of men and families restocking their commercial fishing boats for the chinook opener tomorrow.

Drew glanced through the window, turned back, and then resumed his slouch. I continued to watch, allowing myself to feel that old excitement: the final flurry of last-minute fixes, the cardboard boxes of canned goods rolled down the dock on dollies, the anticipation that this trip out would be the one where you found that pocket of king salmon, so thick all the hooks would fill. The opener could last a few days to a few weeks. A fisherman could make good money in that short window. Or barely any at all based on how long they were allowed to fish, how much the canneries were paying per pound, how thick the fish were in, whether or not they'd put their boat in the right place at the right time. The uncertainty of it, the risk, the possibility, sparked in my chest and cleared my head, just like it always had.

The rhythm of the docks had defined my whole life until I'd walked away from it seven years ago.

"Mom," Drew whined, sprawling across my lap. "I'm hungry."

I let go the breath I'd been holding, about to express my deep exasperation with the fact that being picky was a privilege, another thing out of our reach. Instead, I pulled the Tupperware out again, opened it, and set it in his lap.

Monica popped her head around the corner. She and I had been best friends in high school, although we'd drifted apart since. After high school, Monica had flown south to Seattle and returned with a nursing degree, while I'd stayed home, hung out with the wrong guy, and got pregnant. "Hey, Ellie, he's awake now if you want to come back."

Relief flooded me, and then surprise that I cared so much. "He's okay?"

"More or less." Monica shrugged one shoulder.

"Ready, bud?" I asked Drew, patting his leg, relief quickly being replaced by dread at the idea of actually talking to Pete. He had no idea he was a grandpa.

Drew slid off my lap, knocking the open Tupperware onto the floor. Several chunks of salmon landed on the linoleum.

"Goddamn it, Drew."

I saw the time it took to set the gill net, to clean, fillet, and smoke the fish. All that sleep-depriving work, wasted.

I picked the pieces off the floor and tossed them into the trash can as we headed back to the ER room, feeling horrible at the forlorn look on Drew's face, and worse when his shoulder started to pull again. I gathered up his hand and squeezed it, as if that was some way to explain and apologize for all of it. I would control the anger and irritation better, I promised with another squeeze, as his little fingers wrapped around mine.

My father looked all wrong. Too still and too clean. The hospital bed was angled such that he was sitting upright. His left leg was in a thick white cast from the knee down, and his right arm was in another thick cast from the tips of his fingers up to his armpit, bent at the elbow. His left eye was swollen shut, and that whole half of his face was puffy. His right eye was red and watery but open. His jaw was a swollen lump. His curly dark hair had grown speckled with gray in the years since I'd seen him last, but more startling than that, it was combed and parted, which I'd never seen before.

"Nice hairdo." I sat in the chair across from the bed, trying to ignore the mess of emotions swirling in my chest. Pete slowly tracked Drew with his one open eye, the only part of him that moved. Drew climbed up into my lap, and I settled my arms around him.

Pete ran a hand through his hair, flicked his eye from Drew up to me and then back again. "Monica must've done that before I regained consciousness." Pete's voice was thick and rough, but it flung me back to the secure, happy days of my childhood. Before he'd burned it down to nothing. "Not a very funny joke."

"How do you feel?" I asked. He looked awful.

"Like I should be unconscious."

"Mom?" Drew asked in a reverent whisper. "Is that your dad?"

"Yeah," I said, pressing hard fingers into my forehead.

"What's his name?" Drew was now frozen in my lap, watching Pete watch him. They had the same green eyes, the same nose.

"His name is Pete."

"Grandpa," Pete corrected, his mouth moving toward a slow grin. "He certainly looks like a Baker, doesn't he? If not a little thin," he added, stabbing right at the center of my worry.

Drew whipped around in my lap, his eyes wide and hurt. "You said I didn't have a grandpa *or* a dad. I always wanted a grandpa."

His words cut sharp. I'd tried so hard to be enough. I kept my eyes on Pete. "You have to actually be a father to become a grandfather."

"Not fair, Ellie." Pete closed his eye, held his breath, and tried to shift in the bed. The way he was moving, it looked like he had a few busted ribs as well.

Drew settled his gaze back on Pete. "I see your face, Grandpa, and it doesn't look good."

A quick breath escaped Pete in a laugh that looked like it hurt. "What's your name, kid?"

"Drew." He whispered it full of awe, like he'd been asked the secret password and he knew it.

"Who'd you fight this time?" I asked. I hadn't talked to or seen him since before Drew was born, but I heard things here and there from guys I'd grown up around in the fishing fleet. I'd isolated myself from the fleet since the day I walked away from Pete, unable to watch the rest of them head off onto the fishing grounds after I could no longer join them. At the time, it had felt like sawing off a leg, but in the way of things, it had healed over, and now only hurt when I thought about it. The fishermen in the fleet had given me the room I needed without me actually having to ask. Most had gone from stopping to chat to a singular nod when we passed on the street. Every year new recruits came from down south for an adventurous summer of fishing, or fishermen from other fleets moved to town and joined the ranks, diluting what I remembered and who I knew. But we all still lived on the same small island, and I continued to hear things every now and then. Pete had been fishing out of Sitka about a hundred miles away, or maybe just living there aboard the *Sarah Louise*. He moved in and out of trouble. In more than out.

"I didn't do much fighting. I was the one getting my ass kicked." He attempted to readjust in the bed again, grimaced, and gave up.

"Over what?"

"Herring," he answered vaguely.

I squinted at him. The Sitka Sound herring fishery was the rodeo of the fishing season. It happened every spring when fifty to a hundred tons of herring crowded into Sitka Sound to spawn. Hundreds of boats packed into limited space wove in between each other, waiting for Fish and Game to announce the opening, which typically lasted only a few hours, and sometimes only twenty minutes. A swarm of floatplanes sliced past each other above. The pilots were hired by the boats to direct them to the highest concentrations of herring, dark masses spotted easily from the air.

Just like a rodeo, it was hot and fast, and tensions ran high. There was the potential to pull in six figures in twenty minutes, or not even enough to cover the fuel it took to get there. Everything had to go right, and everyone had to stay out of your way.

Pete was still looking at me. "Miles Holcomb has always been a jerk. Even in elementary school. He used to spit on my artwork."

Drew must've reacted, because Pete's face lit up. "Rude, right? I had to give him the what for, even back then. Do you know what the what for is?"

Drew shook his head once, wide-eyed and slow, which was all the encouragement Pete needed. He managed to sit up a little and lean toward Drew. "Well," he started, focusing all of his attention on Drew in the way that used to make me feel as a kid as if the whole world rotated around me. "It can mean a lot of things, but back then, what it meant was this. You sneak up behind him doing this." He made the sound of a buzzing mosquito. "Yell 'I got it!!' and whap him between the shoulder blades. Hard." Pete smacked the bed with his good hand in demonstration, smiled over at Drew, and shrugged in slow motion. "He thinks you're helping him out."

Drew cracked up, which was the most astonishing sound I'd heard in months. I couldn't take my eyes off the way Drew's face relaxed in delight.

Pete eased himself back against the pillows and worked at getting a full breath.

"Herring was months ago," I said.

He nodded his agreement. "I may or may not have nudged Miles's seine skiff out of the way with mine to make the perfect set. He and his crew were at the bar last night. They've been fishing salmon together since herring. Last night was the first time we crossed paths."

I took a deep breath and sighed. A lot of grievances were worked out like this. At the edges of Alaska, people were used to solving problems on their own.

"You mean you rammed his skiff with yours."

"Nudged."

"What are you doing on a herring boat anyway?" Most herring seiners fished salmon too, and the crew stayed together. You couldn't just jump on for the lucrative parts. It was more of a through-thick-and-thin type situation. "Are you still milking the I-saved-your-life thing with Dean Kluwak?"

Pete's face moved into a lumpy smile. "I did save Deano's life. And if it wasn't for me, he'd have caught a lot less herring this year. It's a win-win as far as I can tell."

"Why are you in Kings Creek?" I asked. He'd given me my space when I'd demanded it, had kept to the other corners of Southeast Alaska and left me this one.

Pete readjusted his casted arm a few inches on his stomach and winced. "The *Sally J* needed a few planks replaced. Cal hired me to do it."

"You came all the way over here to replace a few planks? Hardly seems worth the money."

Pete took a slow breath in. "An extra fifty bucks is an extra fifty bucks." Which is when I realized Pete was in the same situation as me. Both of us circling the drain made me feel as though I was getting closer, faster.

"But, while you're here . . ." Pete trailed off. A look of pure discomfort crossed his face, but this time it didn't seem to have anything to do with his injuries. My back straightened on its own, ready and not ready.

"I owe a guy a lot of money. I could use your help."

Fear struck like a gong against my heart. "Who do you owe?"

"I'm getting out, Ellie."

I closed my eyes. "Who do you owe?" I asked again. "Hank?"

"Hank got run out of town years ago. A bigger operation moved in."

Pete had failed to hold it together in the time I needed him most, by acting exactly like this. I couldn't take it. I stood up, set Drew down on his feet, and found his hand. "We're leaving." I spun back around. "Don't lie, Pete. Drink your life into the dumps, gamble all your money away, but don't lie. That's the worst one."

It had all started innocently enough. A way to distract ourselves in the long winter hours, to take our minds off Mom, the way she'd become so thin, her bones nothing but air such that I could hold her full weight cradled in my arms at the side of the bed while Pete changed out the bedsheets. The way the wind had kicked up as we spilled her ashes into Green Cove on a hard January morning. A great swirling cloud, as if the wind were trying to fit her back together.

I turned eighteen a month after she died. As the heavy winter rains fell steadily, I could barely move, could barely think. I drove in a haze to the high school every morning, unable to do much more than show up. Grief wasn't a heavy cloak, it was a smothering rag held directly over the face.

It was hockey at first. Five dollars bet between us, with a handshake, a lifeline we could throw each other as my father began to float away. If it had stayed like that, we might've survived it all.

Fifty dollars, a hundred dollars. I had been getting a crew share of the profits made on the *Sarah Louise* every summer since I was ten, and therefore had a healthy bank account. Betting brought a bit of the adrenaline rush of commercial fishing that both Pete and I fed off in the summers into that dark winter and made it more bearable.

We would crowd around the television in our small house that felt huge without my mother and get lost in every basket scored, every shot on goal. When betting with each other got less exciting, Pete found a small-town bookie in Juneau. Pete got caught up in the stories of the players, the history of the team, was swayed by the declaration of an underdog. I was more calculated. I pored over stats, studied the guys who set the lines in Vegas, and made my own calculations accordingly, and Pete and I made it through that first winter. We didn't talk about any of it: the way we both avoided Mom's favorite chair, the number of Jack Daniel's bottles Pete stacked up in the weekly trash out on the curb.

That spring, Pete was on the phone with the bookie at least once a week. He no longer consulted me. He placed bets and grew more and more anxious. There wasn't a night that went by without a drink.

And then the mother of a boy I knew in school was diagnosed with breast cancer, and they moved to Seattle, where the nearest cancer center provided chemo and radiation. The idea of it wormed its way into my brain and would not hold still. Why had we not done the same thing? I watched Pete more closely, began to notice the way guilt would explain all his behavior. He had been the healthy one, the one who should've been making the decisions. There had been no talk of Seattle. After the diagnosis, we'd gone out fishing for the season instead.

The slow burn of anger took hold, boiling over one night in the kitchen. I'd been unable to sleep and had come out for a glass of water. Pete was reaching into the refrigerator for the last beer of the twelve-pack he'd started in on at dinner. His red-rimmed eyes and stupid look put me over the edge.

"How could you?" I snarled. "What she needed was to go to Seattle, where there are cancer centers and doctors. But you drove us out onto the grounds instead. What'd you think? That it would just go away? That you could deal with it later? It was your responsibility to make her go!" I screamed.

Pete dropped his head. "Seattle wasn't in the cards," he muttered, and with that, what was left of our family cleaved off with the thunderous finality of a tidewater glacier at the ocean's edge.

We barely spoke the rest of that spring. We got the *Sarah Louise* ready for the season together in silence. I was able to manage until we pulled away from town, until I set the gear for the first time without my mom at the other end of the pit. I couldn't take it. She was gone and Pete was useless. The *Sarah Louise* was full of ghosts.

I walked off the boat the first trip back to town to sell fish. I found an apartment and moved everything I owned out of the house I'd grown up in. I worked odd jobs in town, whatever I could find. Soon enough, the house we'd been renting my entire life had a For Rent sign out front.

Pete continued to unravel in the years that followed. More betting, more drinking, and then came the stories of bar fights. As if he could beat his shame out of someone else. He borrowed money from friends and spun off into a person I did not recognize or care to know.

Drew shifted next to me in the hospital room. While I'd stood up to leave, I hadn't yet left.

"I'm not lying. I'm done gambling." Pete looked out the window. "I'm turning it around, Ellie. It's been long enough."

I closed my eyes. He'd been so solid once. The rock of our family. Until he'd disintegrated into dust.

Pete's face set. Impossible to read. "It was a stupid bet to make. But, we've got some time."

"There's no *we*," I said.

"It's the boat and the permit, Ellie. But we can get it back."

Something exploded in my chest. "You lost the boat?" I took a quick step toward the bed. Drew's face flung upward at the sound of my tone. The air in my lungs would not release.

Pete closed his good eye against me.

Anger tumbled into my veins, hot and then hotter. I kicked the bed. "You asshole."

Pete doubled over at the sudden jolting motion. The bag and tube connected to him swung in a violent arc.

He didn't say anything, which meant he knew I was right.

Fishing boats and permits were typically handed down generation to generation in fishing families in the way of land in farming families. Fishing was what we did, and the family boat and limited entry permit was how we did it. What was Drew to become now? The boat was his future, the way he'd be able to live in his hometown and make enough money to survive. I'd always known the *Sarah Louise* would become mine at some point. I'd always planned to fish with Drew when he was older, to teach him everything he'd need to know to run the boat on his own one day. I'd been waiting for Pete to clear out of the way, knowing I'd likely lost my turn, but banking on the fact that Drew had not lost his.

I barely recognized my own voice when I spoke. "Mom would hate what you've turned into."

Pete winced. He lifted his good hand, palm up, to ward me off. "Just hear me out, okay?" When I said nothing, he continued. "The bookie offered a good deal. I come up with more cash than the boat and permit are worth, he doesn't have to find a buyer, he ends up with more money, I end up with the boat and permit back. He let me keep the permit in my name so I could fish the season because we both know that's the only way I'm going to come up with the money. When I hand the rest of the cash over at the end of the season, I keep the permit and he signs the boat back over to me."

"And if you don't have the money when it's time to pay up, you sign the permit over to him and you've lost both."

Pete ignored this. "I already paid a big chunk of what I owe. Herring was good, and I did alright fishing cohos on my own—" All his words were running together. "Kings open tomorrow, they're in thick, coho too, everything is lining up. 2011 is going to be our year."

"You say that every year." I closed my eyes. "That's not a good deal, Pete. It sounds a lot like extortion. This new guy sounds like bad news. How much more do you owe?"

"Fifty thousand."

"Oh my god." I reached for Drew's hand. He'd inched his way closer to the side of Pete's bed. Why he wasn't frightened by Pete's Frankenstein face, I had no idea. Drew took my hand but didn't step toward me. His thin arm spanned the distance between me and Pete.

Pete met my gaze. "I need you to crew. Kings open tomorrow. We've got until September 20."

A flush of heat prickled my neck. "No way. I am not cleaning up your mess for you. I have a job with insurance. I'm not flushing all that down the drain to bail your ass out. And besides that, there's no way I'm getting on a boat with you. And besides that, have you lost your fucking mind? What about all those years we barely cleared thirty grand? And now you need to make fifty thousand in two and a half months? Kings might be good, but it's not going to be that good. It's never that good. You'd have to have the best summer of your life to clear that much money, which by the looks of you right now, isn't going to happen."

Pete's one eye was fixed on me. He seemed to be looking directly into my mind in the way no one else could. "There's no way you like that office job. How could a kid who grew up fishing survive in a cubicle all day? And Drew looks like he could use some fresh air. How long do you leave him at day care, nine hours a day?"

"Don't you dare talk to me about parenting."

"Come on, Ellie, remember how great our days were out on the grounds?"

"Don't ever talk to me again." I turned for the door, yanking on Drew.

"No!" Drew whined as he stumbled after me. "I want to have a grandpa!"

Chapter 3

The light drizzle of rain was cold on my face as I sprinted the three blocks to work after dropping Drew off at day care. Pete's betrayal snapped like a live wire in my chest. It was almost too big to grasp.

The clouds hung low to the ground. The wet air lay thick in my lungs. I took the stairs two at a time up to the accounting department of the City offices, shrugging out of my rain jacket as I stepped through the door. I said hello to my four coworkers, who alternately frowned or gave me an *oh shit* look at my blatant tardiness. The clicking keyboards and stuffy air and intermittent phone ringing made me instantly hollowed out.

I knew I should keep a low profile, but while I waited for my computer to boot up, I slunk across the room to get a cup of horrible coffee. I opened the mini fridge and found my creamer container empty. Again. Even though I'd written my name across it. While I loved coffee, I detested it black, so I replaced the mug in the cupboard and headed back to my desk.

As a way to Increase Productivity, our boss, Stephen, now required us each to fill out some fucked-up spreadsheet he'd created in which we accounted for what we did in ten-minute increments throughout the day. Which wasn't so bad except that you had to fill in a data field for every single ten-minute block. If you fell more than an hour behind in documenting your time, you'd get an urgent email from Stephen.

In a number of the ten-minute blocks the week before, I'd written *filling out this stupid spreadsheet.* In response, I'd gotten a red slip, which apparently was worse than the orange slip I'd gotten a while back for grabbing an extra box of blue pens out of the supply room and not writing down that I'd taken them.

An icy dread slid down my back when I noticed Stephen watching me type *Absent* in each of the ten-minute boxes for the past two hours.

"Ellie. A minute of your time, please. In the conference room," he said over the heads of everyone else.

I bit the inside of my lip and followed his bald head across the hall to the small, stuffy conference room, avoiding the stares of my coworkers. The minute the door latched behind me, he turned on his toes. "You're late."

I took a breath and rose up to my full height, which almost matched his. "My father is in the hospital. I found him this morning on my way to—"

His face fell into a look of smug satisfaction. "Let's not talk around the subject here, Ellie. You are smart and capable, but you don't like this job. Your mind is usually elsewhere, you've used up all your vacation and sick days for the year and it's only June, and the truth is, I'm tired of dealing with your lack of enthusiasm."

I forced my spine even straighter. "You know I'm a single parent, and you know kids constantly pass horrendous germs back and forth to each other at day care. I can't possibly send him when he's got hoof-and-mouth and there's no one else—"

"It's your attitude, Ellie." His lips tightened. "We have all that scanning you could do across the next three Saturdays to fully demonstrate your dedication to this job."

"You know I don't have childcare on Saturdays."

"That's your problem." The fluorescent light glinted off his greasy forehead.

The clarity I'd been searching for descended, blowing out the thick fog that had been obscuring my view for years. "No. It's your problem. I quit."

Three minutes later, I stood, unemployed, on the wet sidewalk in front of the two-story City office building with the wind blowing my raincoat open. The heavy gray cloud cover had thickened, as if it were a living thing pressing toward Earth.

"Shit," I breathed out. My feet each weighed too much to move, all the clarity gone. Eviction was likely to follow this idiotic move I'd just made. Soon, I'd be begging for a job at the bar. Drew would be home alone at night in a house that would be more like a shed than a house, which would be the only place I'd be able to afford once we got kicked out of our apartment.

I peered out at the sea, down the narrow channel that divided this island from the one closest and eventually opened up into the Sound. I suddenly wanted to be out on the water. A place big enough to hold all the shards my life kept breaking into.

I was no better than Pete. Irresponsible. The thought fluttered against me like lost birds. I had to walk, to move.

I found myself on the gangway that connected the edge of land with the floating docks. It was low tide, which meant my toes piled up in the front of my shoes in a familiar way as I moved down the steep, clangy metal walkway to water level. It had been forever since I knew what the tide was doing. I had worked to ignore the push and pull of the tides for so long, I no longer felt them.

I stepped off the bridge onto the floating dock, where men and women in rain gear wheeled by with hand trolleys full of boxed-up food, sat on decks repairing nets, hammered and sawed whatever was left to fix before they'd head out this evening ahead of tomorrow's opener. The smell of the bull kelp, the wafting clouds of diesel, the clank of tools thrown back in a toolbox. It calmed me in the way of a familiar lullaby.

I stepped aside as a guy I didn't recognize in orange rubber rain gear pushing a cart full of five-gallon buckets, a drill, and other boat gear squeezed through. Likely someone's new crew, up from Kansas or somewhere else flat and dry, who had seen a couple of episodes of *Deadliest Catch*. I could tell by the way he hunched against the rain, too many muscles engaged, that he wouldn't last longer than a season.

Underneath the chaos was the whisper of rain on gray water, the small waves smacking crisply against the wood of the dock. I was dressed all wrong in my office clothes. I'd long ago shoved my Carhartts, ball caps, and stained sweatshirts in a box under my bed.

I kept my eyes down, but felt the older fishermen watching my return to the docks after so many years gone. The fishing fleet I'd been born into wasn't much into talking. Most things were communicated with slight head nods, raised eyebrows, and a twitch of the lips. They would give me all the room I needed for whatever it was I was doing on the docks right then.

I scanned for the *Sarah Louise*. In the long row of boats, my eye caught on the upward curve of her bow, the solid width of her beam. She'd always felt like a sister in the absence of any siblings. I filled my lungs with the wet, salty air, and felt like myself for the first time in forever.

The *Sarah Louise* represented everything my mother and Pete believed in, everything they had taught me to love. I was part wind, part wave, part boat.

The commercial fishing permit and this boat were Drew's future, the family legacy, all I had to give him. The permit enabled one to sell fish to the cannery. The fishery was limited entry, so if we lost our permit, it could be a while or never before another came up for sale. Coming up with the thirty grand to buy a new permit was even less likely. And if he had to buy a boat on top of that, there was no way.

The boat and permit guaranteed Drew's place in the fleet, his place in life. Fishing was volatile, of course; so much depended on luck and the decisions of government officials in dry offices and how hard Drew would be willing to work, but it was a chance at something that I could give him. And if he didn't want it, he could sell up and go to college, move down south, do whatever he wanted.

I had protected myself and Drew from Pete, which meant isolating us from fishing, but I never imagined it would be forever. I'd been too caught up in getting through each day to think much about how and when I'd get us back to fishing. All I knew was that as long as Pete was on board, we couldn't be. In some abstract way, I'd been waiting for Pete to miraculously change, or more likely for him to disappear, or turn up dead.

Promise me. My mother's voice came alive on a gust of wind as I turned down a thin finger of the dock and stood at the rail of the *Sarah Louise* for the first time in more than seven years.

The rain was a steady hum against my hood and shoulders. Everywhere my eyes landed, the *Sarah Louise* handed over a crystal-clear memory. My mother's long braid tucked down the back of her sweatshirt, her quick hands at the cleaning tray, her delight in swinging one slick-bodied salmon after another over the stern into the pit. Pete singing the kindergarten-y, unbelievably annoying morning song he'd used to chase me out of my bunk as a kid. Pete chasing Mom around for a hug whenever he was covered in excessive amounts of fish guts, or any particularly gross boat grime. The idea of anyone else in the troll pit, anyone else at the helm, anyone else making oatmeal in the small galley felt like a betrayal. The memory of how happy we'd all been felt like a hand to the throat.

Take care of each other. My mother's whispered words, her eyes half closed as she squeezed my hand and Pete's against her heart on her final day. I reached out, settled my hands on the cold wood of the rail, and climbed over.

The *Sarah Louise* rocked in the wake of a passing skiff. The smooth arcing motion of boat underfoot brought order to the chaos of my mind, allowed me to focus. This was the rhythm of my childhood, the rhythm of Drew's future. This was something I would not allow my father to take away along with everything else he'd already taken.

Chapter 4

I picked Drew up barely two hours after I'd dropped him off. He was crumpled on the ratty brown carpet two feet in front of the television. I pinched my lips together.

"Drew," Jessica called again from where we both stood just inside the front door. She had a one-year-old on her hip and an infant sleeping against her in a chest harness. I stepped past her. The room smelled vaguely of diapers and an apple core rotting somewhere.

"C'mon, Drew." I reached for his hand. "Let's get your backpack."

He didn't move. "Marshall and Rubble have to find the lost kitten. She might be injured." He kept his eyes locked onto the screen, his shoulder shrugging once, and then again three seconds later, and then again, with a few rapid blinks thrown in and a nose squinch.

"C'mon, buddy." I swallowed down the frustration as I crossed to the row of hooks where he'd dumped his boots and backpack.

"No," he said, eyes still glued to the TV, the pace of his tic picking up. "I need to see this."

Jessica watched us from the doorway.

"Drew," I said, working to keep my voice as even as possible. "It's just a show. You don't need to see it."

"I do!" he wailed. "If I don't watch, they might not be able to find her."

I crossed the room, arms full of boots and backpack, and bent down in front of him. I held out one boot, but he curled up into a ball, feet tucked up under him, eyes still on the screen.

I dug out one leg, perhaps a little too roughly, to slide his boot on. He ducked around me to keep his eyes on the screen as I shoved the other boot on and then each arm into his jacket. He wailed at full volume when I picked him up and carried him out the door.

"Noooooo!" he cried in long, pathetic sobs as we walked down the street.

He went from sobbing in my arms to perfectly still and attentive when we turned up the hill toward the hospital. I tried to let the hot frustration dissipate, but it stayed balled up in the hollow of my chest. I wanted to scream, slam a door, hand someone else this huge responsibility for one whole day so I could rest. Instead, I set him on the sidewalk, readjusted his backpack, held on to his hand, and kept him moving along with me.

The way Drew swung from one emotion to the next, the new one wiping clean the last one without a trace, was exhausting. "Are we going to see Grandpa?" he asked. "Why does everybody have a grandpa and a dad but me? Did my dad get dead?"

I'd meant to have this conversation, had tried it out a million different ways in my head, but I never landed on the right way to say it, and I cringed at the thought of having to further disappoint Drew. I took a deep breath and started picking my way toward it like testing for sturdy rocks when crossing a creek. "I don't know if he's dead or not, buddy. He was headed down a bad road the last time I saw him."

"Why hasn't he ever come to see me?"

We ducked out of the rain under the awning of the ER. Drew's face was turned up toward mine in anticipation. The smooth skin, the open look in his eyes, made something at my core feel unstable. "Why?" he asked again. The sorrow in his voice echoed in my chest.

I knelt so that we were face-to-face. "He was making some bad choices, Drew. A lot of bad choices."

Drew's mouth turned down at the corners.

"But you know the good news? I get to have the most incredible kid in the world all to myself." I smiled until he dropped his head and bit down on a smile.

"Who's that?" he asked, trying to act sly, but his grin betrayed him.

"You!" I laughed as I pulled him tight against me. When his hands reached around my sides, I let this good feeling permeate, drive out everything else. I tried not to wish Drew's dad, Oliver, was dead, but knew that was likely the best possible outcome.

~

When we walked into his room, Pete was dozing in that alert way I'd seen him nap on the *Sarah Louise* a million times.

"Wake up, Pete."

He blinked at the sound of my voice.

"I want the boat. I'll fish the season and pay off your $50,000, and once that's done, you'll sign both the permit and the boat over to me."

Pete blinked again and then squinted at me. He looked old until his face set hard and mad, and then he looked like himself again.

"It's all I have left of her," I added. "And it's all Drew's got. I won't lose it."

The *Sarah Louise* was Pete's home; he'd gambled away everything else. He would render himself homeless and jobless by signing over the boat and permit to me. I didn't care.

"And I don't want anything to do with whatever bookie thug you're associated with now. You'll deal with that." Fear of the underground ways to make money in towns without many jobs, that pulled people under by the ankles, knifed through me, but I ignored it. I would keep myself and Drew out of it. I would maintain a hard, thick line between us and Pete and whoever he was associating with these days. It would be business only. We would fish the season, and then go our separate ways. Completely separate ways.

Pete let the silence stretch between us, one good eye narrowed on mine. In a barely perceptible move, he nodded his agreement.

I took in a deep breath and let it out slowly. "We're leaving town tomorrow at six a.m. You're good at lying. Tell Dr. Stone whatever you need to tell him so that you'll be released by then."

Drew spun around, his face lit up. "We're going fishing?" Relief washed over me, clean and pure, at the stillness of his shoulder, the sudden spark of interest in his eyes. "Just like Sam? And Allie and Jordan?" Three of the day-care kids from fishing families.

"Yep." I smiled down and ran my hand along the cup of his jaw, elation suddenly filling me. I had expected a fight from Drew, and now this. Maybe this was it, the opportunity I'd been waiting for. A happier Drew, no more day care, no more rent, no more cubicle. My past reclaimed, Drew's future opening. Except we had to double what we had typically been able to clear in a season with Mom, Pete, and me, three able-bodied crew, working our asses off. And then the reality came crashing in. This was likely the only opportunity I'd have to fish with Drew before we lost the boat and permit forever.

"What about . . ." Pete dropped his eyes to Drew.

"You fished with me on board from the time I was an infant," I countered.

"Your mom was always there to take care of you."

"Since you are no longer skipper, you'll be babysitter." I knew I was throwing daggers, but I didn't care. It wasn't just his position in the family that I was challenging; it was his position in the fleet, in town, in life.

Pete's face turned to stone. "I will captain my own boat until the day it's yours," he growled. "If we make it that far."

Chapter 5

Drew's hand was tucked into mine as we walked down the hill from the hospital to the docks. He'd been quiet since we left Pete's room, and I was hoping his excitement hadn't been that short-lived. I'd been trying to draw him out with no luck. The clouds were still heavy and low, but the rain had tapered off.

I stopped for a minute as the *Sarah Louise* came into view, trying to get my mind to catch up. I no longer had health insurance, and I was apparently heading out to the fishing grounds with a four-year-old and an asshole in two casts. I knelt to dip my hand into the frigid water. Even in the middle of summer, it was so cold a person could only survive it for a matter of hours.

"Why are you doing that?" Drew asked.

"Feels like home."

"Whose home? Our home? Your hand will be cold now." Drew's face was serious, and his right shoulder poked up at the heavy fabric of his rain jacket.

"No. My old home. The one I used to have before you."

"You lived in the water?" Drew's eyes widened.

I laughed. "Yep. With the whales."

"You did not." The hint of a smile threatened to peek through the flat, tight line of his lips.

"You're right. I lived on that boat there." I pointed. As my eyes settled on the pleasing lines of the *Sarah Louise*, I felt a surge of excitement at the idea of being back in the pit, setting gear, running lines. I could feel again the way the boat moved slow in the morning, wood against wood, in the same manner as bone against bone.

I looked down into Drew's upturned face. "Drew, meet the *Sarah Louise*."

He peered at me. Why was he always so silent? Was it because of something I was doing or not doing? Would this fix it?

"Want to look around?"

"Okay," he said in a way that oozed reluctance.

I lifted him over the rail and pulled myself on board behind him.

"Well, that's a sight for sore eyes."

I turned to see Caroline walking down the dock. She was one of the fleet's legendary women under whose surveillance my generation of boat kids had grown up. She wore the standard orange heavy rain jacket and pants along with the brown Xtratufs everyone fished and lived in. "What's going on here?" She tilted her head to better see out from under the ratty ball cap.

"Looks like we're going fishing," I said, unable to control the smile that was spreading across my face.

"That's my girl." She nodded her approval. "Hey, Drew."

He dropped his eyes.

"You got a suit for him yet?" She meant a survival suit in case we ended up in the water. Even though I knew this was part of it, it wasn't anything I wanted to think about for long. "Sarah's youngest outgrew his last year," Caroline went on. "Be about the right size for Drew. I'll check with her on my way back and drop it off. She's got loads of games too. I'll see what she's ready to part with."

I nodded.

She must've caught the fear that I was trying to hide. "Don't worry, El. Just a precaution. You know what you're doing out there."

I nodded again, trying to convince myself that I believed her. As crew, I had always just done what I was told. As skipper, my father had always been sober and careful, neither of which he could be trusted to be at this point.

Caroline continued on down the dock, but I couldn't get the image of Drew in a survival suit out of my mind.

I shook my head. This was not the way I'd been taught to think. I'd been taught to trust myself in the face of an unpredictable sea. To expect and even invite the unpredictability. And what had I been teaching Drew? That you watched life happen to other people on a screen? That being an adult meant having a short temper and being exhausted all the time?

As the *Sarah Louise* rocked slightly in the wind blowing in from the Sound, Drew flung his arms out wide to catch his balance, his eyes wild. His face crumpled, and he wailed, "I want to go home."

"It's okay, Drew. Just move with it, not against it." What a strange thing to have to explain, how to move with a boat. I reached a hand to him, and he gripped tight as if he might fall down at any moment.

We stepped past the hold, a large section of insulated and lined hull meant for storing iced fish until they could be off-loaded at a tender or cannery. The entrance to the hold was two trapdoors, closed now, that stood a couple of feet off the deck. I could feel the thin iron rungs of the ladder that led down into the hold, hidden now by the door. I could feel the sting of the ice through my gloves as I packed salmon in tight after a long day of catching. Drew and I stepped around the hold and through the narrow wooden door into the wheelhouse.

There was a small head to port; in front of that, a table with bench seats for four. To starboard, a galley with a small countertop, cabinets, a sink, and a Dickinson oilstove that provided heat, a cooktop, and a minuscule oven. Still stretched above the stove was the twine and clothespins my mom had hung up for drying out gloves and socks.

The most forward section of the house was reserved for the skipper's chair, wheel, and instruments. The chair sat in the very center of a series of wraparound windows framed in by wood. There was a ledge between the wheel and the windows where various instrumentation was bolted down: the computer for charts, the compass, the throttle, and the fish finder. On either side of the wheel, running almost to the floor, were instrument panels.

Drew stayed just inside the door as I poked around. No wild running around checking everything out. No touching everything, flipping switches just to see what happened. I bit the inside of my lip. There was no reason to think he would suddenly snap like a rubber band into some replica of me just because we'd stepped onto the boat I loved more than life itself. And why did I want him to anyway? Because that would make it easier for me to understand him, easier to know what he needed and how to supply it.

"Where's the TV?" he asked, his eyes wild.

I closed my eyes briefly. "There's no TV, Drew." Which wasn't exactly true. DVDs could be played on the computer, but I'd be damned if I was going to bring Drew out here to watch shows. If he knew it was a possibility, it would be all he wanted to do.

"I want a TV." His face crushed with the weight of all the changes. "I want Marshall." He began to cry.

I threaded my way back to him through the narrow house. I knelt, taking both his small hands. "You are going to have both Pete and me, all day, every day. No more TV friends. Real friends. And no more day care."

He peered at me through watery eyes. "You don't have to go to work?"

"No." I shook my head. "I'll work right here. You can help."

"What if I don't want to?"

I stared at him for a minute too long. Where was the balance between expecting and accepting? Pete and Mom had clearly established expectations of me without ever making me feel like I should be anything other than what I was as a kid. Through all the hatred and disappointment, it hit me. Pete knew how to do this, and I did not. Maybe he could show me.

Drew dropped his eyes, aware that he'd said something I didn't want him to say. I shook my head to dispel it for both of us. "Then you can stay in here with Pete. Help him drive, maybe. C'mere." I picked him up, crossed the house in a few steps, and set him down in the skipper's chair.

He reached out slowly and rested his hands on the worn wooden spokes of the wheel. "Is this how you fish?" he asked, pushing lightly on the wheel until it gave way a centimeter, at which point he pulled his hands away.

"Yep." I smiled down at him, remembering the way Pete would perch me on his lap and let me steer at Drew's age. I picked him up and settled him on my lap in the chair. I gently wrapped my hands around his and put them back on the wheel. Together, we moved it to starboard and back to port. His body relaxed against mine. "Looks like you're going to get the hang of it pretty quick."

Starboard of the skipper's chair was a set of three stairs that led down to the focsle, the V berth at the bow that held two bunks on one side, one bunk on the other with storage underneath. "Want to see where you'll sleep?" I asked.

"I want to sleep where you sleep." He followed me down the three creaky wooden stairs into the focsle, where I patted the lower bunk on the starboard side.

"This one is where I always slept. Now it's yours. I'll sleep right above you in the top bunk. My mom's old bunk," I added, letting my hand rest there for a minute. Her slow, steady breathing had calmed me on more nights than I could count. I turned to the single bunk on the port side. "This one is Pete's."

"I want to sleep with you." Drew's face hung slack, and tears filled his eyes again.

"Okay. We'll share a bunk until we get used to it. How's that sound?" I dropped down to one knee in front of him. How many changes could I pile up on him at once?

Drew looped his arms around my neck and sat on my knee.

"I know it's a big change, but I think you'll like it."

"I always wanted a grandpa," he said.

How to tell him this grandpa wasn't the kind he wanted? "And I always wanted a Drew," I said.

"And you got one—first try!"

I laughed at his unexpected change in mood. While the roller coaster of parenting was exhausting, the view from the top was pretty incredible. "Amazing how that worked out, isn't it?" I got us to our feet and took his hand. "Let's go check out the rest."

Aft of the focsle was the engine room. I peeked in and found it clean and orderly. Back up in the house, I stepped into the head, a room barely big enough to turn around in with a toilet and sink no larger than my cupped hands. It was also clean. Even though Pete had been letting his life go to shit, he hadn't let the *Sarah Louise* fall into the same situation. Drew peeked in behind me. "Is that a toilet?"

"Yes."

"For little people only?"

I laughed. "Big people use it too."

He scrunched up his face and looked at me like I was crazy.

As I pulled the head door closed and glanced around the house, my heart folded up tight. The more I thought of the new future that had been spinning out in front of me since I'd agreed to fish, the more I wanted it forever.

If we could make the fifty grand this summer, Drew and I would live aboard the boat this winter, fishing winter kings. The following years, I would homeschool him, as Mom had homeschooled me up until high school at the small galley table, so that we could fish most of the year.

With no day care, no rent, a fishing income, and a paid-off boat, a debt-free existence was a possibility. We could explore hard-to-reach beaches and coves, spend time together. I wouldn't be so stressed. In the summer, I'd hire one crew member, and we'd get by just fine, maybe even have a nice pillow of money in the bank that I could rest up against. Just thinking about it was as if someone lifted the corner of the heavy, wet blanket I'd been living under for years. A reprieve. I could see it: a life without daily struggle, time to enjoy these years with Drew, maybe even quit failing so horrendously at this parenting thing.

Of course, it was possible to not catch enough fish to cover the price of diesel across a few months, much less end up with fifty grand at the end of it. It was a roll of the dice, a series of decisions, and a good dose of luck. My stomach ached as Drew followed me up the three narrow steps into the wheelhouse. I couldn't lose this.

My eyes ran across the small, efficient space. I could see my mother standing at the old wooden-spoked wheel leaning against the chair, one leg stretched out long and straight ahead of her, the other crossed over at the ankle. I'd gotten my above-average height directly from her. Both the radar screen and the fish finder screen were blank, but I could see in my mind the green arm of the radar sweeping across the screen in the weak predawn light, the way my mother would start shifting from foot to foot as the fish finder displayed the distinctive boomerang of one fish after another until we found the dark floating cloud that sent us into well-practiced action.

I glanced up at the now silent VHF radios side by side above the chair and imagined the old familiar sound of them squawking in the background as fishermen jested and trash-talked. I could almost feel the boat move as it does in heavy seas, a satisfying weight to each roll. As I glanced from one part of the boat to another, a clarity of purpose settled over me and, at the same time, the absolute uncertainty of what lay ahead.

There was a knock on the hull, and Caroline called out. I stepped out on deck, and she handed over a stack of board games, Uno cards and a kid-size survival suit in a bright-orange bag.

"Thanks," I said, reaching across the rail to grab it all.

"Sure thing, kiddo. I'll see you out there." She smiled until her eyes crinkled and then was off down the docks toward her own boat. "Welcome back."

I looked down at the sturdy-handled bag with the word CHILD printed across the top of it. Inside was a full-body life preserver meant to keep you from freezing to death as you floated for hours or days in the water, either in an inflatable raft or just on your back, alone.

Chapter 6

After a bit of snooping around the boat, it became clear that Pete had been preparing for the opener before he'd crossed paths with the crew that beat him to a pulp. Everything was cleaned, stocked, and in working order. The sound of the drizzle against the wheelhouse was like a familiar blanket drawn over my shoulders.

Drew and I food shopped and began the process of buttoning up our life in town. I told my landlord we'd be out in the morning, which was met with something like relief. He'd been wanting to raise the rent but hadn't out of some sort of kindness toward me. We dropped off most of our belongings at the secondhand store, moved what we would need onto the boat, boxed up the rest, and stored it in Monica's parents' garage.

I bought myself the necessary crew license at the grocery store for sixty dollars and, only because it pleased me so much, splurged to buy Drew his very own kid's crew as well for another five dollars.

Back on the wet sidewalk, outside the grocery store, Drew slipped his hand in mine. It was glorious to not be at work, to be with Drew in the middle of the day.

"Elll-lllie!"

I looked up. The captain of a tender, which anchored up out on the fishing grounds as an alternative place to off-load fish rather than running all the way back to town, was walking toward us. He was an old guy who had been running the tender for as long as I could remember.

He'd also been smiling for as long as I could remember. He was dressed in the uniform of bright-orange rain gear and rain boots. His tangly white beard spaghettied down his chest. "Hey, Will."

"What's the big grin for? Find some bargains in the grocery?" he asked and then laughed at his own joke. Food was impossibly expensive by the time it got all the way out here from the rest of the country.

"Just bought Drew his first crew license." I couldn't help it. Whatever ridiculous look was on my face got even more ridiculous.

"Yeah, little man!" Will put up some knuckles, and Drew shyly made a fist. Will gently touched his fist to Drew's.

Drew twisted away behind me while still holding my hand. "Can I go get a lollipop from Tanya?" The bank was next door.

"Sure, buddy."

He ran off, but then hesitated. Stood outside the door of the bank until someone coming out held it open for him and then slunk inside. Why didn't he try the door? Why so tentative about everything? I breathed out and refocused on Will, who was still grinning at me.

"Heard you were heading out this season," he said. "'Bout time."

"Good grief. It's been about forty-five seconds since I decided."

Will caught sight of someone behind me and yelled, "Van! What are you doing in town?"

I turned around. A man I'd noticed around town a couple of times but had never met was navigating the sidewalk with a loaded-down hand trolley full of boxes. He was tall and thin and wide-shouldered. His dark-blond curls rolled up around the bottom edges of a ball cap. I noticed what I'd noticed before. The way life had piled up at the corners of his eyes. How when he smiled, he looked happy and sad at the same time. He held out a hand to Will. "Hey, man, how's it going?" His words were like molasses, slow and rolling in a thick wave over the edge of the amber jar into the cookie dough.

Will shook his hand. "You know Ellie?"

"Don't believe I do." Van held out his hand to me. When I slid my hand into his, he said, "Nice to meet you." The cadence of it, the way he smiled, as if it were breezy and warm out, as if there were all the time in the world. Some kinked-up muscle in between my shoulder blades let go in his presence.

Will cracked up and shoved my arm. "This is where you say, *nice to meet you too*."

I swallowed. Nodded once. "Nice to meet you too."

Drew came running at us fast with a lollipop in his mouth and another in his hand. "She gave me two," he squealed as he piledrived into my legs.

I hoisted him up to my hip. "That's great, but don't run with a lollipop in your mouth." His face fell. Why did I always do that? Erase the fun. Around me, the air changed. I glanced up at Van, whose whole body had gone from fluid to stone, his eyes pinned on Drew.

"More supplies for the greenhouse?" Will asked, nodding toward the hand trolley.

Van snapped out of it. "Yeah." He flipped his ball cap off his head and resettled it. "I better get to it." He walked off without looking back.

"That was weird, right?" I said to Will.

"What?"

"The way he just acted. When Drew came out."

Will shrugged. "Not everybody likes kids." He grinned. "No offense, Drew. I think you're pretty awesome."

"Who is he?"

"Don't know him well. Lives out . . ." He indicated the archipelago of uninhabited islands west of the island we lived on. "Nice guy. From Georgia or Alabama or something. Drives a heap of a skiff but keeps it running somehow."

Drew squirmed to get out of my arms. I set him back down on the pavement and shook off whatever that just was. I had given up trying to figure people out long ago. "Alright, Will. We've got a lot to get done. I'll see you out there."

His grin returned. "I'll see you out there, right where you belong. I think all this living-in-town bullshit's got you jumpy."

~

That night, I crept into Drew's room. He slept wide open, arms flung from one side of the bed to the other as if life was something to be trusted. I kissed the smooth skin of his cheek, loose and relaxed, and listened to him breathe. How to get him to be more wide open in the day? Was I the one who'd made him so tentative?

He was constantly showing me the options of who I could be, both bad and good. Every day the choice lay before me. All those years on my own with an infant and then toddler and no money and no help. It was pure survival. It was hunger and fear. I vented my frustrations too much, I was never as patient as I wanted to be. Most nights, once he was asleep, I came in to tell him I'd do better the next day.

I perched on the edge of the bed and took Drew's warm, smooth hand in mine and imagined him out on the *Sarah Louise*. No screens, no horrible other kids at day care, just water and air and room to breathe. Hope bloomed deep in my chest. I brushed Drew's hair off his forehead and kissed him, closing my eyes, breathing in the innocent scent of him. "This is going to be better, buddy, I promise," I whispered.

~

At four thirty the next morning, the cloud cover had already lightened to a hazy gray. I carried a sleeping Drew from the truck down the dock through the dark moving shadow of rain. The calls of gulls overhead and the slap of water against the dock made everything feel right. Once on board the *Sarah Louise*, I settled Drew in the bottom bunk of the focsle. I got the stove going and then climbed down into the focsle to stow Drew's survival suit under the single bunk. I froze when I saw mine and Mom's still tucked in next to Pete's. If only the family this suggested were the reality. I tucked Drew's in among the other three and let myself pretend things were the way I so badly wished they were. Mom in the wheelhouse behind me, Pete out on deck, Drew growing up held in the circle we all formed. I shook my head. All I was doing was making my actual reality a sharper knife to wound myself with.

I stood up and quickly moved back into the wheelhouse, where I flipped on the fish finder and started up the computer. I dropped into the engine room, checked the fluid levels, checked the bilge, kept my mind in the safer, top layers, and then perched on the skipper's chair.

Excitement ran up my spine as the engine roared to life. From the skipper's chair, I had a clear view of Drew in the focsle, who remained asleep. When I was a kid, the rumble of the engine helped me sleep. Perhaps he was the same. *Or perhaps he was different,* I chided myself. While the engine warmed up, I took stock of every drawer and storage compartment, mentally making lists of anything we might need in the coming weeks. Debating whether or not I should throw the flask I'd found in the drawer next to the skipper's chair overboard. Twenty minutes later, Pete showed up.

I heard him cussing before I saw him. The clatter of what I assumed were his crutches being tossed over the rail woke up Drew. He sat up, the sleeping bag I'd thrown over him tumbling to the floor.

"It's okay, buddy. Pete just got here is all." I dropped down the three stairs and ran my hand through his sleep-rumpled hair. "Sounds like he might need some help." I tossed the sleeping bag over him again. "Be right back." Drew whimpered a bit and clutched at my hand. "It's okay," I said and kissed his forehead.

Out on deck, Pete was sitting in a heap on the edge of the hold, the light drizzle beading up on his hair. His head hung low, which made his neck look twiggy, a word I'd never before associated with him. He was breathing hard, his body somehow slumped and stiff at the same time. Someone had cut the left arm out of his sweatshirt so he could get his cast through.

"I'm coming," he said without looking over, which was enough to let me know he didn't want my help. Through what looked to be sheer force of will, he got himself to his feet, hopped over on his one good foot, and gathered up his crutches from where they lay on the deck. His face was even more swollen, and a deep purple was spreading around the still swollen-shut eye. He moved through the door while I held it, and thumped his way over to the table, which afforded him a clear view of Drew still sitting up in his bunk.

"Hey, Drew!" he said in a voice lighter and happier than seemed possible for how broken he had just looked. "I couldn't even sleep, I was so excited to head out fishing with you."

I let out a long breath and stepped on deck.

Usually, Pete would be at the helm, the engine idling as I untied lines, but this time I went through the process as if I were alone on the boat, untying the lines and then returning to the wheelhouse to drop the engine into gear and steer us away from the dock without any help from him. He'd felt it, though, from inside the wheelhouse, the extra inches between us and the dock as the lines let go. The boat was as much an extension of him as his hands.

When I breezed past him and Drew at the table and settled myself in the skipper's chair, Pete was wrestling with his crutch, which was caught up in the single leg of the table. The minute my hand touched the throttle, the air in the small house stilled, turned thick. He was right behind me before I had a chance to drop it in gear. His breath hot on the side of my face, the crutches forgotten. "Not a chance." In his measured words was a threat he'd never aimed at me before. But I'd also never attempted to usurp him as skipper. Ever.

A look of intense anxiety settled on Drew's face, and for that reason, I stepped out from behind the wheel.

"Hey, Drew, want to go watch for seals?"

He nodded, likely wanting to put some distance between himself and Pete's anger more than he wanted to go look for seals. As Pete dropped the boat into reverse, it rocked underneath us, and Drew flailed wildly for the edge of the table to steady himself. "Don't worry, you'll get your sea legs eventually," I said as I helped him into his life jacket.

"I'm going to grow more legs?" He flung his eyes up to mine, full of this next horror.

Both Pete and I laughed, which broke at least the surface of the ice between us.

"I'd be jealous if you did," Pete said, a lightness returned to his voice now. "I only have one, and you'd have four. I wonder if they'd be sticky and you could climb up the walls like a spider. That'd be cool."

Drew gave me a confused look as I gathered up a few breakfast supplies and held the door open for him. Pete looked right, and wrong, perched on the edge of the skipper's chair, the casted leg off to the side, checking all his instrumentation while managing the radio and the wheel with one hand. And then he slid open the drawer and pulled out the flask, and it became all too clear what I'd gotten us into.

Drew and I sat out of the rain under the hayrack, a metal roof that covered most of the stern, and split a peanut butter and jelly sandwich as town slipped away behind us. Out in the Sound, the sea spread out gray and choppy, the old familiar challenge that sparked in me a willingness to rise to it along with the slow, sizzling fear that I might fail. The only other thing that ever elicited the same feeling in me was Drew. Everything else was muted, dull, something to endure. This was what Stephen, my boss at the City, had noticed but couldn't name. Accounting in a cubicle was easy, safe, but there was no jolt of life in it, and as a result, it had drained the life out of me.

"Is Pete mad?" Drew had eaten the middle out of his sandwich. Just the crust remained in his hand, a road of jelly from ear to ear. We were moving north now through the Sound. Everything was a shade of gray: the thick cloud cover above, the wispy fog caught in the high branches on shore, the sea, the rain.

"Seems like it."

"Why?" The cool breeze picked up his straight hair in chunks. It had always seemed to me like my mom lived in the wind, the way it tore through powerful and unapologetic. I closed my eyes, turned my face into it to say hello. When I opened my eyes, Drew was watching me, waiting for an answer.

"Pete's done some bad things, and he knows it."

Drew twisted his mouth up and squinted at the far shoreline. I scooted closer and dropped an arm around him. "Hey, don't worry about Pete. We can ignore him for the most part and have a fun time on our own."

"I don't want to ignore Pete," he said in a way that made him seem way too old. "I want him to be my grandpa."

The wind stalled out, and the water took on a flat, ugly look. "I know, Drew." I kissed his temple and pulled him closer. "Hey, do you want to play the seagull game?"

"No."

I wondered how to open up this little human who carried the weight of our barely-getting-by life. How to ease his mind. How to cross this large distance between us.

When I noticed him begin to shiver, we headed back in. Drew settled in the bunk, new dump trucks and Matchbox cars and dinosaurs spread out all around him, along with his good pal, a stuffed dog named Dog. With the clear exception of Dog, I'd bribed him to leave most of his toys at the secondhand store with the promise that he could pick out ten new ones, as long as they were marked a dollar or less.

Pete was still not talking to me, but based on the turns he was making, I knew he was headed toward Dead Man's Reach. We'd anchor up for the night around the corner in Deep Bay, since Dead Man's Reach was too exposed to the wind, and start fishing at dawn the next morning. I rolled my eyes and shook my head. The tide wasn't quite right for Dead Man's Reach, but all fishermen were superstitious. Pete was always willing to take a low haul the first day in Dead Man's Reach to ensure a good rest of the opener with the sea gods or whatever. Which was stupid. We needed to be strategic, not emotional. I sat at the table and flipped open a paperback I'd brought along, but couldn't concentrate.

"I'm going to double-check gear on deck," I said to Pete's back. He nodded in response, keeping his eyes on the sea ahead. "Drew, holler out the door if you need anything."

He was lining up the dinosaurs biggest to smallest and didn't acknowledge me.

The cloud cover hung low over the water, darkening, bringing a blue tint to all the gray. We were in a narrower channel now, weaving between two of the hundreds of islands in Southeast Alaska. The shore was a dark-green mass of hemlock and spruce, all their branches woven together. The rocks of the beach on either side were big and jagged. I filled my lungs with misty rain and felt the muscles in my back relax. It was cool and damp and right. If I could just stay out here, I'd be alright. My life in town had been cleared out so easily. It bothered me that it had taken only an afternoon to erase seven years.

The *Sarah Louise* rocked under me as Pete turned us north toward Strike Cove. I filled my lungs again with misty air. A person's purpose was much more straightforward out here: to keep your head down and work, to fill the hold, to eat and sleep so that you could stand in the shadow of these mountains one more day and keep working. For all the things I felt useless at, I knew without a doubt that I was good at being cold, working in the rain, and catching fish.

~

After Pete tucked us into Deep Bay, I made a quick dinner of spaghetti and went to bed with Drew in the broad daylight of seven thirty, partially because of the early morning ahead, but mostly because I didn't know how to deal with what I'd started with Pete. Boats work best with clearly defined roles. He'd bought the boat eight years before I was born, six years before he met Mom. The permit had always been in his name. It was his signature on the fish ticket, it was he who decided where we fished, the gear we set, and the speed of the troll. Sure, Mom had a say in all matters, but there was no question who to look to when we needed to move as one efficient team.

I climbed into the small bunk and nestled in next to Drew. He immediately flung an arm over me, his breath light against my neck. The distance I'd felt earlier between us melted away and, with it, a huge chunk of my anxiety. What pleasure there was in the two of us venturing off into sleep, flopped together. Why had I so dutifully trained him to sleep alone, as all the books told me I had to? Why had I let someone else decide what was best? I closed my eyes and felt more fully okay than I'd felt in a long time, the small weight of Drew's arm across my chest, his body relaxed against mine.

~

The next morning at three thirty a.m., I extricated myself from the bunk by lifting Drew's head off my thigh and then his knee from my neck. He'd somehow spun around in the night. I'd slept hard, not noticing any motion outside of the *Sarah Louise* rocking on her anchor. I pulled on a sweatshirt over my long underwear top and fleece pants in the dark tight space of the focsle.

The dense cloud cover would start to lighten in half an hour. Gear needed to be in the water at sunup. Pete was already settled in the skipper's chair, buried in the dark of the morning, studying charts on the laptop, coffee going. I filled a mug, topped it off with creamer, and checked out the window. Rain steady against the deck, everything clean and wet.

"Once you pull the anchor, we'll head around the corner to Dead Man's Reach," Pete said. He readjusted himself in the chair one part at a time. He seemed to be holding his breath, looking even worse than the day before. The swelling of his face was just as bad, and now blue-black circles thickly rimmed both eyes.

I looked away. If we were going to make $50,000 this season, we had to fish smarter than we'd ever fished before. "Sound Harbor would be better given the tide."

Pete closed the laptop but didn't look over. "This is still my boat. Until it isn't." His voice was full of gravel.

I set my mug down, straightened up. "I'm no longer a kid, and I'm not your crew. And there's a good chance there's something in your coffee besides cream. We'll fish Sound Harbor."

He turned around at that, his glare cutting through the dark between us. "Don't" was all he said. The word like a slap. Whatever was broken between us broke further.

I walked away without a word. Once I had the anchor hauled and secure, Pete dropped the boat into gear and we headed slowly out of the bay. I moved to the aft deck, filling myself up with the cold morning air, getting the boat ready for a day of trolling. I tried to ignore what was happening between Pete and me and instead focused on the sound of the gulls calling, the murrelets swimming in pairs, disappearing underwater when the boat got too close. The soft hiss of rain against sea, the slow groan of the *Sarah Louise* as Pete corrected course, the smooth, graceful arc of the dolphin's back just off our starboard side.

The dark-green trees looked black as they rose from the water's edge up the steep, mountainous sides of the bay. The dark sky faded to a dull gray. Through the hazy curtain of rain, the mouth of the bay materialized, a narrow opening between rocks that tumbled into the sea from mountains on either side. If Pete turned to port, we'd be heading toward Dead Man's Reach, as he'd suggested. If he turned to starboard, we'd be headed to Sound Harbor.

Pete skillfully steered through the narrow entrance and pointed the bow to the port.

Anger boiled deep inside me. I had a sudden urge to run, to be free of Pete once and for all, to protect Drew from him. But if we didn't stay, Drew's future dwindled to something that looked like my current life. Perhaps he'd fish for someone else. It was easier to hire out as crew as a man. But always better to work for your family until you took over the boat yourself. Without that option, it was more likely he would leave Alaska and find some other life down south. My stomach soured at the idea. This was where he belonged. Out on the fishing grounds, in this boat. Unless he hated it. I thought of his thin wrists, his sunken eyes, Marshall.

I stepped back into the wheelhouse and stood for a minute behind Pete. He took it for what it was—me allowing him to tell me what gear to set based on water color, temperature, hunches, and experience, which he mumbled with one quick glance over his shoulder. One more way we walked in the deep footsteps of forever. Usually it was Mom who popped in to ask, me out in the pit already setting the gear I knew he would choose.

I headed to the stern and lowered myself into the pit, a three-foot depression that ran from one side of the boat to the other, protected from the rain by the hayrack. When standing in the pit, the rail was at waist height, which made it easier to sling fish in over the stern. All the fishing gear was within reach, as were the brakes and gurdies to let the lines out, set them, and bring them in.

I pulled on my insulated rubber gloves; got all the hoochies, flashers, and spoons organized; and then stood in the pit, soothed by the way the engine rumbled under me, by the hectic cackling of seagulls overhead, by the smooth smack of waves against the boat.

As Pete slowed the boat to trolling speed, my body automatically positioned itself in front of the starboard side gurdies, where I'd stood for more hours than I could count. I attached the lead, eased off the brake so that the line would feed out behind the boat, and began attaching gear in the quick, efficient way my body remembered without the aid of my mind. As I continued attaching gear at even intervals as the long lines that trolled behind the boat spooled out, I could feel my mother out on deck with me as she had been every summer of my life, working the gurdies and lines on the port side, or cleaning one fish after another with quick, precise motions, packing them carefully into the hold with ice. I could see the look on her face as the hold started to look more full than empty, the way she relaxed as all of the tension that was left over from town receded. This way of life was so important to her. If Pete had loved her at all, it would've been impossible to gamble away.

"I'm sorry, Mom," I whispered to the wind on Pete's behalf. "I'll make it right, I promise."

Chapter 7

Pete moving around in the wheelhouse caught my eye through the small window in the door. Since there were no fish yet, I scrambled out of the pit to check on Drew.

Just as I cracked the wheelhouse door, Drew shrieked.

"Shit," I said in a quick breath. How could I leave him alone, let him wake up with a near stranger? Of course he was terrified. It had taken months of leaving him at day care before he would let me walk out the door without sobbing.

"Mom!" he yelled as I threw open the door. "I'm driving!"

Drew, still in his pajamas, hair sticking out at all angles, was sitting in Pete's lap, grinning ear to ear, his pencil-thin arms reached out their full length to span the spoked wheel. Pete sat in the skipper's chair, his good arm looped comfortably around Drew's belly, keeping him in place as he adjusted the squelch on the radio with the casted hand.

"Looking pretty straight, buddy," I managed. "Did you have breakfast?" I had loved Pete and I had hated him; it was another thing entirely to feel both at the same time.

"I don't want any," Drew said, his eyes locked on the open gray water that spread out before him.

"I'll put the cereal out for you."

With his good knee, Pete corrected ever so slightly the boat's path through the water as he alternately peered out the window and checked the chart. "We're fine," he said without turning around. "One thing I know for sure, you can't catch fish from in here."

I rubbed at the back of my neck. Drew's face was animated. I'd never seen him sit in anyone else's lap but mine. I put the box of Cheerios in the sink so he could find it easy and it wouldn't spill.

I wasn't back in the pit more than three minutes before the bell rang, indicating the first fish on the line. I was both elated and pissed that Dead Man's Reach had clearly been a good choice to fish. After engaging the starboard gurdy to pull the trolling wire in and securing the ten leaders between me and the fish, the salmon broke the surface just behind the boat. A king. It was beautiful in a way that I'd forgotten. Metallic. Powerful. Fighting the hook with a surprising fury. I was spellbound in a way I'd never stopped to be before. Instead of handlining him in as fast as I could, I watched him for a minute fighting for all he was worth twelve feet behind the boat. And then, a quick flash of brown, and the taut line fell slack in my hand.

"No!" I worked the line fast, hand over hand, until the end of the line surfaced with just the head of the salmon attached. I scanned the surface of the water until I found the offending sea lion swimming away.

Pete flung the wheelhouse door open, the casted foot held off the ground, the good hand balancing him against the doorframe. "Fuck's sake, Ellie." The dull light of morning shadowed his face so that the swollen parts looked even worse out of proportion. "We aren't out here so you can stargaze." Drew poked his head around the side of Pete's hip, taking in the whole scene. Now what was I teaching him? That men yelling at women is perfectly acceptable?

I closed my eyes. Because Pete was right. There was nothing to say. Every fish in the hold was money in the pocket. I'd just tossed fifty dollars over the side. You do not stand around when a fish is on the line.

I turned back, reset the gear, and sent the line streaming out behind us again. Pete went back to his position at the helm with the sharp sound of the door slamming. Another troller cruised by a few hundred yards off our port side. I watched the crewman in the pit working the gear, swinging a king in over the side, like I should be.

When the bell rang again, I quickly engaged the gurdy, unclipped and reclipped the line snaps between the fish and me until I had the leader he was attached to. I handlined him in until he was right up next to the boat and then put all my weight into the stunning blow delivered with the blunt end of the gaff. I spun the gaff around in my hand, drove the sharp C-hook through the fish's head as the sea lion resurfaced only feet away. It lunged straight for the salmon. I swung the fish up and over the stern, my back muscles complaining after five years in an office job. My aim was off. The fish's body clipped the stern. I overcompensated to make sure the rest of him cleared it, causing him to crash into my chest. The sea lion ducked under the boat.

"Ahh!" I yelled over the side at him as I flopped the fish into the holding bin. I delivered the killing blow with the blunt end of the gaff and twisted the hook free.

Usually I waited until I had a bunch ready to clean, but I was jittery and excited to be back at it, and there weren't any other fish on the lines, so I lifted him into the cleaning tray. I cut the throat latch to bleed the fish so that the meat would be as pristine as possible even though I'd likely bruised some of the meat getting the fish on board in such a clumsy way. I cut out the gills, cut a straight line through the white of the belly, yanked out the guts, scraped it clean, and massaged the walls of the belly quickly with gloved fingers, exactly as Pete had taught me when I was seven years old. I sprayed all the remaining blood and parts out of the tray through the opening that dumped over the side of the boat.

Lunch came and went as I pulled in one fish after another. Fish and Game spent the entire summer running calculations, and so did I. The math of it felt like a sturdy post to lean a shoulder up against. The way x number of fish added up to x number of meals for x number of people and x number of months of enough money for us to live on. Biologists spent their time estimating how many fish were likely to be in the waters of Southeast Alaska, counting how many fish were being caught, estimating when to close the fishery to keep fisherman from putting too big of a dent in the population. The fleet was likely going to be able to fish kings for less than two weeks. Then we'd switch to cohos, and possibly be allowed to fish kings again for another three or four days in August. King days were big, though. At around fifty dollars a fish, it was possible to pull in $1,000 a day, and if we found a pocket of fish, that could easily triple. It all depended on how good we were at finding fish.

Cleaning in between catching and packing them in the hold, I fell into the trance of the physical work. One task completed after another, the bounty of my labor lining up. Five fish, ten fish, twelve fish, as the rain worked out its rhythm on the hayrack above and the misty clouds tangled in the treetops on shore. The goal was concrete, my progress toward that goal easily measured.

Not like raising Drew, with elusive goals and hard-to-measure progress. It was so often a matter of searching for some level of patience and control that I wasn't sure I had, finding it, and then losing it in under a minute. This cycle of finding and losing, of yelling at Drew after I'd asked him to pick up his toys for the third time, after he'd lost his boots for the tenth time, left me drained. I would make all sorts of resolutions and then within the hour find myself snapping at him and then trying to make it up with miles of faked patience. The boomerang of it made me feel sick. The way Drew rushed to say, "Sorry, Mama, I'm so sorry," made me even sicker.

The wheelhouse door swung open, and Pete held a sandwich wrapped in a paper towel in his one good arm, propping the door with the hip of the casted leg. He looked impossibly pale and broken.

I hauled myself out of the pit and accepted the bologna sandwich. The XM radio was broadcasting a ball game. I held open the door, and Pete hopped in the uneven sloshing of the boat back toward the skipper's chair. He was tossed into the table, did some gymnastics to catch himself before he fell. Apparently, he'd given up dealing with the crutches in the cramped space of the wheelhouse. The toes sticking out of the cast were swollen purple.

The wheelhouse door swung with the same wave and whapped me hard in the back. I twisted and secured it open with the hook and eye mounted on the outside of the wheelhouse for that purpose.

"What game you listening to?" I asked, disappointment prickling the back of my neck. I stared at him, disbelieving. Even after losing the boat, he was still gambling?

Pete didn't turn around. "I'm just a fan, Ellie. That's all."

I finished off the sandwich in three big bites, staying outside in my bibs and sweatshirt now splattered with fish slime, blood, and scales. Drew was sitting in the skipper's chair, up on his knees so he could see out. "Drew, you good?" I called in through a mouthful.

Drew's face was lit up like that one sunny day a year that graced Southeast Alaska. "Yeah! Grandpa gave me Oreos for lunch. He said, 'Prepare to live!'" Drew pointed a finger straight at the sky. "And gave me the whole bag." The unnecessary Band-Aid over his knife cut that he'd insisted on every day for weeks was gone.

Pete stood next to Drew. He ducked down to talk directly into Drew's ear. "That was between you and me, Agent X."

The smile they shared, their foreheads so close, was thrilling and scary. Drew's reaching out, the smallest of tendrils, and Pete with a handful of knives. Fear arched through me, but how could I say any of that. "Sandwiches, Pete, not Oreos. He'll get a stomachache. You expect me to work out here *and* take care of him? Can you not do the job you were brought out here to do?"

I could barely believe I'd said it. Pete was across the wheelhouse and up in my face, every bit of pain and unsteadiness overridden, before the words were all the way out. He was suddenly coiled like a spring. Despite being in his fifties, decades of fishing had left him as strong as he'd ever been. He smelled of Irish Spring, coffee, and the darkness of whiskey. "You will not talk to me like that."

Despite the way my insides knotted up, I stepped into the small space left between us, looked him in the eye. "You are the one who got yourself into this, Pete. I'm the one who's getting you out of it." My voice was as even and hard as his. "Lay off the booze." We stared at each other as the bell jumped and clanged, signaling another fish. I shoved the wadded-up paper towel still in my hand at his chest and turned for the pit.

The afternoon came and went as I hauled and cleaned one fish after another. Fifteen, sixteen, seventeen, eighteen, and then a dry patch. I worried about Drew stuck in the wheelhouse with Pete, but there wasn't much I could do about it. I listened closely for any sounds of distress.

When hours went by without that happening, I climbed out of the pit and peeked in the window. Drew was perched on the strip of counter space at the base of the windows, usually used for an assortment of gloves and tools and tide books. He was pointing toward something that Pete was peering at through the windows, their faces bent close.

The bell clanged, sending me back into the pit. I pulled in another four kings, sailing us past the $1,000 mark for the day.

At slack tide, Pete moved us across the bay and found another pocket of fish, deep in the cold gray expanse of water.

We fished into the late-evening daylight, pulling the gear and anchoring up around ten p.m., as the dark closed in. I cleaned the final few fish and packed them in the hold. Thirty-five total. A huge day. $2,000. If everyone was catching like this, Fish and Game was likely to close kings soon, and that would be that. The old familiar weight of some proclamation coming down from on high settled over me. It was the way of things, a feeling I'd inherited from my parents more so than landing on it myself. Every day they let you stay out was the chance at more money in the bank, more padding between you and hard times, and when they said stop, you had to stop. We had all agreed to the management of the fishery, more or less, even though I'd heard Pete say more often than not he felt like the puppet at the hands of men in clean clothes.

I tucked up against Drew that night with a stupid grin on my face. Puppet or not, we'd made two grand. I kissed his still shoulder. "It's going to be better out here, Drew, I promise," I whispered.

~

I was back in the pit by four a.m., hauled in fourteen more in the first few hours, and then hit a dry spell. Pete had not said a word to me since I'd shoved my lunch trash at him the day before. I was standing in the pit watching the tide wreak havoc on the surface of the water, pushing and pulling in what seemed like all directions at once, when the wheelhouse door flung open. "Tender's anchored up in Scout's Bay, let's hit it up and get out of here." The door swung shut before I had a chance to say anything back.

I pulled and stored the gear as we motored past a seiner off the cape, hauling his huge net of thrashing salmon on board. In the wheelhouse, I hung my gloves inside out on the twine above the stove. The wind was tossing rain hard at the windows. The stove had the wheelhouse nice and warm. Drew had some sort of dinosaur face-off happening on the table.

"Hey, buddy." I kissed him on the forehead and sat down across from him.

"Hi." His face was drawn and still.

"What's up?" I asked.

He ignored me.

Pete turned us toward Will's tender. Always good to off-load when you were close to a tender. Save yourself a trip to town and time away from hauling in fish. "We'll fish Bently Cove the next few days, see what's going on. Then we'll check out Poor Man's Bay and then loop around to Whiskey Point." He adjusted the throttle, steered into the passing ferry's wake, so we didn't take it on the beam.

"I was thinking Sour Rock after we off-load fish."

Pete said nothing. Drew scrambled up onto the table to chase a carrot that had rolled off his plate in the heavy chop. Balanced on all fours, he overcompensated for the roll of the *Sarah Louise*. He tossed forward, and I reached out and caught him and the carrot. He settled back into the seat across from me as I put the carrot back on his plate, where it was sure to roll off again.

The silence between Pete and I pulled thin and tight, giving me a headache. It was a good thing that Mom wasn't here to see what our relationship had deteriorated into. Drew only mumbled back answers to the questions I asked about the dinosaurs, his shoulder pulling slowly, once, twice, three times. Four times, five times. His barometric pressure dropping, the storm building.

He moved down to the lower bunk in the focsle, where Pete had left a set of wrenches, a hammer, and a power drill for him. I followed Drew down, double-checked that Pete had remembered to take the bit out of the drill, and kissed Drew on the forehead again. He was drilling a dinosaur.

"Hey, mister? You okay?" My mind rolled into all sorts of dark corners. Had something happened when I wasn't paying attention? Had Pete taken his anger at me out on Drew? "Anything you need to talk about with me?" I asked him in a whisper, down on my knee next to the lower bunk.

He shook his head, keeping his eyes on the dinosaur surgery.

"Want to come out on deck with me?" I asked him.

He shook his head, his mouth in a hard, straight line.

"Is it just that Pete's in a bad mood and you can tell?"

He nodded once.

I stood, watched him for a minute, flicked a glance over at Pete, whose back was to us. I'd have to do better than this. It was a small space to have two of the three people actively hating each other.

Out on deck, I got everything ready for the tender. The rain was a hazy curtain blowing across the hard, stony water. It was days like this that defined Southeast Alaska, days like this that defined me.

But Pete didn't loop over the top of Dog Island toward Scout's Bay. He turned us into a narrow cove.

I stuck my head in the house. "What's up?"

"This looks interesting," Pete said, his eyes on the water through the front windows.

"Why isn't the fish finder on?"

"It's not all about depending on flashy screens, Ellie."

"Turn it on," I said. "This is no time to fuck around," I added, forgetting my earlier proclamation to attempt peace. Pete had a theory that when there were no screens distracting him, he could sense the fish. It was bullshit. Ninety-nine percent of the time, he used the fish finder just like everyone else.

He glanced back, his yellow-bruised face and flat look daring me to cross the line. I held his gaze, held my ground, until he reached over, eyes still on me, and flicked the fish finder on. The screen came to life, began its distinctive scan from right to left, illuminating on its first pass a towering thundercloud that meant we were in the middle of a huge mass of fish.

"Holy shit!" I breathed, spun on my heel, and raced back to the pit. I got the gear in the water in record time and caught twenty-six more fish across the afternoon and early evening.

Around dinnertime, I tossed the old buoys we used as bumpers over the side of the *Sarah Louise* as we sidled up to the tender.

"Ellie!" Will hollered as I tossed him a rope. "Fucking glorious out here, huh?" He smiled big and bright as the wind blew rain at us sideways in slapping gusts, the sea and the sky all melted into one reaching gray mass.

"I love it!" I said over the piercing calls of the gulls waiting for handouts or a back turned. And I did, I always had.

The end of Will's beard disappeared into the collar of his wool shirt. He hitched up one strap of his bib overalls. "Working in town's for losers," he added as he reached into the cooler he kept on deck and tossed me an ice-cold Budweiser. I caught it, held it up in a salute, cracked it open, and drank half in one long swallow.

"How's it going anyways?"

"Pete's grouchy as fuck."

He laughed and tossed over another beer. "Maybe that'll help."

"Maybe," I agreed.

~

Once Will and I finished off-loading the fish, I drank Pete's beer so he wouldn't, while Will got the paperwork together.

"Looks like $4,125, Ellie," he reported. "Can Pete make it up here to sign for it? I hear he's banged up pretty good."

"He can make it. I'll go get him."

Before I was all the way into the wheelhouse, Pete asked, "How much?" He'd been keeping Drew occupied and out of the way of the operations on deck.

"$4,125. We need to refuel," I said, even though I knew he knew. We'd left Kings Creek with hardly any fuel on board because neither of us had any money to purchase it. "After fuel, ice, and more groceries, we'll have about thirteen hundred left."

"Kings are in thick," Pete countered, even though his voice suggested defeat. "You hauled in forty today, double the average catch per day of the last opener. We're killin' it. Don't forget to figure that into your equation." He was sinking into himself and pulling me down with him.

Drew had climbed out of the bunk and had thrown himself into my legs. "I want to go home. I want Marshall," he wailed. As the crying escalated to screaming, the shoulder started up.

Pete said, "Sometimes I miss my friends when I'm out here too."

I was too embarrassed to tell him that Marshall was not real, that Drew didn't have any friends.

Drew hung from my pants, his tear-stained face flung upward at me. "Why can't we have a TV?" His shoulder was picking up, drawing and holding Pete's attention.

"A TV?" Pete said to me.

"I want to watch!" Drew's screams jabbed into my brain, escalating the headache.

"Drew, stop. Come help me hang up my rain gear in the engine room." I tried to peel him off my legs.

"NO!" he shouted. Drew collapsed on top of my feet. I dropped my head back, eyes closed for one second, and then scooped him up. He wailed for all he was worth as I carried him down to the focsle. It was one thing to poorly parent, it was another to do it in front of another adult.

I tucked us both in the bunk as Pete headed up to sign. I let Drew wail some more, tried to talk him down without any luck, and eventually held him until he cried himself to sleep. Hot tears leaked from my eyes. Why did I not know how to do this better by now? Drew elicited as much love as he did overwhelm, from deep inside me. One inextricably linked to the other.

When Drew's breathing deepened and slowed, sleep tugging at me, I gave in.

When my alarm went off at 3:45 a.m., I sat up confused. I'd slept through the night? I covered Drew with the sleeping bag, pulled on an extra layer, and climbed the three stairs to where Pete sat steering.

He had coffee going, and he threw me a tight grin from the skipper's chair. I poured myself a cup of coffee, added extra cream, and peered out in front of the boat. Recognizing the narrow, winding channel by the plastic pink flamingos someone had stuck in a tree fifteen years ago, I said, "Fishing Amber Point this morning?"

Pete didn't look over. He nodded once, a slow closing of his one less swollen eye.

I got the deck ready to go in the predawn light. While I'd slept the night before, Pete had refueled in Jamestown and driven us through the night. Two days of fishing after an office job had me sleeping so hard, I'd somehow slept through the refueling. An impossibility I couldn't wrap my head around. I slept light in town, tossed and turned, woke up more tired than I'd been the night before.

Pete hadn't said much of anything other than what gear he wanted set since the day before. On a bathroom break, I heard him laughing with Drew. Instead of rushing back out on deck, I washed the few dishes in the sink, just to be around it. I tried to work out why it mattered, how I could possibly care after all that he'd done to destroy everything since Mom died. Somehow, the unhindered sound of Pete's laughter jumped me over all that and led directly back to where we'd started. Me perched where Drew now sat, Mom making sandwiches, Pete's teasing, Mom's quick comeback, both of them laughing at each other. Each of us puzzled together in this small space.

Drew sat cross-legged in his spot by the windows, looking pleased. He'd apparently boomeranged himself out of the depths he'd reached the night before. Pete was leaned back in the skipper's chair, a wide grin on his face. "Good one, Drew." Pete pointed to a seagull off by himself. "And how about that guy? What's his deal?"

What's His Deal was one of the many games Pete had made up as a way for he, Mom, and I to pass the time. I watched Drew consider the seagull, who was off on his own, and it occurred to me perhaps Pete had drawn him out of the darkness.

"Well," Drew said. "He said that word you like to say, so his mama put him in a really long time-out."

Both Pete and I laughed, and the look on Drew's face was so hopeful, it almost broke me in two. The bell rang and I left them to it.

Within fifteen minutes, we were in the fish. It was lining up to be the best day yet. The bell was clanging nonstop, the lines were full, and I was happier than I'd been in a long, long time. Pete popped his head out at some point, widened his eyes at the number of fish, and yelled, "Whoo-hoo!!!" before hobbling back in. I breathed into his mood swing, relieved to see it. I worked as fast as I could, every hook full, me running from one side of the pit to the other. In this case, Mom would've been on one side running lines while I ran lines on the other. I fell into the old rhythm, handlining, a quick twist of the wrist to spin the gaff, the smooth arc of the shoulder to fling the fish into the boat, the sound of the gurdy reeling in the next. Hook after hook, fish after fish. This was going to work. We were going to save the *Sarah Louise*. We were going to save ourselves.

When the bells fell silent, I set to work cleaning. Pete appeared again, his eyes running over the salmon I'd hauled in, Drew piled up against his legs. Pete tapped his finger at the air as he counted. "Twenty-two! Ellie! It's not even lunchtime!"

My mind rolled out ahead of us, multiplying days by kings by cohos by weeks. It was going to work. We were going to make it. Unless. I looked over at Pete. Unless there was more to the story. There was always more to the story when it came to Pete.

"Who is this new bookie anyways?" I peered at him across the deck of the boat.

"Drives a harder bargain than Hank ever did," Pete said, his face settling into an unreadable mask. "That's for sure."

"What exactly happened to Hank?" Cold iced up my spine as my brain filled in all the possibilities.

Pete shrugged. "Dunno. No one's seen him in two, maybe three, years now. It was strange. He was there one day, gone the next, and this new guy was reaching out to say if you're betting, you're betting with him. He stays hidden, sends guys out to collect and pay out in Sitka, Juneau, Kings Creek, some of the smaller towns too."

"Sends out other guys to cut off your fingers one by one if you don't pay up." I was mostly kidding but also starting to wonder just how sketchy this new guy might be and if I'd already gotten myself and Drew too close to all of it.

"Yeah." Pete looked away. Took a deep breath. "Something like that."

He turned and disappeared into the wheelhouse, leaving me with a spreading hot dread.

Chapter 8

Later that afternoon, Drew stood in the open wheelhouse door and watched me work at the cleaning table. My mind had been circling around this new organized southeast crime syndicate, and it had slowed me down significantly. How far in was Pete? How far would these guys go to get the money he owed them? It didn't take long in the underworld of Alaska before you got mixed up in meth. It suddenly felt as though we were trolling right into the heart of darkness.

I'd hardly made a dent in the stack of fish in front of me. The bell was still ringing, but only every so often. I focused on Drew. Felt all in a rush the way I would do anything to protect him. "Want to come help me, buddy?"

He shook his head, a fearful look skittering across his face as he took in the roll of the boat, the open ocean behind me.

"Maybe just sit here?" I pointed to a small perch outside the pit. "And keep me company?"

He considered me for a moment.

"It's not so bad out here," I added, as I moved a cleaned fish to the group ready for the hold and slid another one into the cleaning tray.

He took one tentative step out onto the deck, his eyes creased with worry.

"You need your life jacket on to be out here."

He disappeared and I figured that was that. I got back to cleaning fish.

Drew reemerged in rain pants, a sweatshirt, and a life jacket.

"Hey, buddy!" I called out, setting down my knife and climbing out of the pit. I yanked on the straps at his midsection to make sure the life jacket was good and snug. I took his hand and led him toward a spot where he could sit out of the rain and be close by. "Maybe you could be in charge of the hose?"

He shook his head and held tight to my hand as we crossed the rain-soaked deck.

"Okay. How about you sit right here, and we'll just hang out while I clean fish?"

He nodded, his eyes bouncing from one part of the deck to the next. "Sit right here, okay?" I tapped a spot on the edge of the pit that was not close to any hooks or knives. Drew sat down and pulled his hands into his lap.

He watched as I picked up the knife and balanced the next salmon in the tray. His shoulder pulled once, twice, when he recognized a fillet knife.

"It's alright. A fillet knife is a tool made for a specific function. Which isn't opening cheese." His eyes snapped to my face, a look like maybe he was about to get in trouble creasing his forehead. "It was my fault that it was out when you were trying to open the cheese. Actually, it was smart to try it. You needed something sharp, and it was right there, but it turned out to be a little too sharp, right?"

He nodded his agreement, his back like a board, refusing the sway of the boat. I bit my lip. A jagged terror that he may not ever like it out here ripped through me. Why was I even doing this? If we somehow made fifty grand, was fishing the *Sarah Louise* going to be one more uncomfortable thing that I forced upon him?

"Want to see something cool?" I asked.

Nothing else about him moved, but his eyes tracked me closely.

"Do you see this?" I pointed at the bulging stomach of the fish in the cleaning tray. "I'll bet he just had lunch."

Drew's face hardened and then cracked as I sliced open the belly, removed the stomach, sliced it open, and pointed at the half-digested herring inside.

He continued to stare at me.

We both turned at the sound of gulls squabbling overhead, their piercing frustration cutting through the droning of the engine.

"You know," I said, taking a deep breath as I finished cleaning the fish, "there was this story once about a fisherman who found a herring gull in town with a broken leg. He made a little cast and fed the bird."

Drew was watching me closely. Mountaintops etched the sky behind him, and I felt a rush of happiness to be right here with him. "The bird's leg healed, but it never left. It hung out around his house, squawked at him anytime he was outside. And when the fishing season started, the bird followed the guy out to the grounds." Drew's eyes widened. "He flew right alongside the boat out of the harbor and out into the Sound. He would perch on the hayrack and talk and flap while the guy ran lines. The gull would take off sometimes, but he'd always come back and hang out on the boat with the guy and his dog."

Drew's posture softened. He was allowing the boat to pull him slightly in one direction and then rock him back the other. "What was the bird's name?" he asked.

"Annie O'Reilly."

Drew squinted at me. "That's a strange name for a bird."

"I know. Want to hear the rest of the story?"

"Yes."

I placed the cleaned fish into the bin and held up the hose for Drew. He wrapped his bony fingers around it one at a time. "Just give the tray a good rinse, so I can clean the next fish."

He scooted himself closer to the cleaning tray, the flowing hose held out with one straight arm. "What if I spray you?"

I cringed. I'd been too harsh, too quick to lose my temper, and here was the result. "It's okay. My rain gear will keep me dry."

"What if I can't get it all out?" He threw a concerned look at the guts and blood splattered all over the tray.

"Just do the best you can. You'll do a good job." I turned away so that he wouldn't feel watched. As I reached for the next fish in the bin that needed to be cleaned, the bell rang. I engaged the gurdy, unclipped leader after leader until I had the right one, handlined it in, stunned and gaffed it, and swung it up and over the stern. Drew had climbed into the pit at the other end to reach the cleaning tray better. Water splashed all over his boots from the hose. With serious eyes, he watched the fish as it flopped and struggled in the sorting bin. I twisted the hook loose and delivered the killing blow. I waited for the freak-out. He raised the hose and tilted his head as he rinsed out the cleaning tray. He said, "What's the rest of the story?" And just like that, we were fishing together.

I let the breath I'd been holding rush out of me. "One day a sea lion hauled out on the back deck. His boat was different from ours. He had a flat shelf at the stern, here." *Ours.* The word felt so right.

Drew looked over with wide eyes. "The sea lion was on the boat? That's not good."

I shook my head. "The dog went crazy, barking and lunging at the sea lion. The sea lion squared up, ready to fight."

Drew kept the hose in the tray, but his full attention was on me now, his mouth slightly ajar.

"And just when the sea lion was about to bite right into the dog's neck, Annie O'Reilly landed on the sea lion's head and pecked at its eyes, which made it dive back into the ocean."

"She saved the dog."

"She did." I smiled. The stories of my childhood rising like smoke into his.

~

At dinner that night, I shoveled spaghetti in while listening for the next bell as we trolled. It was only seven p.m., but Drew had nodded off, slumped against me at the table. I was so hungry, I'd decided not to move him until I'd finished my food. He'd spent most of the afternoon out on deck with me, manning the hose.

Pete sat in the skipper's chair, a bowl of pasta balanced on his casted arm, in a wool shirt he'd cut the right arm out of. "You're right, Ellie," he said. The familiar space of the wheelhouse suddenly felt jumbled and erratic. The noise of the engine rattled between us. "Least I can do is let you decide where we fish."

Drew shifted against me and pulled in a ragged breath. "Better get that kid in bed," Pete said, getting his good leg under him and hopping stiffly over to the sink with his bowl. "Pull the gear when you're done. I'll take the first watch so we can run through the night to Sour Rock. We'll fish there first thing in the morning. That's always been a good spot, and we'll end up there right at sunrise. No sense wasting the night on the hook, given the pressing circumstances."

I nodded at Pete, unable to say anything more. This was what I'd wanted, wasn't it? But he seemed so diminished by it.

I got Drew settled in the bunk, kept the lines in the water until dark, spent another hour cleaning and packing fish, and then climbed in after him around eleven p.m. I'd have three hours to sleep before Pete woke me up for my turn at the wheel. I nuzzled my nose between the wings of Drew's shoulder blades and fell fast asleep.

~

I woke up to something big and heavy striking the bow somewhere close to my head. I flew over Drew's sleeping form and ran up the stairs into the wheelhouse.

Pete was throttling back to neutral, up on his good knee in the chair, trying to see directly in front of the boat, which wasn't possible given the angle and the overcast, rainy night. He was swinging the spotlight in large arcs across the water, but mostly it was illuminating the heavy rain. He didn't look over, only said in a clipped voice, "Dead head. Check the focsle and bilge for water. Right now."

When the towering spruce and hemlock trees on the edge of the beach blew over, the bigger tides often picked them up and carried them out. Most were large enough to ram a hole through the bow of a wooden boat. The loose logs floated at the surface, hard to see in the day, impossible to see at night.

As I dropped back down the stairs, I checked on Drew first, who was still sleeping soundly. "Watch him," I said to Pete over my shoulder, meaning, *Get to him before the water does.*

"I will," Pete said, knowing exactly what I meant.

I grabbed the flashlight secured to the wall of the focsle and scanned for any visible damage or leaking. Nothing. I scrambled back to check the bilge. No more water than normal.

"Ellie!" Pete called from behind me at the same time as another deafening thud sounded off the hull.

I rushed back up the steps.

"I need you out on the bow. We're in a tide rip. There's more. Hurry up, goddamn it!"

I grabbed one of the handheld VHF radios and a Maglite as I sprinted out the wheelhouse door in my wool socks. Pete was already talking as I switched it on. "I need a safe direction to head. We need out of this."

I leaned out over the bow as far as I dared, the wet rail digging into my stomach. The rain was cold against my face, cold down the back of my neck. Even though the possibility was small, we rarely traveled at night for this very reason. The waves slapped loud and irregular against more logs out there somewhere in the dark. My eyes skipped from the oval of the spotlight to the oval of my flashlight. The rain was pounding the surface of the water, splashing up while at the same time falling down. And then the dark sheen of a two-foot-wide trunk, floating.

"Rudder ten degrees starboard!" I barked at Pete, my voice rising at the end. Pete reacted, but it wasn't enough. "Thirty degrees," I shouted into the handheld. This sort of thing had never been my job before. I wasn't sure how to judge, and the night was filled with water, blurring my vision. There wasn't enough time for Pete to correct. I braced as the heavy dark log clipped the bow of the *Sarah Louise*.

Pete cussed on impact, loud enough for me to hear through the walls of the wheelhouse. It had always been Pete out on deck, me or Mom inside following instructions when it came down to something like this. Something like sinking. I fought the desire to be safe in the wheelhouse, following instructions instead of giving them. My sweatshirt hung heavy with rain, hair plastered to my neck and face.

Pete dropped us back into neutral, waiting for me to tell him where to go. The water churned and punched beneath me as I hung over the rail even farther. My mind wanted to race, wanted out, but I forced it to concentrate on what I could sense as much as what I could see in the chaotic water. There was something ahead, twenty feet off our starboard bow. "To port, Pete," I said. He engaged the engine and tentatively moved us to port. "Give it a little bit more," I said in as controlled a way as I could manage.

He did, and the dark mass of log slid by ten feet off our starboard side. I took a deep breath and said, "Back to neutral."

The tone of the engine changed immediately as I returned to scanning the water, my hands cold and shaking. "Hold on," I said into the handheld, praying that there was nothing else out there. "Slow to port," I instructed, my stomach knotting at the idea that there was something else out there we were now headed straight toward. Another black mass, way too close. "Back off!" I yelled. "Turn twenty degrees starboard!"

Pete followed my instructions, and the log slipped past us. I let go of the breath I'd been holding and scanned the water as Pete returned to neutral. "Slow to port," I said again, shoving at the way my own fear wanted to rise up in the black night. Pete shifted back into gear, and the water started moving slowly underneath me. Another black mass floated by in silence, then the sea opened up wide and clear. I stayed out to make sure it remained that way. Eventually, the sky was orange and I was shivering and Pete was knocking on the glass at me.

When I stepped back into the wheelhouse, soaked to the bone, Pete was restowing our three survival suits next to the bunk where Drew still slept. My eyes locked onto the small one. Pete hobbled his way back up into the house, laid a hand on my shoulder, and squeezed. The first time we'd touched since the winter Mom died. "I wish she could've seen you get us out of that," he said, a tired smile on his broken face. "You did great, Mo."

Chapter 9

Pete got the coffee going while I changed into dry clothes and dropped the gear in the water. We fell into a rhythm over the next three days, a reprieve from whatever had been gathering between us. Lines in the water by daybreak at four a.m., in bed by eleven p.m.; thirty-nine kings, forty-two kings, thirty-five kings. We bought ice and groceries with the money from the first sale. I was pushing my body to its limits, but it felt true and proper. Town life was sloughing off me and Drew.

Pete had taken to dropping a hand to Drew's shoulder to calm it. Drew had been spending more time with me on deck. We'd be ready to sell fish again soon, and this time the check would be for somewhere around ten grand. Pete was monitoring the radio day in and day out, waiting for any news from Fish and Game. It seemed likely they'd give us another four or five days before they closed the fishery. If we kept up the pace and everything continued to line up, we could potentially be sitting on twenty-five grand before Fish and Game closed kings and we started fishing cohos. Kings were worth three times per pound what cohos were, and each was twice as big, so we'd need the remainder of the season to make the rest of the money catching cohos, but we'd be in good shape entering the coho fishery.

On the fourth day, when I climbed up the stairs in the early-morning hours, Pete said, "You don't look so great."

I sloshed coffee and creamer into a broken-handled mug. The thick liquid slid down my throat and enabled me to feel a little more ready to step out into the cold, drizzly rain.

"You don't look like a million bucks either," I said. "I had terrible dreams."

"Me too," Pete said, peering out at the hazy line between water and sky, his good hand loose on the wheel. "That we didn't catch any fish today because you got the gear in late."

I downed the rest of my coffee and threw him a look of pain before I stepped out on deck. I forced my cold, complaining muscles to lower me into the pit, to set the gear and haul the first fish, but I couldn't find my rhythm. The sea mimicked my jarred movements, flowing up and over itself, forming a thick chop on top of the steady rollers. The fish were off the bite, not hitting any of the gear that I continued to switch out on my own, eliminating the step where I typically checked in with Pete, trying to find what might draw the fish in. Pete left me alone while he did his part studying the fish finder, charts, and tide tables.

Sometime after lunch, Pete drove us into the fish and I got the combination right. A syncing of our skill sets instead of full dependence on his, as I began to pull them in, one sleek silvery body at a time. Around noon, the fish disappeared, and the air felt different. Drew was back on the hose on the other side of the pit, taking his job very seriously. I kept my eyes on the sea, felt it gathering.

"Look!" I said, pointing at the humpback spouting twenty feet off our starboard rail. The harsh burst of breath rose high in the air. The misty gray plume blew straight into us.

"That stinks!" Drew yelled, eyes light and smile wide as he wiped his arm across his face and looked out beyond the stern where it blew again. "He needs to brush his teeth," he said, turning back to his hose when the fluke flashed, signaling a deep dive. I laughed.

Drew looked up, the entire front of his life jacket soaked. I smiled down at him as I wiped the sweat, rain, and whale breath from my forehead. "I love being out here with you, Drew."

He went back to his task of rinsing all the guts and blood out of the sorting bins and cleaning tray, his tongue pinning one corner of his lips in concentration. Less than a half hour later, a short, sharp wave smacked the side of the boat, out of rhythm with the others.

"Drew?"

He looked up at the change in my tone.

"Time to go in, 'kay?"

"Okay, Mama."

I helped him out of the pit and held his hand across the deck.

Pete looked up as we came in.

"I don't like the look of things out here, I'm pulling the gear," I said.

Pete nodded over his shoulder, then turned his attention back to the harsh consonants of the weather forecast coming from the marine radio that was confirming what we both already knew.

I hauled and stowed the gear, then ducked back into the wheelhouse to check the weather report before I started cleaning the remaining fish. "Supposed to get worse?" I asked.

"Yeah. Winds out of the south. Thirty-five, up to fifty."

I stepped up next to him and peered into the blurry swirl of rain and sea.

"What do you think?" he asked.

I stared at him. A clear shift of authority. Him handing it over. Marbled Inlet was long and thin and the best anchorage in a strong south wind. Coot Bay was much closer, but more exposed. I watched the wind on the water, gauged the waves, calculated how much time before it became intolerable, thought of Drew's small body, realized for the first time that perhaps I had been a part of Pete's calculations all those years, and said, "Let's head for Marbled Inlet."

Pete nodded once his agreement.

"Let me just finish up cleaning and packing, and then I'll take the wheel. You can go put your foot up," I offered. His broken leg wasn't supposed to bear weight for another few weeks. He got around the boat with a hop swing involving his one good leg and his one good arm, but he'd get tossed and catch himself with his bad foot often enough that his toes, where they stuck out of the cast, were swollen up like angry purple-red sausages.

"Great idea," Pete said, his voice a little tight. He reached down to help Drew, who was scrambling to get up into his lap.

"Can I drive, Pete?"

"Grandpa," he corrected.

~

An hour later, Pete hobbled his way down the three stairs and passed out in the focsle bunk. I dug out some coloring books for Drew, got him set up at the table, and then settled myself in the skipper's chair, feeling satisfied instead of lost. Fish nestled in the hold, more days like this one to come, potentially, after the storm passed through. I leaned up against the idea that Pete and I together were going to right his wrong. I watched Drew's still shoulder as he bent over his coloring book. Maybe this was what he needed all along. Maybe this would ease me, and therefore him.

~

Forty-five minutes later, Drew made his exasperated sound as he slid out of the booth seat to chase yet another crayon that had rolled fast enough to jump the lip of the table. The waves continued to stack up tighter, and Drew was scrambling around the wheelhouse, chasing crayons more than he was coloring. When the coloring book slid off the table and across the floor, I said, "Why don't you put the crayons away and work in your workshop?"

Drew moved down to the bunk and opened up his boat machine shop, fixing one imaginary stranded member of the fishing fleet after another. Pete's rhythmic breathe-snoring competed for attention with the sound of the rain beating against the wheelhouse windows and the omnipresent rumble of the diesel engine.

The wind spent the next hour building faster than I thought it would. Drew played, but looked up at me more often as the wind heeled us hard to port and the roll of the boat became harder to anticipate.

I tried to appear as relaxed as I could, reminding myself I'd seen foam converge into straight lines across building waves a hundred times before. I double-checked the distance to Marbled Inlet and let my eyes linger for a minute on the image of the bay on the chart, overlapping that with the memory of the steep, sheer walls, the way the bay tucked up behind them, shielded from the wind. It would be better than Coot Bay. I'd made the right decision. I glanced at my watch. Only, we'd be in Coot Bay by now, instead of out here in the weather.

The wind was now topping out above forty knots. Perhaps we should've taken our chances dragging anchor in the less protected bay. I shook my head. A good skipper makes quick decisions. I knew that. I took a deep breath in and let it out slowly. We were making ground, plowing our way toward safety. I glanced over at Drew, who met my eyes with a question in his.

"We're good, buddy," I said to both of us, echoing Mom's long-ago voice in my head. In all those storms we went through together, she did nothing to fight the wind or the motion of the water. She seemed happiest, in fact, to let it define everything.

What should've been an hour trip stretched into two as we made our way diagonally through the wide channel toward the north end of Shaw Island where Marbled Inlet lay. As the wind and waves built, I struggled to keep the wind in the sweet spot. Not too close to the beam in order to control the roll, and not too close to the stern, which would walk the stern in the following seas. I planted my feet wide and used my tall, solid frame to keep the wheel steady, to keep us on course as best I could as the boat labored at a snail's pace. I kept checking the chart and my instruments to reassure myself that we were still moving forward. A deep well of fear that I had never known before having Drew darkened the edges of my vision. If anything ever happened to him . . . My mind exploded into small ineffective pieces.

The wind continued to build, gusting up to fifty knots now.

"Mama." Drew's voice was thin. "I don't feel good."

I couldn't let go of the wheel to go to him. "It's okay, Drew, this happens sometimes. Is it your belly?"

"Uh-huh," he whimpered from the bunk, Dog squeezed tight to his chest.

"It'll get better once we're anchored." There was a good chance we'd still be bounced around on the hook, but it would be a lot better than this.

As we neared the north end of Shaw Island, I had to point the bow more to the north, which made the wind hit us directly on the stern. It was nearly impossible to control the boat in the following seas. We picked up speed, but the boat sloshed and spun under us.

I flinched when the large black Maglite hit the floor and rolled with great speed from one side of the wheelhouse to the other. Pete was immediately hauling himself up the stairs, squinting, curls flattened on one side. He took one look out the windows, and his cheek twitched.

I stole quick glances at him as he ran his eyes over the instrument panel and screens, then peered out into the mass of wind and waves, combing the hazy shore, looking for a familiar landmark. His fingers flexed at the end of his cast, an involuntary searching of his hand for the wheel. A sharp need to hand it over ran through me, to be done with the responsibility of it all, but then something even bigger followed. The knowledge that I was working toward a new role and I would fill it. Another gust of wind and rain heeled us harder to port, and Drew cried out.

"It's okay, buddy," I said to him over my shoulder. "We'll be there soon." I cleared my throat against the slight waver that had made it into my voice.

Pete tightened his fingers over the terminal end of his cast and flattened his mouth into a tight line. "Looks like you're a couple miles out from Marbled?" he asked, his eyes full of the same single-mindedness I felt. There was no getting out of the situation we were in, there was only getting through it.

Pete's eyes returned to the chart plotter, and I knew his mind was running through different scenarios, weighing the decisions that had already been made, considering decisions still ahead. He met my eyes, and I understood we would get through this one minute at a time, just like we'd gotten through plenty of other situations out on the fishing grounds. Drew cried out again, the fear in his voice reaching out like a hand, wrapping its cold fingers around my throat.

Bracing himself against the wall, Pete hop-jumped back down the stairs. He piled in the bunk headfirst in a way that caught Drew's attention. "You ever heard of a roller coaster, Drew?" Pete asked. "People down south build these huge rides just to feel like this. To see if they are as tough as fishermen like you and me." He laid down as calm as could be, and Drew curled up next to him. "I used to tell your mom this story of William the bottle-nosed dolphin. He gets in trouble a lot. Do you want to hear it?" Pete asked as Drew threw an arm across Pete's wide chest and buried his face against Pete's neck.

The *Sarah Louise* dug in as we climbed the next steep wave and then slid down the backside of it. There was a moment of reprieve in the deep trough between waves before the boat shuddered violently as the bow smashed into the next wave, and we powered up and over it. The boat strained under my feet. All I could think about was the back of Marbled Inlet, the innocent curve of Drew's neck, the way the wall of mountains surrounding the bay on three sides would shelter us from the open water that seemed deeper than it ever had before.

Chapter 10

"Mama!" Drew screamed just before he puked.

Pete's soothing words sounded far away as he cleaned up Drew, rinsed the puke bucket, and set it back within reach. I closed my eyes, the muscles in my back and arms locked against the way the boat wanted to slide off course, as if I could physically keep us on the shortest route toward safety. Outside was a mass of gray water and gray sky and blowing rain in between. When the next explosive wave slammed down over the stern, Drew screamed. The boat lurched in and out of control. Pete's tone continued at a strong steady pace, a mumble of words that settled both me and Drew.

I checked the chart for the hundredth time. Drew threw up again. The smell, combined with a quick, sharp toss of the boat to starboard, made my stomach seize. We were close. I squinted through the smear of rain and sea, trying to make out the narrow entrance. I thought I saw it, and then wasn't sure as the clouds blew through so low it was impossible to tell water from sky. The dull gray of the summer night was further disorienting.

The low clouds shifted, and the entrance was there, ahead. I widened my stance and gripped the wheel, bracing for the turn. "Hold on," I yelled. The entrance was narrow, the timing of the turn important to keep us off the rocks on the far shore.

"Keep an eye on that far side," Pete said.

"I know," I yelled back. Pete was up and moving around down below. I fought the wind, trying to keep us on course, as close to the shore as I dared, in order to make the turn as quick as possible. The rocky shoreline to our starboard side disappeared and reappeared behind the dense curtain of blowing rain.

Pete was out of the bunk, standing next to me holding Drew, both feet firmly planted, his voice pulled tight and thin as he strained to see out the front windows. Drew's arms were wrapped tight around Pete's neck, his legs around Pete's waist, his eyes searching for mine. "Mama!" he screeched and lunged for me.

"I can't hold you right now, Drew." He sagged against Pete with my refusal.

The turn needed to be early enough to compensate for how hard the wind would blow the boat toward the far north side of the entrance once we turned broadside to it, but I needed to leave myself plenty of room to clear the rocks on the close side.

Drew heaved. Pete hunched them both over the sink behind us. Drew puked again.

The long, narrow spit of the south side got closer and closer as I held course. My mind focused and everything else disappeared. We needed just a little more speed to counteract the outgoing tide.

My heart fisted as we climbed to the top of the next wave, and then I cranked the wheel hard starboard. There was a moment of stillness, a break from the tossing, before the wind hit the *Sarah Louise* full force on the starboard beam. The boat heeled violently to port. Pete lost his balance and was thrown into the table.

"Keep the throttle forward, Ellie! All the way forward," Pete yelled, clambering back to his feet, with Drew still in his arms. The *Sarah Louise* dug in, already at full throttle, the motor pushing us forward, but the wind was moving us steadily sideways, straight for the rocks.

I kept the wheel hard starboard, but the *Sarah Louise* was losing to the wind and tide. We were running out of room. I'd turned too late.

I tightened my grip on the wheel. *No! No! No!* The *Sarah Louise* and I struggled together to keep us off the rocks. The straining engine vibrated through the whole boat as it fought for ground against the wind. The jagged rocks on the north side got closer and closer. I kept the rudder hard starboard, aiming the boat toward the slightly calmer water one hundred yards ahead, where the bay opened up. I could see it, the shelter from the mountain, before a wave of water slammed into the windows with so much force I flinched at the possibility of broken glass.

I stood up on my toes as if the weight of my body could help the *Sarah Louise* move forward faster than we were being blown sideways. Through the blurry flow of water on the wheelhouse glass, I could make out the sharp ridges of rocks rising out of the water to the port side getting closer and closer.

We were among the rocks now.

Pete dropped down the stairs with Drew still in his arms, and returned with Drew's survival suit and two float coats. My mind fought the idea of cold water. Of Drew, floating. "I can steer us through," I hollered to Pete.

There was a flash of red in my peripheral vision along with Pete's words, too loud now. "Feet first, Drew. Feet have to go first." And then the rough sound of Drew being zipped into his survival suit. In nineteen years of fishing, I'd never abandoned ship.

I turned the wheel slightly to port to steer us around the closest rock. The boat's speed increased as it began to move with the wind. I was no longer aiming for the inside of the bay, I was steering us straight for shore. If I could beach it without putting any holes in the boat, there was a chance we could get the boat off the beach on a higher tide once the storm passed. I squinted into the howl of Drew and the howl of the wind, the frantic churning of the motor. We were two hundred feet off the beach, and for a second, there seemed to be a clear path to it.

Until the nearest wave was sucked out to sea to reveal the top of a rock directly in front of us. The impact crushed my ribs into the wheel. I felt the wood of the stem crush the same as my rib cage. We skipped, airborne for a moment, and then a second impact. My lungs would not take in or expel air. The edges of my vision darkened. I lunged for Drew in Pete's arms behind me. I wanted only to protect him, to keep him from whatever was coming next.

"No," Pete said, clear and sharp, inches away, shoving a float coat at me. "The inflatable first."

I spun, knowing he was right. It was the only way to keep us out of the cold, thrashing water. I whipped on the coat and pushed through the door to find the deck at a steep, slippery slant. The bow of the boat was caught on the rock, and everything was sliding toward the stern. The wind whipped my hair into my eyes. It tore at all the lines, everything shrieking in some sort of wild, unplanned chorus.

I moved as fast as I could across the inclined deck, sliding a little with each step, sick with the knowledge that there may only be a matter of minutes to get the inflatable in the water and get all three of us off the boat before it sank. With shaking hands, I wedged myself, grabbed at the knife attached to the chest of the float coat, and cut the line that held the inflatable raft in place on the hayrack over the pit. The wind immediately picked up the far edge, threatening to rip the inflatable off the hayrack and toss it overboard.

I screamed as I jumped for its bowline. Lifting my left arm caused such an intense pain, I thought I was going to black out. After missing with my left, I caught the bowline in my right hand. The wind tore at everything and the rain slammed against every surface. I tugged at the inflatable with my good right arm until the wind caught it again, and it crashed down on the deck.

Drew's "Ma-maaaa!" ripped through the open door of the wheelhouse and swirled around, mixing with the wind and the rain as I dragged the inflatable over to the rail, my left arm now useless. A large wave lifted the *Sarah Louise* off the rock. We hung there in the trough of the wave for a minute, the deck evening out before the wind and waves caught it, tossing us, but not as bad as before. There was an odd sluggishness to the movements of the *Sarah Louise* with the added weight of water in the bilge. We'd be on the bottom soon.

I lifted the bow of the inflatable over the rail with my one good arm and then shoved the rest of it over with my shoulder. The effort dropped me to my knees. The pain took on color. There was the snake of the bowline running past my head and over the side as the chop pulled the inflatable away from the boat fast. I'd forgotten to tie it off.

Pete's casted foot crashed down, pinning the line until I had it back in my hand.

"You first, I'll hand Drew over," Pete yelled directly into my ear, through the wind. I used the rail to pull myself to my feet, then tied the inflatable off. Pete had Drew in his arms, chest to chest. Drew's eyes were frantic, jumping from me to the dark, roiling water everywhere and back to me. There was so much fear in his next scream that it cleared my head.

The inflatable bucked in the water below me. I gripped the rail and tried to time my jump, but I lost my balance and fell in. I fought the up-and-down and side-to-side motion of the inflatable until I had my knees wedged in as securely as possible and then reached up for Drew, the pain in my chest wild in its cage. The inflatable bounced off the hull, surging up and down, and jerking when it reached the end of its tether. Waves slapped against the hull of the *Sarah Louise* arrhythmically, spraying salt water up, while rain came at me sideways. I was tossed in one direction and then the other. I grabbed at the bulky red of Drew as Pete lowered him down. I had his legs, and then I didn't as I was tossed with a quick and sudden force to my right. I caught the side of the inflatable at my waist, my head dunking into the cold sea.

"Drew! DREW!" I sputtered, spitting out salt water. The surface of the water chopped at steep angles around me as I plunged my arms in, searching for him.

Chapter 11

"Ellie!" Pete called from above. He'd not let go. Drew dangled in Pete's grasp, casted arm at an odd angle, both hands tight around Drew's small chest. I reached up and Drew was in my arms. We slid to the floor of the inflatable, and Pete dropped in next to me, cutting us free from the *Sarah Louise*. He grabbed the oars, trying to clear us of the heavy motion of the boat as quickly as possible. He groaned in pain as he pulled with his broken arm against the water, fighting it to get us to shore. I wrapped myself around Drew's rigid form, found his ear, and whispered over and over, "It's okay, Drew, we're alright."

Several minutes later, the inflatable ran up against the dark, rocky beach. Pete dropped the oars, jumped out, and pulled us out of the reach of the surging waves. He climbed back in, pulled Drew and me against his chest, and finally, finally, Drew's rigid body softened between both of ours.

When a sharp gust of wind blew rain hard against us, Pete and I instinctively tightened our embrace, which is when I noticed Pete was shaking with cold.

I pulled back. "You don't have a float coat on."

"Couldn't get it over the cast." His one-armed wool shirt clung to his chest, and his lips were blue.

"Shit, Pete."

"I'm fine," he said. He reached behind us and unclipped the emergency dry bag, forever stored in the inflatable. I sensed the rag doll motion of the *Sarah Louise* still out on the water but couldn't bear to glance over.

I gathered Drew into my arms, and he clung to me, his small body lost in the bulky survival suit. "There." I pointed to a huge hemlock with low-hanging branches where the forest met the beach. Pete was already hypothermic, and Drew and I were likely not that far behind.

I held Drew's weight as much as I could on my right side and slipped and stumbled toward the trees as the rain ripped up the beach all around me. I ducked under and crouched in the dry cave the branches made. His eyes were wild, full of the fear I felt but could not acknowledge. Not yet, not here. We needed to be dry. We needed somewhere to go.

"It's okay, we're okay." It felt as if I were breathing in knives. Through the thick neoprene, Drew's shoulder jerked, whiplashing his head. His eyes blinked in rapid succession and his nose twitched. The cycle repeating and then repeating again. It was the worst I'd ever seen it. I pulled him to me, heart to heart, in the way the nurses assured me calmed him as a newborn. Except now there were layers and layers between us.

"Where's Grandpa?" Drew said as I pulled at the zipper to check that he was dry in his suit. "Mama?" He twisted against me, trying to see out toward the beach, his shoulder pulling a steady rhythm.

If I could just wrap myself between him and the whole world. "Grandpa's fine. He's coming." My fingers searching for anything I could reach without unzipping so far that more water got in. I ran a rough hand around his collar, over his shoulders. "Do you feel wet anywhere?"

He ignored me. My hand was wet, so I couldn't tell. I pulled at the neck of the suit and peered inside. "Drew. You've got to be dry."

He tossed his head, trying to get away from me. I zippered him back in, deciding he wasn't soaked, and the longer he was unzipped, the more likely he was to end up that way.

Pete limped toward us, carrying the emergency dry bag, slow and unsteady. On the boat there was always something to hold on to, to aid in the hopping. Now, the cast slipped and slid on the uneven rocks of the beach. He kept his head bent to the task of staying upright, covering ground.

He'd managed to drag the inflatable ten feet up the beach, well out of reach of the grabbing waves, and tie it off to a thin alder. He appeared in fragmented pieces in between the thick, heavy branches as he made his way to our semidry cave of hemlock. He looked worn down to almost nothing, his wet clothes hanging off his thin frame, the pain a silent shout with every step.

Behind him, the wind caught the *Sarah Louise* broadside, pulling her farther away from us before wedging her up onto what looked to be a shelf of land just offshore. In a shuddering sigh, she slumped. She was open and exposed, tipped onto her port side, unrecognizable. I stared at the exposed section of hull, the part that should be underwater, and felt the enormity of what I'd just done. There was a gaping hole where the planks along the hull had been splintered and torn away when she was pulled off the rock. Either the stem or the keel or both were certainly damaged by the initial impact of the rock, and there could easily be other holes on the port side that I couldn't see from my vantage point.

Pete ducked under the branches. His face was skeletal, drained of blood and life. If he'd been at the helm, we wouldn't be here now. If he'd been at the helm, we'd be setting the anchor, figuring out dinner, falling asleep behind the protection of a solid mountain of rock.

Pete half crawled, half dragged himself over to where we sat and reached a pale hand dripping with rain to Drew's head, searching out his eyes. Drew's neoprened arm reached toward him. Pete bent and gently touched his forehead to Drew's.

"I'm sorry," I whispered to both of them.

Pete shook his head as he sat up and peered into the bay through the branches, but it was impossible to see very far through the rain. "Did you see any other boats in the bay?" He was unrolling the top of the emergency dry bag. Every year since I turned ten, it had been my job to check the batteries, food, and clothes it contained before the season started. "Ellie," Pete said to get my attention. "Where did you last see any other boats? We've got to get off this beach."

My mind was syrup, producing slow, thick thoughts that were impossible to push through.

Pete twisted the volume knob to turn on the radio. His hair dripped and his face was slick with rain. There was the bright-sounding beep of him switching channels. Drew softly whimpered against me. I wrapped him close, an ancient pull to protect his body with mine. I struggled to focus my mind. "Two seiners when we pulled the gear, another troller off Point Jack, but we weren't close enough for me to see who it was. No one in the past hour."

Pete stalled out as he brought the radio up to his mouth. How did you address yourself on the radio if you no longer had a boat? My mouth filled with a sour taste.

"Vessels near Marbled Inlet, this is the *Sarah Louise* on 16, over," Pete said into the radio.

I held my breath, focused on the way Drew was mostly dry inside the survival suit. There would be no building a fire, no plane sent from town, in this weather. It would be hours before the Coast Guard cutter could get here. How long did we have? I didn't know.

The radio crackled to life. "*Sarah Louise, Sarah Louise, Katie Anne.*"

Pete dropped his head, a small smile of relief at the edge of his mouth. "Yeah, *Katie Anne*, switch to 88?" Pete switched channels.

"You run out of booze or something, Pete?"

"Silas, you anywhere close to Marbled?"

"Tied up in Kake. You still out in the shit?"

My stomach knotted at what he was about to say over the radio to the whole fleet. It would make it real. I'd sunk the *Sarah Louise.*

"It's been a day, Si, but we're alright." Kake was the closest village, but too far away to ask Silas to come get us in this weather. "*Sarah*

Louise, out." Pete set the radio down and ran a shaky hand through his soaking hair.

"The homesteader," I said. The thick sludge of my mind beginning to move.

Pete looked up. "What?"

"Remember the story? Wasn't that here? The old guy who chased the Forest Service floatplane out of the bay with a twelve-gauge?"

Pete's face registered the memory. Very few people had met the homesteader, but we'd all heard about it. The seasonal Forest Service tech called it quits and headed back to Minnesota the day after the incident. It was all anyone could talk about in the bar for weeks. "I thought it was farther north," Pete said. He used both hands to readjust his casted leg against the gray sand. His toes were sliced and bloody from the mussels we'd just walked through.

I picked up the radio and switched it back to channel 16. "Marbled Inlet homestead, Marbled Inlet homestead, *Sarah Louise* on 16, over."

Drew shifted and his elbow caught me in the ribs. I hunched over, unable to breathe in or out as I rode the crest of the pain. Once it set me back down, I swallowed and raised the radio. "Marbled Inlet homestead, this is the *Sarah Louise*, do you read me? Over."

The rain had intensified to a steady pounding against the beach. A static of noise that matched the static of my brain.

The radio remained silent, and then a deep, scratchy voice came through. "*Sarah Louise*, this is Marbled Inlet homestead, switch to 88?" I switched over and caught the tail end of his gruff, "Marbled Inlet."

I depressed the button. "We're on the beach. North side of the entrance."

Pete's eyes caught mine in the heavy silence that followed. The radio crackled to life again. "On my way."

Fifteen minutes later, a sixteen-foot open aluminum skiff with a windscreen emerged out of the curtain of rain in the middle of the bay. The bow threw up a large, curling wave on either side of it. Pete crawled out from under the hemlock as I gathered up Drew, who had fallen into an eerie silence. My right arm supporting Drew, my left hanging limply, I hobbled toward Pete at the edge of the water as the rain pounded against everything. My side was a rubber band pulling tight against my effort to stand up straight.

Once he spotted us, the homesteader turned the skiff, running fast up to the beach and then throwing it in reverse and killing the engine as the starboard side slid up onto the beach at an easy angle.

Pete and I waded a few steps out into the water to the edge of the skiff. A strong gust of wind blew me off-balance. Pete caught me with an arm around my waist. His stance was wide and steady, his cast fully submerged underwater.

"Give me Drew, climb in, and then I'll hand him up," Pete yelled into the wind.

I nodded as he took the weight of Drew. I held on to the skiff with my one good arm as a wave lifted the water from my shins to my thighs, freezing the skin beneath.

An older man dropped a wide, powerful hand over the starboard side. When he pulled, something popped in my chest, and a garbled scream rose up and out of me and I instinctively shook out of his grasp.

"Mama," Drew wailed in response. I reached for the man's hand again, dug into the pain, and together we dragged my caved-in body on board. The older man reached over the side and took Drew from Pete and then handed him to me. I pulled him against me as I hobbled my way over to the chair next to the operator's chair, both covered by the windscreen. With the assistance of the old man, Pete was soon on board.

The small, compact white-haired man shoved the boat free of the beach with an oar as Pete eased himself down behind me. I readjusted Drew in my lap, trying to see his face. He kept his eyes squeezed closed. I wiped the rain from his face, frantic at the way he seemed to be slipping away.

"Drew," I said. "Are you okay?"

He flicked his eyes open.

"Drew?" I asked again. His eyes jumped around, not landing on anything.

The old man was suddenly next to me. His white hair was cropped close to his head. He held his arms out from his body, slightly bent at the elbows, as he peered at Drew. "Is he hurt?"

"No," I answered, my voice unfamiliar to my own ears.

"Is this all of you?" His forehead creased. "No one else on board?"

"We're all here," I said.

"What happened?" he asked, looking from me to Pete.

I couldn't think of any words, and I just shook my head. Pete didn't add anything, so the old man dropped into the driver's seat. He started the engine, threw it into gear, and spun us away from the beach in one quick orchestrated set of moves. As the stern of the skiff dug in, I turned back to look at the *Sarah Louise*. It tore at me to leave her there, on her side, broken and abandoned. I closed my eyes and bowed my head to Drew's, focused on the feel of his breath at my neck.

The outboard, the wind, and the rain were loud enough to keep the homesteader from asking any more questions as we sped toward the back of the bay. He killed the engine, beached the skiff, and pointed at an almost invisible small opening in the trees where a path started.

"Fire's going," he said. "Are either of you hurt?" He looked from my hunched form to Pete's casted extremities. "I mean, worse than you were already?" I shook my head and stood up. "How bad did you hit?" he asked.

"High on the starboard side," Pete answered. "And a dead-on hit to the stem. I don't know how bad any of it is." Pete belly-slid himself over the rail, his cast plunging into a foot of water. He reached up for Drew, and I handed him over, the sharp pull of pain in my chest almost dropping me to my knees. I ignored it, got myself over the rail, and slid down to my feet in the water. "I'll be in shortly," the man yelled, moving back to the controls, the engine roaring to life. "Follow the path there."

Pete waded to shore ahead of me, Drew balanced in his arms. Where the woods met the beach, we found a wooden walkway, fishing net stapled to the boards to give more traction. Pete limped ahead of me. "Let me take Drew," I said, and he handed him off without a word. His cast was a dull thump against the snaking path of water-soaked boards. The diffuse light of the late evening darkened as the canopy closed in, high above us.

The house was tucked up under the trees and off the beach, not visible by air or water. The path ended at the front door. Pete's good hand rattled against the doorknob, his fingers unable to close over it. I reached around him and turned the knob. "Hurry, Dad. You're way too cold."

Pete stumbled inside a wide mudroom, and I followed, closing the door behind me. I slid to the floor immediately, Drew limp against me. The knife in my side was hot and beginning to twist.

Pete bent down, and together we freed Drew of the bulky survival suit. As soon as he was out, Drew leapt toward me. I wrapped him up tight in my arms, and he buried his face in my neck. Pete's thick hand cupped the back of Drew's head. "Hey, Drew," he said.

Drew lifted his head.

"You know what I noticed out there, more than anything else?" Drew watched Pete closely, his thin shoulder pulsing. "You were so brave." Pete went on. "I couldn't believe it. I've never seen anything like it in all my days." One corner of Drew's mouth moved toward a tentative smile as Pete settled a wide hand on Drew's pointy shoulder, as if to absorb some of what Drew's body was trying so hard to shrug off. "Let's see what we've got in the dry bag, your shirt is getting wet from Mom's float coat," Pete said, reaching for the bag. I'd forgotten to add dry clothes for me and Drew to the emergency dry bag. At some point, the list of failures would get too long, become too heavy to lug around.

Pete pulled a pair of my old high school fleece pants out of the bag along with a long underwear top. "That'll work for Drew," I said. We worked together to get Drew's clothes off with only two good arms between us. My old clothes didn't smell like mold somehow. I rolled up the pant legs and sleeves until they sort of fit. Once Drew was dressed,

Pete pulled out the rest of the clothes. I remembered suddenly the way I couldn't bring myself to take Mom's extra set of clothes out of the dry bag that last season Pete and I had fished without her. It had seemed a sacrilege. Impossible. Instead, I had washed them and put them back in. It seemed Pete had continued to wash and replace not only hers but mine year to year.

I reached for Mom's thin, long underwear top, her blue Taku Fisheries wool pullover, her gray fleece pants. The float coat had kept the middle of me dry, but my pants, a wide circle around my neck, and from the elbows down were soaked. I turned away from Pete and peeled off my wet clothes. The slight twist of my torso felt like razor blades. I stayed bent over, taking short, shallow breaths as I stepped into the pants and then sat down for a break before pulling the long underwear top and pullover on. Once I was dressed, Drew climbed back into my lap, and then it was her and me wrapping our arms around him.

"It's cold," Drew whimpered.

"Let's find the woodstove." I got to my feet slowly, the pain now radiating out from my chest, climbing up the back of my skull. Pete was wrestling a pair of fleece pants over his cast. "I'll be there in a minute."

"Does he live alone? Did he say?" I asked as I moved toward the door into the house.

"Seems pretty quiet. Lights are on, though."

I took Drew's hand and pushed through the front door, which opened into one large square room, divided into two smaller rooms by furniture and function: a kitchen and a living room. In the middle was a large crackling woodstove.

"Hello?" I called. Never a good idea to startle anyone in the backcountry, much less walk into their house unannounced. The immediate heat of the room felt so good, it brought on the tears I'd been fighting to hold off. There were two rocking chairs in front of the woodstove. Once I determined no one else was around, I crossed the room to the nearest one, dragged it as close as possible to the stove, and settled myself and Drew in it. He turned in my lap, pulled his knees up, his left shoulder pulsing out his anxiety. The anxiety I'd just fueled exponentially. I looped my right arm around him and settled my chin on his head. He took a deep, slow breath in, a slight pause before the next tensing of the shoulder. "Okay," I said into that pause. "Okay."

The kitchen took up half the room with polished wood floors and clean counters. The other half served as a living space with a rug, a couch worn thin from use, and a large TV. There were no books on the shelves that lined the wall next to the couch. Instead, a messy assortment of flashlights, boot sealant, matches, tide books, binoculars, loose papers, and a fishing reel. The room had the orange glow and thin smell of propane lights.

Pete balanced himself in the doorway and then hopped over to the rocking chair next to me. "You alright, Ellie?"

I nodded, unable to bring myself to look at him. Drew's breathing dropped into a slow, steady rhythm as he collapsed into sleep. I tried to figure out what time it was. Late, by now. As Drew's shoulder relaxed, one sliver of me relaxed along with him.

"Your toes look horrible," I managed to say to Pete as he lowered himself into the rocking chair next to mine. It was the easiest of all the things I needed to say. They were a bloody mess.

"You did great, Ellie," he said. "Hell of a thing."

"I sank the boat."

He shook his head. "It's beached, not sunk."

"I missed the turn." My head ached as the needles of pain in my ribs radiated into my skull.

"You made a decision when you needed to, that's all. From there, you just deal with it as it comes. No way to tell how much an onshore wind will counteract an outgoing tide. Jesus, Ellie, we're fishermen, not magicians. Coot Bay might've been worse. Stop beating yourself up over everything. The world will beat you up plenty, without you adding to it." Pete's rough, calloused hand wrapped around my forearm. "Besides, we all three made it out."

I closed my eyes as the tears rose. When the first one escaped, Pete said, "Your only job when the shit goes down like that is to make sure everyone gets to shore. You did that."

"I would've lost the inflatable if you hadn't been there."

He leaned back in the rocking chair, adjusting his battered body, his hand still resting lightly on my arm, his voice more tired than I'd ever heard it. "That's how family works, Ellie. We're much better off when we're in the shit together."

There was the creak of the outside door and then voices in the mudroom. "Hello," a woman's voice called out. She came through the door in sock feet and fleece pants, arms loaded down with firewood that she dumped into the bucket next to the woodstove. I had a vague sense that she was old, but mostly she was ageless. As if she were leaving her mark on life instead of the other way around. She brushed wood chips off her shirt and came straight over to me. She knelt next to the rocking chair and laid a hand over mine on Drew's back. With a searching look, she asked, "Is he alright?"

I answered with a nod, not trusting myself to speak. She squeezed my hand ever so slightly, a gentleness I'd not felt since Mom died. A second round of tears gathered behind my eyes, ran down my face.

"Tea?" she asked, getting to her feet, patting my hand before she moved away. "I imagine all three of you are near hypothermic if not there already. Let's get you warmed up from the inside."

I nodded, and the woman's wide face pulled upward toward a smile. She ran both hands through the kinky gray curls that puffed out wildly in all directions from her head. "I'm Charlotte. You met Danny," she said, crossing the room to the kitchen.

I wiped quickly at the tears and turned at sounds of stomping feet in the mudroom. Danny opened the door, followed by Will's friend Van. His tall, thin frame towered over Danny. I sank back against the rocking chair, shame rising to a hot boil and blooming across my cheeks.

"This is Van." Danny pointed with his thumb. "Lives in North Bay but cut a path over here pretty quick. Though I don't like to admit it, he's pretty useful."

"We've met," I said. My eyes met Van's, and something like anger crossed Van's face, I was sure of it.

"He's—" Van started, dropped his eyes to Drew, and then had to clear his throat. "Your boy, he's alright?"

"Fine." The danger I'd put Drew in was mortifying. It was one thing to judge myself, it was another to see the horror of it reflected in a stranger's gaze. I wanted Van to go away, leave me to it.

Danny was shuffling around the shelves in the living room, pocketing one thing and then another in what was turning out to be very deep sweatpants pockets. "You hit right at the waterline on the starboard side. I circled back to look," he said, still rifling through the shelves. "Appears we could patch it and move it onto the beach on the high tide at midnight. Keep it from sinking the rest of the way. Soon as I find my damn headlamp. Charlotte!"

"I hit low also," I said. "Might be waterlogged." If I put a hole in the stem or keel with the initial hit, the whole thing was full of salt water. In which case, there would be no salvaging it.

"One way to find out," Van offered. I avoided his eyes.

Pete worked to get himself to his feet. "I'm coming."

"Me too." I used my good arm to push up from the rocking chair. Drew slipped a bit in my weak arm, causing him to cry out as I sat down quickly to catch his weight in my lap.

Charlotte appeared at my side, lifting Drew, settling him against her in such a confident way, he turned his head into the curve of her neck and closed his eyes. My mind unhinged. I allowed myself a moment of imagining Drew in the arms of his own grandmother, me in the safety of my own mother's presence. "You aren't going anywhere, except to bed with this one," Charlotte was saying as I blinked myself back into reality. "Come on, you'll take our room. I'll bring your tea in when it's ready. Me and Danny will sleep in the kids' old room."

Danny had apparently found the headlamp he was looking for and headed back out to the mudroom. He laid a hand on Pete's shoulder as he stepped past him. "No offense, Tiny Tim, but you aren't going to be any help at all."

Unable to bear any more, I allowed Charlotte to pile up extra blankets and turn back the thin sheet and quilt on the bed, all while still holding Drew. Once I slid under the covers, she gently laid him down next to me. "Thank you," I whispered as she stepped back out into the living room. Drew dropped off into sleep, my hand on his chest, the steady beat of his heart underneath.

Chapter 12

I woke to hushed voices, a strip of dim light coming through the bottom of the closed bedroom door, a full cup of tea gone cold on the stand next to the bed. Drew was sideways on the bed, face down, his head pushed up into my armpit. I ran my hand over the cobblestone of his back. Pete was right. This was all that mattered. This was the point upon which the world turned. I saw again the look on Van's face. What did he know of risk? Living out here, alone. Life as simple as it possibly could be. Heat, food, peace, and quiet. What did people without kids know about the deep, scary underside of existence?

Through the door, I could hear Pete's cadence, Van's words melting into each other, and Danny's deep voice. I was going to have to face it sooner or later.

I pushed myself up to a sitting position, and the pain pooled in my chest. Swallowing against it, I eased my feet to the floor. The small room consisted of two dressers, two nightstands, and the bed, all hand-built of wood such that inside smelled like outside.

I stood and straightened myself up slowly. Drew didn't move. I bent to kiss his smooth cheek, heard the soft rumble of his breathing, and tucked the covers around him. I slid through the door and squinted into the dim light of the propane lanterns mounted on the walls. Charlotte used the table to push herself up to standing. "There she is. You want some coffee?"

"Yeah, thanks, I can get it," I said, but she was already across the kitchen filling a mug. Guessing at the color of the dull light pushing in through the kitchen window, I asked Pete, "What time is it? Four?"

"'Bout." Pete's one good hand was loose around his coffee mug. His hair was wet and pasted to his head, which meant he'd gone along after all. Van's hands were chapped red around his coffee cup, a sign he'd just come in as well. He was hunched over, supporting himself on two elbows.

Danny patted the empty chair next to him, and I sat down in the most casual way I could manage with all eyes on me.

I was as mortified that I'd gone to sleep instead of back out with them as I was that I'd wrecked the boat in the first place. That's not what you do. You don't lie down. You stand up, dig in, and move forward.

I looked from Van to Danny to Pete. They were going to tell me I'd punctured the hull low enough that I'd flooded the whole boat, in which case it was unsalvageable and we'd need to drag it out deeper and let it sink to the bottom. Or they were going to tell me that the damage was only up high and they'd managed to float it up onto the beach with the tide. In which case, we now owned a boat that needed extensive hull repair that I didn't know how to do. Pete could repair anything on a boat, but not with two broken limbs. Even if he could, we didn't have the money to buy the materials we would need for the job, much less hire someone else to do it. I'd sunk the boat with $10,000 of salmon in the hold that would warm up and ruin in the next few days. We had $1,347 between us. Either way, it was over.

"No one's going to tell me?" I said eventually. Not that it mattered.

Charlotte set a cup of coffee in front of me before she settled herself into a chair at the table.

"We got it beached," Pete said. "Or, they did." He nodded at Van and Danny. "I stood around totally useless."

"The good news . . ." Van looked tired, but more than that, he looked like he'd been run over by life, which made it slightly less awful that he was witnessing my demise. His eyes caught mine for a second.

They were the iridescent color of sunlight on salmon. His accent shaved off the hard edges of words such that they rolled out smooth and easy. "With the boat hung up on the shelf like it was, all the water that got in ran to the back end of the boat—"

"Stern, goddamn it," Danny said with no malice. "He's a helluva mechanic, but he doesn't know shit about boats. He's a farmer."

Something like a grin passed across Van's face. "Tractors, boats, same thing." He turned back to me. "The other good news is that you remembered to cut the engine." He leaned back in his chair.

"I did?" I had no memory beyond Drew's fear, the punch of rock into wood.

Van hooked one lanky arm over the top of his chair, his other elbow resting on the table. "It was doused pretty good, but no intake of salt water as far as I can tell. I gave it a cursory freshwater rinse by hauling a few buckets, but you'll need to change all the fluids, the alternator, get it running good and hot as soon as possible to dry it out." The way his words slid into each other, the slow cadence, created a certain calm in the midst of chaos. I wanted him to keep talking, to make that place of calm even bigger.

"There's no damage to the keel?" I asked. "The stem?" If I'd punched through either, the engine would be flooded, not doused.

Pete looked even more weary. "There's damage to the stem. But, as long as we don't hit anything else, it'll probably hold the rest of the season and we can replace it this winter." His words hung in the air. At this point, it was hard to imagine there would be anything more than a tomorrow, much less a this winter.

My foot began to tap in a quick, erratic rhythm under the table.

"We appreciate everything you've done," Pete said to Van and Danny. "It's more than enough." Pete was releasing them in the way of the backcountry. You come together to help until things have leveled off, and then you get back to the demands of your own life, which have no doubt piled up while you were helping someone else.

Danny sat with his back straight, his white buzz cut immaculate. "You can't even get into the engine room, and as far as I can tell, your girl Ellie there needs a few days to rest. Busted up ribs hurt worse than buzzed-off fingertips."

"I'm headed to town later today," Van said. "You're welcome to come along, pick up what you need to get that engine going and whatever you need to fix the hole."

"Only one? How big?" I asked Pete. My mind made it small, but I'd seen it through the driving rain and heard the splintering. It wasn't small.

"Four four-foot planks."

I squinted, attempting to release the pressure that was building in my head. I turned to Pete. He looked so old. A flash of empathy struck me. He was facing the loss of the same thing I was, this time at my hands. "How much time would it take to replace the planks, Pete?"

"I'm afraid not, Mo." He shook his head in a way I'd never seen before. Slow and defeated. "We can't do the work. Look at us." His black eyes had faded to a sickly yellowish green. The thin bones of his face pushing through. "You need to get in to see Dr. Stone about those ribs, and I can't even walk. You haven't even looked her over, Ellie. I have. We're done."

I was suddenly wide awake. Giving up wasn't what we did. "The hell we are, Pete."

His eyes flashed at my tone, and relief flooded me. The spark wasn't out.

"I've watched you replace planks," I said. He never gave in. I wasn't going to let him start now.

He drooped in the chair. He shook his head again in that same crushing way. "I can't even get up a ladder."

"I can."

He shifted his casted arm, supporting it in his lap, and met my eyes. "You can't swing a mallet with broken ribs."

"They're only bruised."

"Bullshit." He sat up slowly, narrowing in on me, which meant there was a chance.

Now everyone's eyes were on me, but I didn't care. I would right the wrong. Both mine and Pete's. "How much to buy what we need for the repairs—to the hull and the engine?"

Pete's jaw set, the muscle balling. "Two, three grand."

"How long for me to replace the planks with you explaining every step?"

Pete paused a beat. "A day to gather supplies and tarp. Four to five days on top of that to replace the planks if nothing goes wrong. But there's more to it—"

"How long before a tide big enough to float the boat off the beach?"

He looked away. "Next Saturday. One week."

So, he'd already checked. "And when's the next big enough tide if we miss the one next Saturday?"

"A month out." If we were stuck out here for that long, we'd never make the fifty grand by September 20.

I bit at the corner of my lip. "We need a baseball game, two-to-one odds."

Pete's eyes cut to mine. "No, Ellie."

"We need a game today or tomorrow. As close to two to one as we can get."

Pete glared at me. "There are plenty of other options."

"I'm going to guess that you have ruined your ability to get an advance from the processor or to charge anything to your account at NAPA?"

Pete tilted his head as he took a breath and blew it out. "They might give you one."

"They'll know I'm fishing with you."

"We could ask around the fleet, see if anyone has an alternator, a starter, a few batteries lying around, some extra fir or oak for the planks—"

Just the thought of it made my face burn. "No, Pete. We've got to do this standing on our own two feet. What's the most lopsided matchup today or tomorrow?" I leaned across the table toward him, tamping down the rising unease at the idea of getting in deeper with this new bookie, but this seemed the only road out, and I was desperate to right my own wrong. It would be a clean, simple bet. I'd done this before a hundred times. Baker was a common enough name. There was a whole sprawling family of unrelated Bakers in Juneau. The bookie wouldn't connect me to Pete.

"Ellie. Drop it." Something I'd never seen before flickered on Pete's face. Was it fear? Or just the most bone-crushing weariness?

"I know you know."

Pete let out a long, slow breath. "I know because I'm a sports fan," he said in a voice gone flat. "Not because I still bet." He watched me. Weighing the options until he closed his eyes and said, "Cubs versus Padres."

"What's the pitching lineup?" I could feel the heat rising in my face.

Pete didn't say anything, just looked at me out of a face gone old overnight.

"We've got $1,300," I interrupted. "I'll buy what I can for the engine today, and I'll put the rest on the game. Two-to-one odds will give us what we need to buy the rest."

"If you win," Pete said. "Otherwise, you owe a guy money you don't have."

"Which is no different than the situation we're currently in."

Pete's top lip twitched.

"We'll launch on the tide in six days," I said. "Which gives us a little more than two months before September 20." I said a silent prayer that kings would still be open in six days. If not, we'd be relegated to cohos, making a fraction of the money we'd been making so far. That was if I could win us enough money to fix the boat in the first place.

Pete was shaking his head. "We'll also need oil, new filters, transmission fluid. Hydraulic fluid—"

"Which is why I'm going to double our money."

"I don't like this." Pete stared hard at me. "It's changed, Ellie. It's not the small-town gig it was with Hank when we first started."

"It's our only choice." I stood up to refill my coffee and glanced over at Charlotte, her face unreadable.

Danny tapped a finger against the table. I wondered if he could feel the way the heat was rising in the room also. "Why don't you take my skiff into town, Van? She'll die of pain if you spend three hours beating into town in that shitty skiff of yours. I'll take yours over to Kake." Van nodded as Danny stood. "I'm sorry I can't help you folks out much more from here. My son's crewman quit, so I'm going fishing for the next few weeks."

Pete stood, wincing as he weighted the casted leg. He reached out a hand for Danny to shake. "Thanks for all you've done."

Van asked, "You good to leave in half an hour? Might as well get going. If I lay down now, I'm liable to sleep the whole damn day."

"Yeah, sure," I said, trying to get a full breath in my lungs. I shook Danny's hand as well. "Thank you, both," I said, glancing over to include Van.

"Nothin' to it," Danny said in response.

"I need to grab a few things from the house," Van said.

Pete sat back down, sullen. "I don't like this, Ellie."

"How's it work now? Who am I calling?"

Pete looked away. He exhaled heavily. "It's all very secretive. Cops caught on a number of years back when the guy from down south ran off Hank, took over, and turned it into an empire. Cops have been trying to shut the whole thing down since, so the top guy stays hidden. You call a number, give them your bet, they'll have a guy in Kings Creek to meet up the next day to pay out or collect. You don't show up, because you owe him money you don't have, he'll start looking for you," he said in a voice drained of color.

"Has he ever done anything sketchy to you? Except for the extortion, which, granted, is a good deal for both you and him, if you look at it in a certain light."

Pete agreed with a head nod.

"Anything else? Has he ever threatened you? Manipulated odds?"

Pete looked down. "No."

"He's paid out in full every time he's owed you?"

"Yes."

"Alright, then," I said, catching his eye, trying to hide my own discomfort. "It'll be okay. It's our only option. Remember how good I am at this?" It was how I'd bought a truck that first year out on my own, how I paid for yearly cancer checks, how I'd padded out my savings account on top of whatever shit job I could find in town until I started throwing up somewhere in week eight of the pregnancy and continued throwing up almost every day until Drew was born. I'd lain on the couch, unable to work, blowing through my savings, refusing to gamble even though all I was doing was watching sports. The baby flipping and kicking made it impossible to pick up the phone and place a bet. I would not do to the baby what Pete had done to me. I would stay aboveboard, no matter what it took. And now look at me. I closed my eyes against the thought. Told myself it would just be the once, to get us unstuck, to create the situation where we had a chance to do something more with our lives, and trusted myself to stick to it.

Pete nodded. "Only place the bet if Sammy Gladstone is pitching for the Padres. That kid's got heart," Pete added.

I sighed into an old frustration. "Heart's got nothing to do with it, Pete." It was a numbers game. Math. Not heart.

"Does Drew like pancakes?" Charlotte interrupted us. "That much bread makes me bloated, but the kids used to love them. I made them at least three times a week when they were growing up."

"Drew loves pancakes." I smiled what I hoped looked like an apology for invading her space.

When I went into the room to grab extra layers, Drew was softly snoring. I ran my fingers through his fine, straight hair and kissed his forehead. I thought briefly about waking him up, taking him with me. I thought about the possible trauma of another boat ride so soon, how much he loathed being dragged around on errands in town. I thought about the stupidity of spending the last of our money buying engine supplies before we knew if we'd be able to fix the rest of the boat, and then I thought of even one day wasted and the press of September 20.

The thought of Drew and Pete spending the day together felt more right than wrong.

I took a slow breath, bent over Drew, and kissed him again. "I'll be back soon, little man."

Twenty minutes later, Van and I headed out of the bay in Danny's skiff. I could not pull my eyes from the *Sarah Louise*. They'd beached her upright, mostly, but she'd settled in at an awkward and broken slant. The smooth slope of her bow looked like a useless gesture without the water underneath her. I closed my eyes. "I'm so sorry, Mom," I whispered into the heavy drone of the outboard as we sped through the opening of the bay.

~

Three hours later, I was weak from the pounding of the skiff. Even though the chop was small, I'd felt every wave between Marbled Inlet and Kings Creek. I tied the boat up to the public dock in town with shaky hands. The rain was steady against the thick timber of the dock. Van cut the engine and hopped over the side. In an awkward silence, we turned toward the ramp that led up to the street. I scanned the docks, afraid word had already got out within the fleet.

"Three hours enough time?" Van asked when we reached the street.

I nodded. "Yeah, sure." We parted ways, and I headed down the familiar sidewalk, huddled inside my float coat, bent against the rain.

"Ell-lllie!" Will was sitting on a bench outside the cannery, drinking a Coke.

"You just off-load?" I asked.

"Yep. Now I need a bag of chips." He stood and fell in step with me as I walked in the direction of the convenience store. His belly strained against the snaps of his thick rubber raincoat. He'd cut the bottom six inches off his rain pants in a ragged line that exposed the ankles and half the shins of his brown Xtratufs.

"That beard is getting impressive again," I said to keep him from asking anything I'd have to answer with the truth. His entire chest was a fluffy, wiry white-and-gray nest.

"Keeps me warm." He threw me a sidelong glance and continued, his big feet slapping against the pavement next to mine.

"Which you need because it repels the ladies."

He laughed loud and long. "Where'd you guys ride out the storm?" he asked. "We got all ripped up out in Henry Sound on our way in to off-load. That one got me worked up. Thought I was going to yack for the first time in twenty-two years."

I slowly straightened up so that he wouldn't notice anything amiss. The last thing I wanted was for the whole fleet to hear about how I'd wrecked the boat eight days out after seven years off the grounds. It would be the one thing I'd be remembered for forever. I glanced over at Will, forcing a smile. "Marbled Inlet. Good anchorage in a south wind like that." I hated myself for not being truthful. And to Will, of all people.

"It is," he agreed.

"When you headed back out?" I asked.

"'Bout forty-five minutes. How should I spend my last little bit of shore leave?"

"You could try drying out your socks."

He grinned. "Lost cause."

"See you around, Will," I said and hoped that I would. That he would be tossing me another Budweiser soon from the deck of the tender as we off-loaded thousands of dollars of fish. That I would be able to push through whatever had broken in my chest, that I'd be able to make my hands do what Pete's knew how to do in time for the tide in six days.

"So long, Ellie." Will raised a weather-beaten hand as he pushed through the door to the convenience store, and I continued on down the sidewalk to the auto parts store.

~

After carefully pricing out what we needed at the auto parts store and at the shipyard, I walked back toward the library, chewing the inside of my cheek. It was going to be closer to three grand than two. Plus, we were basically out of fuel and groceries, having only stocked the bare essentials of both when we left town due to us both being broke.

"Hey, Ellie," Mrs. Hannah called out. Her white hair was tucked close behind her ears, and her wide waist was accented with a belt.

"Hi, Mrs. Hannah," I answered as I headed toward the farthest computer.

"Still remember those presidents?" she asked, her wet eyes twinkling.

"Of course I do." I smiled. She asked me this question every time she saw me. In fourth grade, I'd been the only student willing to rise to her challenge to memorize all the presidents in order for extra credit, which had pleased Mrs. Hannah to no end. After she'd retired from teaching, she'd become the town librarian.

I settled at a computer and waited until she busied herself with something else so she wouldn't suspect how low I'd fallen from my exceptional performance in fourth grade. I read through the stats of both men slated to pitch that night. The Cubs were favored to win and had Alex Moon on the mound, last year's Cy Young Award winner. The Padres were going to have Sammy Gladstone on the mound, a loose-limbed rookie. I closed my eyes. I'd have to take the Padres. It was a stupid bet. I'd be smarter to pay a portion of my credit card debt with my half of the $1,300 instead, but it would cover such a small amount of the total, I might as well throw the cash overboard.

I took a deep breath and stared at the screen full of stats along with Sammy Gladstone's headshot. I looked in his eyes. "I'm counting on you," I whispered to him.

~

Back out on Main Street, I paced in front of the convenience store. Was I really going to do this? I'd never once bet more than I had. This was really stupid. Pete-level bad decision making. Potentially devastating.

"Hey! Heard you and Pete are fishing again! Is it true?" Anders Jensen, a longtime troller in the fleet was crossing the street, grinning.

"Hey, Jensen. Yeah, a couple of has-beens floating around out there in the rain."

He cracked up as his huge hand cupped my shoulder. "Glad you're back out there, kid. Pete's no good without you. Where you been on the radio?" In high school, I never missed an opportunity to jump in on the trash-talk chatter among the fleet on the radio in the evenings or on long runs back to town. I loved the way we all stayed connected over miles and miles of open water and untouched wild land. Thick invisible threads that we all wove this way and that into a haphazard pattern, strong enough to keep us all afloat.

"Been raking 'em in over the side. Got no time to chat with all you wing nuts."

He hooted, punched me in the arm the way I'd seen him kid around with his own boys who were about my age a thousand times. I balked at the knifing jolt through my rib cage and then played it off so he wouldn't ask. "See you out there, El," he said. "I'll be the one catching all the fish you're looking for."

I gave him the flat, sarcastic look he was expecting and then gave myself a minute to let the pain settle back to a simmer as Jenson headed down the sidewalk. I walked past the front door of the convenience store twice more, huddled deep in my float coat. "Fuck it," I said, turned back, and stepped inside.

Ryan sat on a stool behind the checkout counter where he always was. He glanced up from his perpetual *People* magazine and pulled off his readers. "Hey, Ellie. Where's Drew?"

Ryan had known me since I was in middle school and had an addiction to Twizzlers.

"With . . . Pete."

His face went slack. "For real?"

"Can I borrow your phone?"

He waited for me to say more and then seemed to take in the way the last week had wrung me out. He pulled the landline phone off an underneath shelf and set it on the counter. "I'll give you a minute." He stepped out from behind the counter and busied himself at the far end of the two rows of snacks and essentials that made up the store. I dialed the number that Pete had scribbled on a torn off section of paper. By memory.

"'Lo?" a heavy voice said on the other end.

"I want to bet the money line on the Padres tonight."

"Who's this?" Something tapped wildly in the background. A pen against a table. If he connected me to Pete by my last name, he might not take the bet. It was a cardinal rule you couldn't place a bet to pay off a bet. That was you betting the books' money, which meant you deserved whatever he wanted to dole out.

"Someone who wants to bet the money line on the Padres tonight," I said a little louder to get over the tapping.

"That's not how it works, sweetheart. I don't take bets from people I don't know." His deep voice was the opposite of Hank's. It suggested dark, rainy night trouble, whereas Hank's voice on the line had always suggested something akin to a walk on the beach searching for sea glass.

"Please—" I started, but he interrupted.

"Well, now, that's something new. Someone on the other end of the phone, begging."

"Ellie Baker."

"Huh," he said.

"From Juneau," I added to skate through as a member of someone else's family.

"Juneau," he repeated, a little too slowly.

"Twenty-five hundred on the Padres," I said. If he didn't let me place the bet, it was over. If I bet all we had and won, it still wouldn't be enough to cover the cost of the repairs plus fuel and groceries to get us back out on the grounds. I'd never before bet more than I had to my name. My hands began to shake.

"Ballsy bet," he said. I breathed out the breath I'd been holding. "Sammie's been pretty erratic on the mound. Been getting into some trouble off the field."

When I didn't say anything, he chuckled in a *I can't believe it* kind of way.

"Nine a.m. tomorrow," he said. "I'll have a guy at the corner of Third and Cedar. You'll hand over twenty-five hundred when you lose, or we'll hand over $5,000 if you somehow, on God's green earth, win." He hung up.

When I stood up, the muscles in my side locked down tight over my ribs. "Thanks, Ryan," I called as I hobbled outside, back to the sidewalk. The world swung on its axis, on the verge of spinning out of control.

The ramp was almost flat with the high tide. It clanged and clattered as I stepped onto it and then again when I stepped off onto the docks. The rain had all but stopped, and the cloud ceiling had lifted to reveal a bit more of the mountains across the water.

Van looked up from where he was stacking boxes of supplies to tarp over for the ride back. His mouth pulled into a half smile that shot through me, more surprising than the cold slap of a rogue wave. He stood up, his eyes a light iridescent green in the gray light, worn out at the edges but something else entirely at the center. Was he glad to see me? Was I glad to see him? I looked away, noticed a box full of books.

"What'd you do, rob the library? Mrs. Hannah doesn't let anyone check out that many at a time."

He covered the boxes with a tarp. "You know Mrs. Hannah?"

"Everybody knows Mrs. Hannah." I nodded my head toward the box. "That probably took a lot of sweet-talking."

"My specialty," he said with a grin that made the rest of the world fall away.

"Gross. She's a hundred."

He laughed. "How was the visit to Dr. Stone?"

"It's just bruised." I was too embarrassed tell him I didn't have eighty dollars to pay for a visit or the hundreds an X-ray might cost without insurance since I'd quit my job. Or how I'd avoided my PO Box, where a bill from the ER surely sat. It occurred to me how often I'd been shaving at the truth since Pete had shown up in my life again. I had that old feeling of getting dragged into no-man's-land, the same as that first season fishing without Mom, watching Pete and our entire life unravel.

"Probably ought to have it checked out," Van said, slow and steady. His eyes clear and kind, now.

"It's just bruised," I said again, this time letting some annoyance seep into the words to make him stop.

He turned back to tuck the tarp in around several other boxes from the hardware store. "More greenhouse supplies?" I tried to ease up, change the direction I'd shoved us in.

"Yeah. Winters . . ." He trailed off. "I need more food. Running behind, though. Meant to start a lot earlier." He turned away, making it clear he didn't want me to ask. "You got supplies being delivered from NAPA?"

I shook my head. "Waiting to make sure the Padres win tonight." I'd tried to buy engine parts after the phone call, but something in the guy's voice on the phone and the buzzing in my chest made me not able to bring myself to spend the money we might have to use to appease a bookie who was a big enough deal to keep himself hidden while I tried to figure a way into the rest of what I might owe him. I stepped into the skiff.

"And if they don't?"

"They have to." It came out like a thin curtain I was sure Van could see through. I busied myself at the stern line, but he kept watching me. "Ready to go?" I asked.

He yanked a few times at the tarp to cover up a box on the edge of the pile, tied off the last corner, then moved to the console.

I untied the skiff from the dock and watched town fall away behind us as it had a little over a week ago when I'd felt confident enough to try taking the helm from Pete.

~

We were back in Marbled Inlet by three p.m. The bay was a blue-gray sheet pulled tight at the corners, the thick cloud bank hovering like a block of concrete just above the sharp mountain peaks.

Van backed off the throttle. I pulled off my earmuffs. "Want some help unloading?" I asked.

He glanced over, looking doubtful.

"I got one good arm," I added.

"You look sort of yellow at the edges."

It was unclear whether my mind or body was more exhausted. "I'll be fine," I said automatically.

He turned back to the water in front of him as we sliced through the calm bay. "I'm taking you back to Danny's, where you can lay down."

I wanted to protest. Who was he to make decisions for me? But I couldn't. I felt yellow at the edges. I climbed over the bow when he beached it in front of Danny's path and gave a weak push to get the boat off the beach, but it didn't matter, he had the oar out and was pushing off the beach in a way that was actually effective. I turned toward the path, pulled by the idea of Drew back in my arms.

"Mom!" Drew came racing toward me as I stepped inside the front door. His mouth and chin stained red. "We made a huckleberry pie!"

Charlotte had on an apron and was washing up bowls in the sink.

I bent down, and he looped his arms around my neck. His shoulder pulsed into my cheek. "You were gone a thousand hours."

"I know, buddy. I missed you." I wrapped him up in a hug despite the searing knife at my side. "Is there any pie left or did you eat it all?"

"I ate it all!" His eyes brightened, and something in me loosened. "Just kidding. Pete ate two pieces, though. How come I can't have two pieces? He didn't even do any work. He just laid there all day." He swung his arm over toward the couch, where Pete was lying down, his foot propped up on the end of the couch. His toes were swollen up tight, and his cast looked soggy.

He was looking at Drew, his arms up, palms out. "Why you gotta be like that? I don't rat you out. C'mere!" Pete pretend swiped at him.

Drew squealed and piled into my legs for protection. I dropped one hand to his back, the other to cup the back of his head. Drew's happiness in that moment was mesmerizing. I wasn't sure I'd ever seen him quite like this. I felt the edges of our worn-out closed circuit expanding to include others. What if Drew could have a life full of people who loved him?

"You make the call?" Pete asked. His crutches were leaning up against the wall in the corner. He must've collected them from the boat. Or, more likely, Danny or Charlotte had. It made me uncomfortable how much we were relying on them.

"I took the money line on the Padres for twenty-five hundred."

Pete pushed up on an elbow. "Almost double what we have if you have to pay up?"

"Right."

Pete's eyes stayed on me as I combed fingers through Drew's hair.

"Pretty sure he believed I'm a part of the Juneau Bakers."

Pete nodded slowly, still watching me. Drew pulled away and disappeared behind the counter where Charlotte stood, then climbed up into the chair next to her. She handed him a towel and a wooden bowl to dry. I was about to explain to him what to do when he gave it a thorough wipe and handed it back to her. She smiled, murmured something, and handed him a plate. I winced, afraid he'd drop it. And then wondered if I'd taught him to be tentative by not trusting him. In my strung-out town existence, to hand him a plate was to risk a half hour of cleaning up shards when all I wanted to do was lie down on the couch.

As Drew used his belly and one hand to balance the plate while he wiped it dry, his tongue pressed into one corner of his mouth, I saw clearly the dark cave we'd been living in and how close the exit had been all along.

"This is the last thing I wanted," Pete said from the couch. "I want to be done with all of it, Ellie." He rubbed at his chin and looked away. His eyes looked beaten.

Drew came running back into the living room, followed by Charlotte, who was drying her hands. Drew leaned up against my legs and laced his fingers into mine. "The bread is rising, Mama, don't touch it. Charlotte says I'm a good helper in the kitchen."

She smiled over at him and then at me.

"You've been so generous," I said. "Thank you."

"It's been so long since there was this kind of energy in the house." Charlotte smiled until her eyes crinkled up and then sighed. "Always wanted grandkids."

"How many kids do you have?"

"Two." Charlotte kept her eyes on Drew. "Brent lives over in Kake, and Melissa fishes with her husband out of Ketchikan. Don't hardly ever see her. They stay busy. She doesn't want any kids, and Brent doesn't seem too inclined that way either." She continued wiping her hands methodically with the towel in her hand.

"You raised them both here, in Marbled Inlet?"

She nodded. "Been here thirty-five years now. Got the land as a homestead, back when you could still do that." She tilted her head. "You going to rebuild on the beach there at the entrance?"

"Depends on who wins the baseball game." A wave of nausea washed over me.

Drew was staring up at me. "You don't look right."

Charlotte peered at me. "Why don't you lie down? Drew and I have some kneading to do."

As I crossed the living room toward the bedroom, the woodstove popping, Pete said, "Game's at seven."

~

At 6:45, Pete, Charlotte, Drew, and I were piled on the couch. Van sat on the floor, his back propped up against the couch at one end. Charlotte had started the generator and found the channel, and now we were watching the players line up for the national anthem. I had imagined we'd be listening to it on the radio, but Van had laughed at me when I mentioned it. Danny got more channels than I knew existed.

Drew sat in my lap, asking which team was the white one and why they wore belts and why the one guy had a beard and the others didn't. Charlotte had made a delicious venison stew, which everyone filled their bellies with except me. I'd been too nervous to eat much.

"So how's this work?" she was asking now.

"If the Cubs win, we owe the bookie $2,500. If the Padres win, he owes us $5,000," Pete explained.

"Seems like a bad deal for him," she said.

"Cubs are favored to win. By a lot," I said. "It's a pretty safe bet for him."

Pete grunted as he shifted on the couch.

"Bold move," Van said, raising an eyebrow at me, looking more entertained than concerned. I tried not to notice the way his broad chest pulled at the sweatshirt he was wearing. I had not noticed a man since watching Drew's dad disappear into the fog after saying words I didn't mean. And now what? I was noticing some guy who was clearly on the run from something living hours from town with barely enough to eat? I shook my head.

"Or stupid," I said. "I don't have twenty-five hundred." I had to admit, Van's lack of concern bolstered me. As if he didn't doubt I'd be able to handle whatever happened. I tried to settle into that feeling myself, but it evaporated when I noticed the worry deepening Charlotte's face. She likely had plenty to worry over without me adding to it.

"What will you do?" she asked.

"Give him the $1,300 I have and figure it out from there. We could probably sell parts off the boat—"

Pete gave me a wounded look and then focused back on the screen. "Batter up!" he called out as the Cubs took the plate. I studied Sammy Gladstone as he flopped his big feet and used his bird neck to check behind him for god knows what as Rodriguez took the plate. Sammy brought the ball into his glove in slow motion and settled steely eyes on his catcher. He shook off the first two signs and wound up. If he only knew how much was at stake.

Rodriguez connected with a piercing crack, and the ball sailed over the back wall. I dropped my head into my hands. When I looked up, Van was watching me. "Last I checked, there were nine long innings in a baseball game," he said with a slow, easy grin, his words all running together.

By the bottom of the second, it was still one–zero Cubs. The Padres were at bat, two outs, man on first, and Billy Stanford stepped up to bat. He made the sign of the cross four times, tapped the bat against each insole once, eyed the pitcher, and slowly raised the bat.

Pete was leaned forward as close as he could get to the TV while still perched on the couch. "This is it, El, he's got a .274 batting average, his mom has been in the hospital. He's playing for her."

".274 isn't so good, Pete," I said, but he was ignoring me.

Alex Moon checked over his shoulder in a sly glance, causing James Holder to scoot back toward first. Moon turned back to Stanford, brought his arms to his chest, and threw fast and hard.

"Home run! Home run!" I was up and hobbling around before Stanford got his feet underneath him and took off toward first.

"Sit down!" Pete yelled. "I can't—oh my god, home run!! Home run!" He launched off the couch and limped over to me. Drew galloped circles around us, and just like that, Pete and I were back on the same team.

~

By the top of the sixth, the Cubs were up by two runs, and Sammy was coming apart. I took a break and stared at myself in the bathroom mirror. I looked as old as Mrs. Hannah. When I got back to the living room, Sammy had given up another huge hit, and the Cubs were now up by three. I paced in the kitchen.

By the bottom of the ninth, I was perched on the arm of the couch, barely breathing. The score was now Cubs 7, Padres 4. The Cubs pitcher, Moon, still pitching in the ninth for some reason, had wobbled a bit on the last pitch. When the ball was returned to him after the runner was safe at first, Moon rolled his shoulder and a grimace crossed his face. "What was that?" Pete asked. There were two outs, and the bases were now loaded.

Moon stepped off the mound, tucked his arm up, and rolled his shoulder again.

"Is he hurt?" I asked, watching the star pitcher shake his head and flex his back. "That doesn't look right." His coach walked slowly out to the mound.

"Don't take him out," Pete whispered. The camera panned to the relief pitcher, who was warming up. "Oh no," Pete muttered. "Not that guy."

I sat, eyes glued to the screen. The Cubs coach exchanged a few words with Moon and then signaled to the relief pitcher. Moonie jogged off the field.

Pete squinted, unable to tear his eyes away. "That guy is one of the best closers in the league."

The relief pitcher took the mound, fresh and focused.

The Padres were at bat, bases loaded, two outs. A bowlegged man with a bit of a belly stepped out of the dugout and grabbed a bat. If he struck out, I was in a whole new world of trouble.

"Brian Demacus?" Pete said. "I've never even heard of that guy."

Every muscle in my body tensed up as Demacus took a few practice swings.

Demacus stepped up to the plate and dropped into his batting stance. He was too low. Charlotte leaned forward on the couch. Van was still sitting on the floor, back propped up against the couch, looking as relaxed as ever.

Demacus swung, missed, spit in the dirt, and knocked the bat against his shoe as the ump made the call and the commentator yelled, "Strike one!"

I needed to get up, run, be outside, away from this. Instead, I stayed on the end of the couch, eyes glued to the TV.

The closer wound up, Demacus swung, missed. "Strike two!" the announcer yelled.

"Oh no," Charlotte muttered. I looked over and caught Pete's eye. He had come alive. His clear eyes flooded me with that old familiar feeling: It was just him and me on that edge of life, where we both liked the view. I unclenched the grip I had on the couch. I took a deep breath. *Here we are. Here we go.*

The closer checked the runner on first over his shoulder. He pulled his arms into his chest, cranked his left leg, and threw a curve ball. Demacus swung and connected. We were all on our feet before the ball had left the bat.

"It's gonna clear, it's gonna clear," the announcer was yelling.

"Go, go, go!" Pete was hopping on his one good foot, his good arm circling in the air as Demacus dug in on his way to first.

"Shepard has a good bead on it, looks like he might snag it before it leaves the park," the announcer said. The ball hit the outfield wall at the same time as Shepard, and then both bounced to the ground.

The runner on third hit home, and the second runner was right behind him. Charlotte grabbed my arm, neither of our eyes leaving the screen.

Shepard looked shaken, and the ball was rolling away fast. The rest of the outfield was converging to save the play. Shepard got to his feet, but his throw was way off. The shortstop dove to catch it, but missed. The second baseman scooped it up, and threw it home as Demacus laid out for the slide. I caught my breath.

"SAFE!" the announcer yelled. "He's safe!"

"He's safe!" Drew yelled, jumping up and down, flinging himself all sorts of ways at the same time. "He's safe!"

Charlotte joined in the crazy jumping, making Van and Drew crack up.

"Whoo!!" I yelled, and then Pete's good arm was around my shoulders, his cheek against mine. "We're back in the game, Mo! You did it!"

Chapter 13

In the predawn of the next morning, my entire torso convulsed with each pull of the oars, the pain hot and radiating as I rowed out to Danny's skiff, but I didn't care. The glow of having won the craziest fucking bet ever had not worn off even a little bit.

The mountain behind Danny's house rose straight off the water, the green trees so dark and thick they looked black. At the top of the mountain, large patches of snow hung on despite the long hours of summer sun.

The rain was light, just a dusting that felt good against my face. Danny had collected my rain gear from the *Sarah Louise* the day before along with Pete's crutches, clothes for all of us, and Dog. I left my hood off and settled into the rowing. In the same way I'd learned to do with the raw ache of missing my mother, I pushed the physical discomfort into the bottom corner of my brain, imagined it folded neatly and put away. There, but not in the way of whatever else I needed to do.

Once at the skiff, I climbed over the rail, tied the inflatable off to the buoy, and untied the skiff. I'd always loved the way the sound of an engine starting hints at all the possibilities hidden in the simple act of pulling away from town. I slipped on ear protection, dropped the skiff into gear, and felt the stern dig in.

~

Three hours later, as I walked up the dock in town, I got a couple of arm pumps and good-to-see-you-backs. I nodded and waved in a way that suggested I was tight on time so I wouldn't have to describe the *Sarah Louise* on her side. The enormity of what I'd done washed over me, again. I'd never felt so destructive. I checked my watch: 8:50 a.m.

As I walked toward the corner of Third and Cedar, I decided I wanted to see this guy before he saw me. From Second Street, I cut across a tidy lawn and then picked my way through the debris in the Holcombs' overgrown yard. Becky Holcomb had been one of my best friends in middle school. The playhouse where we'd smoked our first cigarettes that was falling down back then was falling down worse now.

I sat with my back to it, out of sight of the house but with a clear view of the corner of Third and Cedar. The rain was picking up, loud against my hood. A thick man I'd never seen before walked up Cedar from the direction of town. He had on work pants and a rain jacket with the hood pulled up. He turned down Third, stopped, lit a cigarette, cupped his hand around it to keep it lit, and looked directly at me. He certainly looked like someone who had killed people. I tried not to think about *The Godfather* or any other mafia movie I'd seen. *He's just a man,* I told myself. Probably grew up around here. But I knew that he hadn't. The set to his shoulders was different. His body was not carved out of cold rain.

Our eyes locked, and a heavy fear filled me. He nodded his chin once upward with a flat, hard look on his face, clearly signaling the lameness of my hiding spot.

I got to my feet and walked over on legs going numb.

"We're not the kind of organization you can fuck around with." His fleshy cheeks were scarred by acne, his face still set in a sneer. "That does not work out good for you."

I forced my back straight. Made my voice as strong as I could. "I placed a fair bet."

He shook his head, took a slow drag on his cigarette as the rain misted us and the street held still. "I've got a message for you. And Pete.

From the top." His words like barbs sinking deep in my skin. "You try this shit again, and there will be consequences."

He reached under his rain jacket and handed me an envelope. "Five grand."

I slid the envelope into my pocket, nodded once, and walked quickly down the hill to Main Street, trying to shake the way his pointy eyes had drilled into me, but I knew in the way that you just know, he didn't live according to the rules the rest of us did.

~

I pushed through the front door of the shipyard store, my scalp tingling like I'd just narrowly escaped something. Caroline called from an aisle. I immediately straightened up as she walked over.

"How's it going out there? You and Pete getting along? Drew taking to it?" She shifted the basket of odds and ends to balance on her hip bone.

"Drew's fine. I—" My eyes were suddenly filling and I couldn't look at her.

"Ellie?" The concern in her voice drove a wedge of ache for my mother right through the middle of me.

I dared a quick glance, trying to blink away the tears. I wanted to tell her all of it, right then. I wanted the soft edges of her words to rub out the hard angles of all the bad decisions I'd made. I wanted to tell her I could hear all the bad decisions like the pounding of the feet behind me and was unsure which was going to catch me first. I wanted to loop my arms around her neck and tell her I had five grand in my pocket and that maybe we'd stay ahead of all of it, maybe we'd be okay.

She smiled, the smooth skin over her wide cheekbones accented by the deep wrinkles at the corner of her eyes. "Whatever it is, you'll figure it out. You've got the grit of your mom, no doubt about it."

I nodded, afraid if I said anything, I'd say all of it, and all the horrible truths of my situation would be lying on the floor between us.

Jimmy from the *Sword* squeezed around us with a nod in the narrow aisle and began to search the shelves close by. Caroline dropped a hand to my forearm, gave it a squeeze, and continued on down the aisle.

~

I moved so slow loading the skiff with lumber and supplies that a couple of greenhorns took pity on me. I hated that I had to step aside and let them do it while I struggled through the short, shallow breaths my ribs allowed. It took much longer to get back to Marbled with the skiff loaded down. I'd also bought several bags of fresh fruit, cheese, veggies, chocolate, and anything else I imagined Charlotte might like and not often get. At the fuel dock, after filling up, I bought two extra jerry jugs of gas for Danny's skiff as a thank-you for letting me borrow it.

Once back in Marbled Inlet, I killed the engine and rocked in the water in front of the *Sarah Louise*. She seemed to be in an even deeper slump on the beach than the day before. I felt as though I had injured a family member. I just wanted her fixed. I wanted things back to normal. I wanted to fish. I wanted my mom and my dad back, and I wanted to keep Drew immersed in the life I loved and safe from anyone who would ever do him harm. The way Pete and then Charlotte had drawn him out made me certain we could not go back to work and day care. He was better out here. I was better out here.

Six days, six days, I repeated to myself. I needed to stay on task. Get us back out fishing on the next tide. I beached the skiff in front of the *Sarah Louise* not too far from an ATV Pete must've borrowed from Charlotte and Danny to get himself out here. I'd bought Advil in town and taken a handful, which had dulled the pain in my chest to more of a kitchen knife stab than a steak knife stab.

The sound of hammering came from Van's house somewhere deep in the woods across the narrow arm of land, muted by the dense forest. I walked up and ran my hand along the length of one of her lowest planks toward the bow. The rain was an even, steady beat against the beach, against my body, against the *Sarah Louise*. Standing at the bow, I could see clearly where the stem, the singular strong piece of wood that ran horizontally from the tip of the bow to the keel, had suffered a hard hit. There was a deep gouge as if someone had taken an axe to it. As if I had taken an axe to it. Pete had insisted on using purple heart when he'd replaced the stem years ago. An expensive choice, but clearly a good one. The strength of the wood had kept us from sinking.

"I'm sorry," I whispered to the *Sarah Louise* as my hand fell away. I ducked under the bow and squinted into the rain at the huge piece of plywood nailed to the hull. I imagined the ripped and jagged hole underneath. I leaned my forehead up against the hull. The cool, wet wood calmed the gathering dread.

Chapter 14

I squeezed my eyes shut, the enormity of the task at hand like a whole new storm to live through. Planks had to fit the curve of the hull and every other plank around it perfectly. That last bit between planks was filled with a mixture of cotton, rolled oakum, and cement to keep water from seeping in. Any mistake would leave leaks or weak spots that could sink us slowly, or all at once. Corking the seams had always been my job. I'd be okay if we got that far. Pete had always been the one to replace the planks. The main reason I was good at corking was because Pete was exceptionally good at replacing planks. The seams were always exactly the width they needed to be.

Unease ate at me when I noticed the generator that had been hauled out here for us to use, even though I knew none of this was going to be possible without power tools. There was a gray plastic tote next to it. I peeled the lid and peeked in. Full of borrowed power tools.

A thumping overhead caught my attention, and seconds later, Pete was peering down at me. "Charlotte's got Drew making playdough."

"We can't leave him to her, you know."

"I agree. I went back to get him a few minutes ago, and they both about cried. I used the extra time today to get ready for the engine work." He tossed down several large blue tarps and then strong-armed his way down a ladder propped against the hull, keeping all weight off his broken leg. "Hand off go okay?" he asked once he was on the beach.

"Yeah."

"I still can't believe you won." A jagged smile crossed his face. "You always were better at it than I was." He looked away, and I felt what he didn't say next. That we should just fly to Vegas and bet our way out of this hole. That we should play the odds, that we were sure to end up back on top without killing ourselves trying to rebuild a broken boat and then catch more fish than was humanly possible in the next two months. He gave me a minute to consider it. No, I shook my head. We would do this the real way, the hard way, the true way. Pete nodded slowly at the wind, the languid wash of waves on the beach agreeing.

"We're borrowing all this from Danny?" I asked, walking over to the tub of tools.

"Before he left yesterday, he said to borrow what we needed. I believe he felt bad leaving a couple cripples out here to rebuild on his beach, alone."

I walked down to the beached skiff. I had gotten really good at hiding any trace of need. I didn't like the idea of flying it like a bright-red flag now. But it was true. With only half of Pete and half of me in working order, it took us forever to unload the engine supplies from the skiff. The planks were heavy and needed to be carried up above the tide line. I decided to deal with them later. They'd be fine in the skiff for a bit longer.

I dug the Advil out of my front pocket and tossed it over to Pete.

"Busted ribs hurt way more than they should, don't you think?" He unscrewed the lid and shook a handful of red pills into his palm. He popped them all into his mouth at once.

"That oughta do it," I said, barking out a laugh as he swallowed them down.

"Don't tell me you took the recommended dose of one."

"Whoever decided on that dose isn't a fisherman."

Pete laughed. "My point exactly." He whipped his hood on and looked up at the towering hull above us. "Alright. Four planks, four-foot sections, a day each, and one day of corking." He looked over.

"We could shave some time off to give you a day of rest. You look like you need it."

"No time for that," I said, realizing all I wanted to do was sleep for days and days. I blinked away the feeling, focused on pushing through just like I always did, but I felt thinned out. "It's almost five o'clock now. We've got five days left, and we need to dump the fish and tarp before we start." The idea of dumping all the fish I'd spent the last days hauling in, cleaning, and packing made me want to cry. But if we let them rot in the hold, we'd have a whole other huge problem on our hands.

Pete squinted at me. "Tide's at six p.m. on the seventeenth."

The bone-deep exhaustion broke over me, forced me to put a hand to the hull to stay upright. "I don't know, Pete," I was saying suddenly. "Sounds impossible."

Pete turned his head so that he was looking at me out of one eye more than the other. "That doesn't sound like you."

I pulled at the knots in my neck. "You don't know me anymore, Pete."

Pete pressed his lips into a straight line. "You were never afraid of anything."

"Youthful stupidity. Things changed. I became an orphan. I had a kid."

He looked as though he'd been punched in the kidney. "An orphan?"

"There's more than one way to leave, Pete." I ran my eyes back up to the plywood patch and blew out a breath. "Dump the fish first?"

He swiped a hand over his face. His voice was flat when he spoke again. "Yeah." He walked over to the ATV. While he dragged the inflatable over, I climbed up the ladder, one rung at a time, and pulled on my chest waders and insulated rubber gloves. I tossed the thawing fish up onto the deck in a way that drove the knife in my ribs clear through my chest and out the other side. I packaged up the pain, contorted myself around the bulk of it. Pete was on deck after a while, carrying each king by its tail in a way we never did and tossing them over the low side of the slanted deck into the inflatable. Two hundred fish, four full inflatable loads, dumped at the water's edge with the two of us struggling against the weight. It was all wrong. The rough handling of the fish we were so careful not to bruise otherwise, the tossing them back in the sea instead of pulling them from it.

The long line of floating dead kings carried by the outgoing tide eventually attracted a sea lion and then another. A couple of harbor seals popped their heads up to see what the commotion was all about. A pack of seagulls showed up, which called in a hundred more as they scooped up anything the sea lions left behind.

Pete turned his back to it. "Let's get the tarps up to keep us dry while we work. There's a few more in the focsle." As I started up the ladder, he added, "And bring me the five-gallon bucket I left in the engine room."

Once inside the slanted wheelhouse, standing on all the wrong surfaces, I gathered up the tarp from under the forward bunks and the five-gallon bucket. In the galley, I grabbed a granola bar and a bag of almonds and dried cherries.

After an hour of pushing through every movement I forced my body to make, we had a tarp ceiling over the bow of the boat, held up by alder branches cut and limbed from the edge of the woods. I'd pulled the plywood off both holes in the hull, and Pete and I were looking up at them. Everything was tinged blue under the tarp, and the rain pattered against the top side of it.

"First step," Pete said, settling onto the rocks of the beach under the tarp. "Wreck it out." He pulled his flask out of the side pocket of his work pants and took a couple of long swallows. He lay flat on his back on the rocks and dark sand and used the five-gallon bucket to elevate his broken leg.

I sighed, hating the idea of making it worse before making it better.

He held up his good arm and pointed at the gaping dark hole in the hull. "You'll need to cut out an additional six inches fore and aft of all edges to clean them up. Wreck out any plank above and below that looks damaged."

"We need to get Drew," I said. "We'll sleep on the boat. We'll make it work somehow. We can't put Charlotte and Danny out any longer."

"He's fine for now. I'll go get him soon," Pete said. "I just need to lay here a minute. Go slow while you wreck it out," he added. "Don't make any extra work for us than you have to." He reached again for his flask.

I started the generator and dragged myself up the ladder. Snapping my ear protection in place, I started up the saw. The sound of the blade took me back to the docks in the spring. Sandhill cranes overhead, the humpbacks returning from their wintering grounds in Hawaii, the dark burning off earlier and earlier every morning. My favorite time of year, better than Christmas. Everyone buzzing on the docks, saws and sweat applied to spring boat projects long put off because of too much rain, too much dark. The anticipation that this was sure to be the year in which it all lined up. Everyone showing their cards, pessimistic or optimistic about whether or not the fish were in, the likelihood of being in the right place at the right time, whether or not the cannery was paying top dollar, if the price of diesel would inch up a lot or a little. The dice were rolling, not stopped on anything yet, which meant it was still possible they would land exactly where we all hoped.

I took a deep breath and plunged the saw into the side of the *Sarah Louise*, making the damage worse, this time on purpose. I'd only ever seen Pete do this, and it felt horrible.

I pulled off my ear protection when Pete and Drew appeared below me. Drew looked weary.

"Hey, buddy!" I hollered. He looked so small peering up at me from under his hood. I wanted to climb down and hold him, but for the next five days, I could not waste even a minute. "Pete will stay down there with you while I'm up here working."

Drew's face crumpled. He collapsed into a heap on the small dark rocks, and I wanted to do the exact same thing. I turned away from him too quick and had to fold into the pain in my rib cage.

Pete set up bull's-eyes, and eventually talked Drew into a rock-throwing contest, which lasted about ten minutes before Drew was in a heap again. Then Pete had him building a seaweed mountain, and then they were both exhausted. When I climbed down the ladder forty minutes later, Drew was red-faced and whining, and Pete was red-faced and angry. The minute my feet touched the ground, Drew started crying. "I want Marshall." He made the sentence last four times longer than it should. I bent down in front of him and took his hands in mine. "Drew, I have to fix the boat, and Pete has to help me. You are going to have to entertain yourself some."

"No!" he cried louder. *Five days, five days, five days.* It repeated in my head like a dripping faucet. Every minute I was not working was another minute lost to the tide. I closed my eyes, stood up. "Yes, Drew. That's it. That's your only choice."

"I want to go home!" he wailed, setting a handful of kittiwakes skittering off the beach.

I looked up at the sky. "We need to get the wood out of the skiff," I said to Pete. Mostly to get him to stop watching me fail with Drew, who dissolved into a pool of torment on the beach at my feet.

"You'll plane them over in Danny's workshop," Pete said over the noise of Drew.

Frustration pulsed through my veins as I picked up Drew. "No, Pete. We can do it right here. Somehow."

Pete rubbed his good hand hard across the scruff of his three-day beard. His eyes were whiskey watery. "Ellie, most people ask for help when they need it. And then accept it when it's offered. It's dry in there."

Drew's crying now included huge gasps of air, and he struggled to free himself from my arms. I set him down, and he stomped off to climb up on a rock down the beach, his arms folded across his chest, his back turned toward me.

"Yeah, well, we're not freeloaders. I'll do it out here."

"I'm taking him back up to the house." Pete limped over to the ATV. "This is ridiculous."

"No, you're not."

He started up the ATV and revved the engine loud enough to preclude any further conversation. He drove up to the rock Drew had perched himself on and reached out a hand, which Drew took immediately and climbed up in front of Pete. With the casted arm anchoring Drew in place, he drove off across the beach.

Pete returned a half hour later as I was adding gasoline to the generator and threw me a sour look as he swung himself off the ATV. I glared back at him.

"We need help, Ellie. Get over it."

"You're the one who got us into this fucking mess, Pete. If it wasn't for you, I wouldn't have been out in that storm trying to judge the turn. If it wasn't for you, I wouldn't be living in town accruing debt. If it wasn't for you, Mom would probably still be here." My hands fisted at my sides.

Pete froze, straightened up evenly on both feet. "Go ahead, say it. You've been needing to, so just say it."

I felt the blood rushing to my face as years of pent-up frustration and betrayal boiled to the surface. "Why didn't you make her go to Seattle? It might've helped. It might've made all the difference."

Pete's face was like ice. "It was complicated."

"What could be more complicated than doing whatever possible to keep the person you love around longer? I can't think of a single reason to not do it, except cowardice."

Pete flinched like I'd swung at him. He swallowed hard. "She refused to go." Pete said it carefully, like walking across glass.

"What?" The word came out in a whisper of breath.

Pete closed his eyes and glanced up before he looked back at me. "I didn't want you to know. I couldn't understand it myself, and I didn't want you to feel like I did. Betrayed, on some level. Sit with me," he said, his voice as broken as I suddenly felt.

Pete eased himself down onto the rocks of the beach, and I sat down in a daze next to him. "She was given a thirty percent survival rate. Dr. Stone wanted to send us to Seattle for chemo, which we were going to do until we looked into it and realized how little of it our insurance would cover. Not to mention the cost of staying in Seattle for weeks or months. I wanted to sell the boat and permit to cover the cost. We didn't own anything else. We rented, had an old truck. Your mom refused. She said she wouldn't trade your future for hers."

"What?" I could barely get the word out. "I would've gladly given up this for her."

"I know, Mo. Me too. I begged her." He looked at me, his eyes full of all the hurt I carried around. "I found a buyer, even. But she said no. All she wanted was one last season out on the boat with you and me." He ran a hand through his hair. "I hated myself. We had health insurance. I thought I was being responsible. I never imagined it would be so useless. I kept thinking if only I had a more stable job, if only I'd been a better fisherman and been able to save more money. If only I'd gone to school and gotten some degree and a job down south, we would've been more prepared." He turned to look at me. "That night in the kitchen when you were so angry, so certain it was my fault she didn't get the treatment she needed, you were right. In so many ways, it was my fault. I couldn't bear for your anger to be directed at your mom. If I couldn't save her, I wanted to save your memory of her."

The words floated around me, not lining up, anger gathering like a storm at the edges. "So she died to save the boat, and then you gambled it away?"

Pete wrapped his good hand around his casted hand and dropped his head. "She probably would've died anyway, Ellie."

"That's not the point." It felt good to be angry. It seemed to be the only way to hold off the black bottomless hole that I was tipping into.

When Pete looked up, his eyes were red and heavy. "This boat haunted me. I hated that I had it instead of her. But fishing is all I know, so I kept doing it. In some ways, I think throwing the permit and title down on that game was my way of trying to force myself to start over."

When he saw the look on my face, he added quickly, "I know, Ellie, I know. But I thought you were done forever. I didn't know you had a son. I didn't know you missed it. You walked away."

Hot tears rolled down my cheeks and off my chin. I dropped my face into my hands.

"Ellie." Pete reached out toward me, but his hand floated useless in the huge space between us. "In that first year, I felt so betrayed by her choice even though I could see what she was doing and why she was doing it. We should've told you the truth. But you were so young when it was happening, and afterward, I couldn't bear for you to feel the level of betrayal I did, so I just let you hate me instead."

I had to move. I had to get out. I got to my feet and ducked under the tarp. The rain like ice against my skin. Pete called out to me, but I was so far away. Back to that summer before I understood I was about to lose everything. I was seventeen, excited and wholly unprepared for the huge life decisions that lay ahead. If only she had been there for an extra six months, an extra two years, an extra decade. If only I'd had a compass I could come back to, course correct according to.

Deer are silent until death is imminent, and then they scream as if they'd been just barely holding it in all those quiet years. It pierces the forest, bounces off trees, and scatters the rain. I could feel it rising in me.

~

When I walked through the front door of Charlotte's house a lost hour later, the world felt far away. As if I had not much to do with it anymore.

Pete was hobbling around a pile of our belongings that had been gathered on the couch. "Mom!" Drew yelled when he saw me, clearly much better off than when I'd last seen him.

He slid off his chair next to Charlotte at the kitchen counter and ran to me. I picked him up and held him close, feeling the rightness of it. Knowing I'd do anything in the world possible for even one more day of this, of him.

He squirmed out of my arms. "Look at our playdough castle." He grabbed my hand and pulled me toward the kitchen table, where a huge, drippy mass of white playdough had been left to dry. I wiped at the rain and tears on my face. "Looks great."

Drew took me on a lap around the table to point out the turrets, the drawbridge, and the watchtower. I'd never heard him say any of those words before, and they sounded strange on his lips.

"Charlotte, this is . . ." I stopped when I caught the hard set to her face.

"It's no trouble, you know," she said, an edge to her voice. "A boat on its side on the beach, when there's plenty of room here for all of you." Her eyes flashed annoyance before she noticed Drew, who was watching us closely, his shoulder pulling once, his face starting to crack. "Don't forget to show her the crocodiles you put in the moat," Charlotte said with a smile, steering him effortlessly back into his previous excitement.

"Right," said Drew. He turned to me with serious eyes. "DON'T put your fingers anywhere near HERE." He pointed with a straight arm at the front of the castle.

"Got it," I said and slid my hands in my pockets, which made Drew nod once, approvingly.

"I just don't want to put you out," I tried to explain to Charlotte. She had on a housecoat, and her tight gray curls frizzed away from her head, making a halo of sorts.

She waved her hand in between us. "Drew—" she started. "I miss—" She took a deep breath, her eyes hollowing out. "Ever since the kids left, I get so lonely out here." I felt her loneliness and my own of the past five years entangle and start to pull me under.

I bent down awkwardly, the pulsing in my side spreading through my whole body. Once Drew and I were face-to-face, I ran my hands down his arms and grabbed both hands. "Buddy, would you like to spend more time here with Charlotte while I work on fixing the boat?"

"Yes," he said gravely. "She needs help with the dishes."

"You'll tell me when you get tired or want a break?" I asked Charlotte as I struggled back to standing.

"Of course," she called over her shoulder as she dropped a hand to Drew's back and the two of them headed into the kitchen. "Drew and I will eat meals together, and he'll go to bed when he's tired, and if he needs you for something, we'll come find you."

Pete was standing in the living room, where he'd been listening. He looked as shaken as I felt. I met his eyes. "I'm exhausted, Pete."

"I know it, Mo. Lie down for a bit. Let me get us started. You need rest."

My body could barely move through the thick sadness that had settled over me. For Mom. For Pete. For me. I was at the door of the bedroom without any memory of having crossed the room. Pete was behind me turning off the light.

I woke up to Drew in the bed next to me. His hair against my face, his spine against my chest. I dropped my head to his as all of last night came back to me. How could she have gambled away even the smallest fraction of a cure? Who cared about fishing in the face of that? Perhaps she had not felt about me the way I felt about Drew. I lay on my side, arm over him, trying to make things distinct in a dark room.

Chapter 15

I woke up a few hours later. The rain against the windows made Drew's body stretched against the side of mine even more cozy. My watch read five thirty a.m. I closed my eyes, but I was too tired to sleep, and so I lay with Drew, my arm traveling the steady waves of his breathing, my mind on a million paths at once, the same scene playing in the background: Mom and I cleaning fish next to each other in the pit on my seventeenth birthday that last summer we fished together. We had spent my whole life refining the motions of catching, cleaning, and packing fish in relationship to each other. Each pushing the other to move just a bit faster, a bit more efficiently, while working side by side. But her actions were slow, as if every movement was an effort to push against time closing in on her.

That day, in particular, I could feel how hard she was working, the way the vise was tightening. When she lay her knife down, I looked up. We were only a few feet apart, but she felt unreachable. Our bodies rocked in unison as the *Sarah Louise* rolled over one wave and then the next, as the seagulls fought somewhere overhead, hidden by the thick cloud bank that swallowed up the top of the poles. In the narrow band between sea and cloud, the smell of diesel and fresh fish and salt surrounded us. "Ellie," she said. My heart scraped clean with just the one word. "There are only moments of clarity. The rest is so gray. Remember that, okay?"

Drew mumbled in his sleep and rolled away from me. It was almost six a.m. now. I peeled off the covers so as not to disturb Drew and pulled on Mom's clothes from the dry bag, its contents scattered on the floor. The sharp pain of my body the only interruption in the slow syrup of my mind.

In the kitchen, Charlotte sat in the dull light of a single propane lamp, her hands around a coffee mug, staring out the window into the morning. She was dressed in work pants and a wool shirt, and the smell of outside hung around her as if she'd already been out and come back in.

I eased into the chair next to hers. She took one look at me and covered my hand with hers.

"How does it work, Charlotte?" I asked in just above a whisper.

"What do you mean?" Her voice matched my own. A small ripple in the still morning. She picked up my hand and laced her fingers with mine, which undid me.

"My mom." I swallowed against the tears that were coming anyway. "She died before Drew was born. I have so many questions."

Her eyes were full of kindness.

"It's so hard," I said, just barely audible.

"It is," she whispered, nodding.

"You're so patient with him."

"You could be too, if given the chance."

Pete stirred on the couch in the living room. He rubbed quick circles over his eyes, a move that threw me directly back into my childhood. All those years of predawn mornings after late nights of cleaning fish. He'd always woken up that way. Intimacy isn't always a grand gesture. It's often in all the small ways we anticipate each other.

He stood up, still in the same clothes as the day before. He gathered up his crutches, leaned against the wall, and thumped his way into the kitchen. His casted arm jutted out at an odd angle so that he could wrap his hand around the crutch. His fingers were red and swollen up tight. "Morning, Charlotte," he said, and then to me, "Ready?"

The moment stretched between us long enough that he stopped rustling around and turned back to look at me.

"I can't do it, Pete." The space between us pulled tight as he waited for me to explain.

"I just need a day, maybe two. It's too much to push through." The surprise on his face mirrored my own. Had I really said those words? Had I ever allowed myself this? Not since Drew. Not since Mom. When there's no safety net, you cannot allow yourself to fall.

"Yeah, good idea," Pete said, watching me carefully. "We both know those ribs aren't just bruised. You take two days. That still gives us two before the tide. We'll power through it together, okay?"

"Thanks, Pete," I whispered as he thumped over and wrapped me up tight in a one-armed, one-casted hug. I dropped my head to his chest, testing the strength of him as safety net.

"Love you, Mo," he whispered back.

"Mama?" Drew said from the doorway of the bedroom, one of Dog's legs tightly gripped in his hand.

"Morning, buddy," I said as Pete released me.

"Can I have cancakes?"

"Sure. We could make them together?" I ventured.

Drew's eyes widened. "Charlotte says I'm good with the spoons. I did it right when we made the pie."

"The measuring spoons," Charlotte filled in as she got down a jar of flour and pulled eggs out of the refrigerator.

"Do you mind?" I asked.

She gave me a look like I'd better not ask again. "I've got more kindling to split. The pancakes are up to you two this morning."

Drew ran to a corner. "Charlotte says this is my step stool, and you have to level it off, Mama. No heaps." He and Dog wrestled an old set of three wooden stairs over to the counter. The planks were worn down to a shine by years of little feet.

Pete followed Charlotte out the front door, and I felt the strength of them both even after they were gone. "Okay, how about you do the spoons, and I'll do the cups and eggs? Do you want to stir?"

"Yes!" Drew ran in place on the top step, his hands balancing him on the counter, Dog still gripped tight.

"What should Dog do?" The easy morning light illuminated this kid, this messy miracle of us.

"He'll watch!" Drew propped Dog on the counter, where he was sure to get covered in flour and egg, and I practiced not caring.

"He'll be good at that."

"Do the eggs!" Drew commanded as he went back to running in place. This was a different kid. A shiny new confidence under the surface of the old nervousness. How to coax it out? For one, I would not tell him to hold still. I bit my lip to make sure it happened.

"Maybe you should do the eggs?"

Drew stopped running and looked panicked. "I'll do it wrong." He would definitely do it wrong. There would be a million small bits of eggshells. I took a deep breath. Promised myself a nap after breakfast. Charlotte would be back and could take over watching Drew.

"How about if eggshells end up in the eggs, we'll go fishing?"

Drew's face crumpled.

"For eggshells," I quickly clarified. "I'll show you how."

"Okay." Drew's face cleared.

I found a bowl and a frying pan. The pancakes ended up with too much baking powder and not enough salt and some eggshells, and they were the best pancakes I'd ever had. We were sweeping up flour as Charlotte came back in. Drew had just started whining about wanting to watch TV, and my side felt like concrete as she swooped in and asked Drew if he could help her stack some kindling and then she'd teach him a magic trick only she and her kids knew, and he was out the door and I was crawling into bed in the middle of the day for the first time in god knows how long, feeling horrible and happy in equal measure.

I woke up sometime that afternoon with Drew standing over me. "Mama, I know magic. Can I show you?" His face was lit up.

"Ellie, I made up a place for you to rest on the couch. I'll put some water for tea on," Charlotte called.

I ignored my first instinct to refuse and called out instead, "Tea sounds perfect."

"Mama!" Drew said impatiently.

"Okay, alright. Let's see it." I pushed up to sitting, breathed into the wall of pain. Drew held up three linked silver rings.

"All connected . . ." he said in a spooky voice.

I nodded. Worried because I couldn't see any breaks in the rings where they could come apart.

He collapsed the rings between his hands, fluttered his fingers, dropped the rings, let out a strangled sound, and scooped them back up. Fiddled with them some more behind his back and then held up one ring in one hand, and two in the other.

"Wow," I said, actually impressed.

"Want to see again?"

"Yes, totally. Can you teach me?"

"Nope. I'm the magician, not you."

I laughed, not caring how much it hurt. "Can you show me again on the couch?"

"That's quite a magic trick," I said to Charlotte as I hobbled over and settled myself in the pillows and blankets she'd spread out for me. She handed me a plate of smoked salmon and bread and a couple of Advil.

"Does a hot water bottle sound good? Probably not for the ribs, but I imagine your back's all tied up tight too."

It felt so good to be mothered. It felt so good to allow myself this comfort, this help. I pushed away the ticking clock of the upcoming tide, the likelihood that Drew and I would go back to our dreary town existence where no one made me hot water bottles. "Yes, please. Sounds amazing," I eked out over the emotion rising in my throat.

I acted surprised a hundred more times while Drew the Magician separated and reattached and separated the three rings. The hot water both inside and out eased my muscles and mind until Pete popped in and asked Drew if he could come help him in the workshop, and Drew raced off as fast as his feet could carry him, leaving Dog sprawled on the floor in his wake.

I closed my eyes as their voices disappeared behind the closed door. Felt the way I'd come to a screeching halt here on this couch after so many years of running. One layer after another after another caught up and soaked me in memories. Oliver playing his guitar on the couch, head tilted back, his voice somehow gravelly and smooth at the same time. The same long, thin fingers as Drew, the same look in his eye that named me as the center of his world. He'd spent whole days writing songs about me, about our wild, chaotic love. The world was our stage, we were the stars, and I had no idea life could feel that way and thought it would last forever. Austin, Texas, had sounded exotic at that point in time to me. A boyfriend who was looking out for the two of us, romantic.

He just had to make enough first to front the band, to get his foot in the door. He'd come up to Alaska to make big money fishing, had hurt his back his first season out, and it still bothered him, so he'd been hunting big money elsewhere ever since. He wasn't getting ahead yet, but had a plan to make his dreams, our dreams, a reality. He didn't want to move to Austin just to have us both work in restaurants. We'd move with cash in our pockets, if not in the bank, he'd said, his eyes full of the neon lights and stages he desired as much as he desired me. I was up for it, of course. Anything different from the life with Pete I'd walked away from, anything exciting, anything with him next to me, us carving our own unlikely path. A guy he knew was going to cook the meth. He promised he'd never touch the stuff. All he had to do was front the money, and they'd split the profit. There was going to be a lot of profit. I'd begged him, "Anything else, please, anything else." But there wasn't anything else. There was land for miles and a seascape to lose yourself in, but there were few jobs and fewer opportunities, unless you stepped over that line that seemed to get closer and closer with each dream dreamed up and then gone stale.

With the hot water bottle coaxing out one memory after another, I saw the confidence in his shoulders, felt the magnetic pull of him, the look in his eyes like I was enough, could feel the way he wrapped his body around mine, the only way either of us could fall asleep. The way the future that Mom's death had drained all the color from started to fill back in with him by my side. And then the slippery slope of him losing rather than making money, spending more time in Juneau than with me, the cagey look that gathered around him, same as it had with Pete. And then his growing paranoia, his being up all night, his body thinning out. Then the positive pregnancy test, and I knew what I had to do. He didn't understand when I told him so definitively that I was done, that he had to go. I never mentioned the baby.

In the still of Charlotte's house, I allowed myself to feel it again. To watch him slam the car door in the ferry parking lot later that night, catch my eye through the rain-smeared passenger side window. The hurt in his eyes plain to see. I cleaved in half in that moment that he walked away. The part of me that loved freely left with him. The part of me reserved for the sole protection of the secret growing inside me stayed put. When he was across the parking lot, I climbed out to feel the rain against my skin, to watch him sling his duffel over his shoulder, to hear the clang of his feet on the metal walkway into the three a.m. ferry to Juneau.

Why had I picked someone just like Pete? All big dreams and bright eyes and a proclivity toward vices. Because I loved them both. *Love,* I corrected myself. In a fierce way that I had worked hard to bury. Maybe walking away wasn't the best strategy. Maybe sticking it out was better. I would never walk away from Drew. But I had turned my back on the two other people I had ever loved as much as him. Had Mom walked away, in a sense? Or had she just lived out the days allotted? I thought back to that last summer. She hadn't been closed off. She'd been the opposite, really, open and sparking with joy as always. Just more and more tired. As I turned over the months of that last fishing season in my head, looking for judgment or self-recrimination, I couldn't find any. She made a decision when she needed to and then dealt with whatever came after with bravery.

I nestled deeper into the pillows, closed my eyes. The tide in four and a half days pressed in on me like the hand of a giant, but for now, I held still, ignored it. Allowed my body and my mind a small sliver of time to undo the damage, to stitch themselves back together. I closed my eyes and let myself drift.

When I woke up a couple of hours later, I had a freight train urge to be with Drew and Pete. The house was quiet and still, but through the window in the kitchen, I could see that the lights were on in the workshop next to the house. I eased out from under the blanket on the couch, tentatively breathed in as deep as my ribs would allow, and got to my feet. I took a few more Advil, hit the bathroom, and pulled on my boots, still in the daze of a midday nap.

~

The workshop was a tall, airy corrugated metal building. Inside, the rain on the roof whispered in the background. Pete was dumping a five-gallon bucket of water into a fifty-gallon drum that was precariously balanced on top of the propane crab cooker. I could feel the ache of his body in mine as he forced his broken arm over his head to empty the bucket.

"Look, Mama," Drew called out from the back of the workshop. He came running, holding up two sticks, one cranked at a hard angle. "Pete made me drumsticks!"

"Grandpa," Pete corrected as he glanced over his shoulder at me. "We'll use this setup to boil planks so they are easier to bend when it's time to bolt them in place. The planks will be too long to fit, but I couldn't find anything better. We'll get them mostly boiled, which isn't very good, so you'll have to put some muscle into bending them into place without snapping them in two. Possibly impossible, but you'll figure it out."

I closed my eyes for a fraction of a second as the days, hours, minutes, left to finish what I hadn't even started pressed into me. My hand instinctively covered the ribs that pulsed with my increasing heartbeat. Pete's face was crumpled with concern. "Sorry, El—we'll get to this when we get to it. You need to rest for now. Did you sleep? Looked like it when we peeked in on you."

"Look, Mama," Drew said again, holding up his crooked drumsticks.

I bit down on my need to point out that, with drumsticks, he was likely to bang on all sorts of things that shouldn't be banged on and said instead, "Pete's pretty crafty, huh? Did you show him your magic trick?"

"It was amazing every one of the forty-two times," Pete said and then added, "Charlotte was needed for the greenhouse project. Me and Drew decided to get the cooker set up and then see if it gets hot enough to bend some wood for a drum." His voice was so clear, his eyes so alert. I wanted to thank him for drinking less, for making what I knew to be a herculean leap back toward the father I needed him to be, toward the grandfather Drew so desperately wanted.

Drew reached up and rested his hand on Pete's where it was wrapped around the handle of the crutch, and I felt the tears rising.

"Looks like it's getting close," Pete said, hooking Drew's fingers in his pinkie. Pete raised his eyes to mine and then looked away quickly. "Maybe we should make you a whole drum set," he said, his eyes running over all the buckets and boxes and scraps of the workshop, his mind whirring in that anything-is-possible-with-me way that I loved as a kid. "Think you'll be ready by tomorrow?" he added in stark recognition of the reality of our situation, even though his face betrayed him. The rain picked up against the side of the workshop like the arrival of an old friend.

"I love you, Pete." It surprised him as much as it surprised me.

"Dad," he corrected, the corner of his mouth pulling toward a smile. "You love me, *Dad*."

Drew's shoulder pulled once, twice, with the rising emotion, his hand still resting on Pete's crutch. "Dad," I corrected.

"Grandpa," Drew corrected as well, with all the gravity in his voice of shifting tectonic plates.

The smile spread across the rest of Pete's face. "Finally."

~

I carried the blankets and pillows into the bedroom to lie down again. I awoke to Pete, Charlotte, and Drew clearing dinner plates. How had I slept through the sound of Drew's voice at dinner? Typically, his voice was like a four-alarm fire, my whole body responding to it. The whole day felt like an alternative reality with the mom in me allowed to take a break. I emerged into the living room squinting. Charlotte was at the sink, and Drew was looking sheepish, leaned up against Pete's side, where he sat in a chair around the table.

"What's up?" I asked Drew, running my fingers through his stick-straight bangs to clear them out of his eyes as I sat down in the chair next to Pete.

"Charlotte has asked for a concert, and Drew has obliged," Pete explained. "Although, suddenly he's plagued with second thoughts." Drew's shoulder pulled once and then again under his thin shirt. While I was still in my mom's clothes, Drew was back in his own.

"She'll understand, buddy, if you don't feel like it," I said. Drew had never been one of those kids bursting to put on a show. Sure, a magic trick in front of just me, or apparently, now, in front of just Pete, but never anything in front of a crowd. But he had a determined, fearful expression etched into his face.

Pete reached for his crutches, where they were balanced against the wall. "Should I get you all set up? We've got these individual drums built, but a man needs them arranged just so into a set." Drew looked down. I could feel the way he wanted to break out, how afraid he was, how impossible it seemed. His shoulder pulled again. And again. I wanted to break in, to control the situation, to say *no, no, never mind,* but I glanced over at Charlotte, who was watching Drew with something like admiration, and it occurred to me that this was him becoming himself, that he didn't need me to direct, to control. He needed me, us, to hold the space in which he could grow to trust himself. I stared at Charlotte. This was what she'd done, just today, by leaving me alone with a hot water bottle and enough blankets and pillows to keep me in place. This was what Pete and Mom had been doing all my life until the three of us were flung apart. This was what Pete was doing right now.

"I could be your singer," Pete offered. Drew raised his eyes and bit his lip. Pete held his hands out, palms up. "I'll just follow your lead, how about?" Drew's eyes widened back toward fear. "Or you can follow mine. We'll just see what happens?" Pete added. Drew's forehead remained creased in worry, but he hooked his fingers on Pete's crutch, and together they moved toward the door. "Give us a few minutes to get set up, then come on over," Pete called to me and Charlotte as they disappeared through the door.

"I saved you a bowl of spaghetti," Charlotte said. "Your boy had two bowls. I thought you were going to be out of luck." She pulled a covered bowl out of the oven, still warm, and set it down in front of me. Drew had never done much more than pick at dinners before we left town.

"Thank you," I said. "For everything."

She caught my eye and smiled. "I haven't been to a concert in years."

I laughed. "Me neither."

Charlotte and I traipsed over to the workshop as I scarfed down the bowl of spaghetti en route. Toward the back end of the workshop, Drew sat on an upside-down five-gallon bucket, gripping a crooked drumstick in each hand. He had his head down, but kept flicking his gaze up as we approached. He had on a duct-taped pair of too-big headphones, likely Danny's. Pete rustled about, arranging in a semicircle around Drew various buckets, pieces of metal, and two drums they'd made with wood and some sort of thick plastic sheeting. When everything was set, Pete hopped off to one side, and balanced himself, a crutch in each armpit. "Ready?" he asked Drew.

Drew nodded.

Pete yelled, "Go!" and then covered his ears with both hands and started singing horribly off-key and loud.

Drew let loose, his arms flying, his face focused on making the most noise possible. I could see Charlotte laughing but couldn't hear her even though she was right next to me. My hands flew to my ears, and so did Charlotte's. Drew's face turned red, and he bounced off the bucket, but never stopped moving as he caught himself and stood instead, arms whipping, making sure not to neglect a single piece of the junkyard trap set. He stopped as quickly as he had started and bit down on a smile. I whooped and hollered, and Charlotte was laughing so hard that tears streaked down her face. Drew looked over at Pete, who was cracking up, clapping, and whistling.

"I think that deserves a big piece of huckleberry pie," Charlotte exclaimed, wiping at her eyes.

Drew could no longer contain his smile. He looked over at me to ask if that was okay, and I nodded. He shot out of his seat and took the hand that Charlotte offered. As they left, Charlotte was recounting her favorite parts of the performance, and Drew was smiling and twisting and kicking his feet. "Looks like we might have a drummer in the family," Pete said, easing himself down on the five-gallon bucket Drew had been sitting on, his leg jutted out and his casted arm balanced awkwardly in his lap.

"I had no idea he had that in him," I said.

"Kids are full of surprises," he said, rubbing a palm over his face. "That was pretty awesome."

"Can I ask you something?"

"Yeah, course." He looked a little weary but gave me the *let's have it* sign with his good hand.

"Would selling the boat and permit have covered whatever the insurance didn't and the trip to Seattle?"

Resignation slumped his shoulders. "Not all of it. But close."

I leaned into the workbench behind me, looked down at my feet. "Was she not happy?"

"Happy gets harder to define as you get older, as you've probably discovered."

"With us, I mean." My voice was just barely louder than the rain brushing the roof.

Pete sighed. "I've asked myself the same question a thousand times." His shoulders drooped even more. "You remember how quick your mom was to laugh, though?"

"At you, mostly." I smiled and huffed out half a laugh.

He nodded. "Life gets so much harder after you bring a kid into it. Don't get me wrong. She loved you, loved every one of those seventeen years she got with you. She said she trusted that you could take it from there. She wasn't someone who assumed life would be, or should be, easy. She took it as it came, and when this came, the decision seemed pretty clear for her."

I stared out the small window in the door, wishing the gray weren't so gray.

Pete went on. "I took it personally for a long time, let it destroy me, honestly. I felt responsible for putting her in that position because I'd chosen to be a fisherman. I'd chosen to have a family, and when it came down to it, I did not provide what was needed—better health insurance, more money." His face pulled tight. "I think the only reason she agreed to go out with me in the first place was because I owned a boat." A sad, airy sound came out of him. "I had to convince her the rest of me wasn't half bad either." He tilted his head. "You know she loved fishing, Mo. With you and with me."

"She would've hated living in town. Or down south," I said. "Married to a lawyer."

He laughed now, for real. "Am I the lawyer in this scenario? Can you even imagine?" He pushed up onto his good leg and reached for his crutches. We turned to head in.

"She wouldn't have been so impressed with your expensive lawyer shoes and swanky apartment."

He shook his head. "She would've run off with the next guy in a ratty T-shirt and a camper van. Good thing I didn't go to law school."

~

The next morning, I got up when I heard Pete moving around. Checked my watch. Four thirty a.m. I tucked the covers around Drew and watched him sleep a minute, the ease of yesterday bright between us.

The pain in my side was its own heartbeat, flooding my body with an ache that took my breath away, and I crumpled onto the edge of the bed. "Shit," I breathed out. Tried to gather my strength. I'd have to push through. It was Thursday. We had three full days and likely two full nights of work before the tide at six p.m. on Saturday that would either float or reflood the *Sarah Louise*. I couldn't make my mind contemplate anything beyond that. Perhaps because everything beyond that was as impossible as everything between now and then, perhaps because I couldn't bear it if the *Sarah Louise* sank for good this time.

I found the edge of the pain and tried to hold myself there. Let my mind unfocus, detach, in order to get to my feet and walk out to the kitchen, where Pete was making coffee.

"Ohh," he said when he turned to look at me, crutches gripped in his armpits. "You look like you're about to puke."

I nodded, eased into a chair at the table. "It'll pass. Maybe some coffee?"

He stumped over and dipped his head to examine me. "Take another day."

"The tide waits for no man," I said.

"It might wait for a woman. Moons and goddesses and all that?" Pete scrunched up his face and raised his eyebrows.

I snorted, and it doubled me over.

"Seriously, Ellie, go back to bed. You can only push yourself so far. Charlotte is going to take Drew today, which will give me time to get through the engine work. We'll start the hull repair tonight."

"That'll leave us two days to do four to five days' worth of work."

"We'll stay up all night. That's four days' worth of time. Just rest right now, Ellie, you're a wreck."

I didn't have it in me to argue. Charlotte's house had become a place outside of time. A time outside myself. All I wanted to do was curl up with Drew, spend a slow morning tending to all the invisible threads between us I'd not had the time to tend to. The encroaching tide, the money we owed the bookie in two months, the way the planks of the hull had to fit together exactly in order to not break or leak, all of it felt like a tidal wave gathering over my head. I nestled in next to the hot furnace of Drew and closed my eyes to all of it.

When I woke up, the bed was empty and the smooth sounds of Drew and Charlotte floated in from the kitchen. My watch read ten a.m. I focused on small breaths so as not to stretch my ribs any more than necessary, easing into an upright position and getting to my feet.

"Hey, buddy," I said, making my way to the table, where Drew sat eating toast.

"Charlotte is making more playdough. Want to build something with me?"

"I do." I couldn't resist staying inside this newfound space just a little bit longer. I'd head down to the boat by noon, I told myself. I swallowed down the fear rising. "What should we build?"

"Marshall's lookout tower. You can do the telescope that goes on top. It's in Adventure Bay. This is my second breakfast." He pointed at his now empty plate.

"Kid's growing," Charlotte said as she finished the last whip of her stirring spoon and set a huge metal bowl full of flour-colored playdough onto the table. "Drew help me tape down the wax paper."

"How do you make playdough? I didn't know that was even possible."

"Oh, it's easy. Flour, water, salt, a little oil, cream of tartar. I used to have food coloring to make it more interesting, but it's been years. Let me make you some coffee."

"I can do it." I added water and grounds to the percolator and set it to boil as Charlotte spread the wax paper over the table and Drew secured it with erratic lengths of tape.

Once that was done, Drew flipped the bowl over and pried the enormous mound of playdough out. He patted it with a flat palm and said, "Come on, Grandma, you can make the windows."

"Ohh . . ." she said, her eyes catching mine over Drew's head. She shook her head to let me know she hadn't suggested he call her *grandma*. Drew sat on his tucked-up feet in a chair, still patting the playdough with a firm palm.

"Drew." I walked over and ran a hand down his back. "Charlotte isn't actually your grandma—"

He whipped around to face me, a few sharp intakes of breath that always preceded crying. "But I want a grandma. I finally have a grandpa, and now I want a grandma," he whined. It pierced through me, everything that could've been but wasn't. I beat him to the crying. I wiped hard at my eyes but didn't try to hide it from Charlotte.

Charlotte looked from one to the other of us. "Well, I imagine you had a very special grandma, and I'm sorry you didn't get to meet her. I could never take her place, but, since no one else calls me Grandma, I would love it if you did. Which means I need a name for you that no one else calls you." She pursed her lips, and then her face lit up. "How about Werd?"

He stared at her with wide eyes.

"That's Drew backward," she explained, her eyes full of mischief.

He cracked up. "Okay!"

"Now, who is Marshall, and what kind of windows does he have in his lookout?" she asked, getting us all back on track.

I loved her so much in that moment, I couldn't get a breath in or out. My eyes blurred with another round of tears, so I got up and made myself another cup of coffee. Behind me, Drew was standing up in the chair. "Marshall is a hero. He has a whole circle of windows. It's not always just him alone in the tower. There has to be room for others to look out too."

I settled into the chair between Drew and his new grandma and listened for the first time to Marshall's various adventures in Adventure City, even asked a few questions to which he readily supplied quick answers. Charlotte made wraparound windows, and I made one heck of a telescope. Drew alternated between focused shaping of the tower and running his feet on the chair with his hands pressed into the table as it all came together.

"Seems like an ideal place to raise your kids," I said in between Drew's Marshall stories.

Charlotte looked up. "Oh. It wasn't like this." She swung her hand over the playdough. "Except every once in a while. You know how there's those lightning flashes of feeling like you're doing something right, but mostly it's a lot of trying to convince yourself you're not doing it all wrong?"

It was my turn to widen my eyes. "Does everyone feel like that?"

She shrugged. "I don't know. Wasn't anyone out here but me." Her mouth quirked up into a smile. She shrugged again. "Probably." She sighed. "Endless daily tasks on a homestead. Like life on a fishing boat, I imagine. Danny fished alone and then with the kids once they got older. I stayed home, ran the place, fixed what broke, which was always something. It was hard. Worth it now that I look back, though."

"What made you decide to come out here?" I asked.

"Love." She shrugged. "Stupidity."

I laughed and then had to hold my breath to get through the added pain in my side.

"Danny and I are both from Illinois."

"No way." I tried to imagine Charlotte in flat land or in a city, but it didn't work.

"Didn't know the first thing about homesteading. Or oceans. Went straight from the church wedding to the cross-country bus that dropped us at the ferry terminal in Bellingham. Still have my one small suitcase I brought with me. Under the bed you're sleeping in. To remind me."

I peered at her. "To remind you of what?"

"Hope."

My face must've fallen because she looked up quickly. "Did I just make it sad? Didn't mean to. When I look back, it's not sad. I mean it is, but it's also happy and lonely and not lonely and exhilarating and exhausting." She sighed. "Once you have kids and things get more complicated, life becomes all the things at once, like a fire hose to the chest. Would be easier if it could somehow stay being one thing at once, like when you're a kid."

I sat there wrapped up in Mom's clothes and Charlotte's presence and wanted to talk to her forever. About everything. "It usually feels like everything all at once, but right now, I just feel content."

She smiled at me across the distance of our years, and I felt for the first time in a long time the way a mom can be ahead of you on the path, turn back to check on you to be sure you are alright, and that's all it takes to fill you with the comfort of someone ahead who is looking out for hazards, who has already made the choices at the Y's, who knows the berries to eat and the ones to avoid, if you want to ask.

We worked in silence for a bit. Drew completely absorbed in making the tower the correct height, his tongue pinning one corner of his mouth in concentration.

"Where's the door go, buddy?" I asked him.

"Right there." He pointed. "You make it, Mama?" He had playdough smears across his shirt and forehead.

"Rounded at the top or square?"

His eyes locked on mine, all business. "Rounded. And there's a loopy slide to get from the top to the bottom quick."

Charlotte shot me a *good luck* look. I laughed in the small little gasps my ribs allowed. "I'll do my best."

Drew patted my hand with his tiny playdoughy one, and I wanted to never ever leave this kitchen. I glanced at the clock on the wall: 1:15 p.m. I swallowed. "Drew?"

"Uh-huh." He didn't look up.

"I've got to work on the boat for the next few days."

Charlotte nodded her agreement, perhaps in recognition that she too could feel the way time was running out.

"Think you'll be alright here with Charlotte?"

"Yeah," he said with all the brazenness of a teenager, except his shoulder pulled once, then again.

"Just a couple days, okay?"

"Yep." He pressed his lips together in the way that I knew helped him keep from crying.

"There's a second ATV under a tarp behind the workshop," Charlotte said. "Keys in it."

~

I pulled on warm clothes and a raincoat and within minutes was standing up on the ATV to take the bumps in my legs, steering out onto the flat, wet sand, across the wide expanse of beach, and up to the *Sarah Louise*.

I had to take the ladder one rung at a time because it hurt to engage my core to lift my foot on the side with the busted ribs. Given how hard getting up the ladder was, I had to turn my brain off before it spiraled out into all the other much harder tasks that lay ahead. I started to build a wall around the discomfort just like I did when I got too cold or too hungry on the boat or too lonely in town. I found some footing on the uneven deck and started across, the sound of Pete in the engine room far below me.

"Hey."

I jumped.

"Sorry," Van said. "Didn't mean to scare you." He stood in the doorway, one arm stretched to hold the door open, one foot propped against the part that should be upright. All the muscles of his arms and chest that had been previously hidden under sweatshirts were on display in a distracting faded T-shirt.

"I, ah—" Rain beat against and ran down the steeply slanted deck between us.

He grinned. Waited.

"What are you doing here?" I finally got out.

"Helping Pete with the engine work. That tide's coming up quick." He tilted his head, squinted a little. "Feeling any better?"

"Good as new."

He raised his eyebrows at that.

"Pete down there?" I gestured toward the interior of the boat behind him.

"Yeah." He widened the space between his body and the doorframe while holding the door that was poised to slam shut and take off a leg due to the slant of the boat. I hung up my rain jacket on the hook outside the door out of habit and climbed through, contorting my body so I didn't touch his, but nonetheless igniting something at my center I thought was long extinguished. My eyes darted up to his. Something skittered across his face that was impossible to read. I ducked my head, and hurried down into the engine room, where Pete was crouched, tools spread out all around him. My heart beat up into my throat, and I was breathing hard.

Pete turned as I approached. "Oh good," he said.

"I'm going to finish wrecking," I said. "And then you'll show me how to take the measurements for the planks, and then I can plane the first board tonight, put it in the cooker, and bend it in early tomorrow morning. While it's cooking, I'll start on the next one. Two today, two tomorrow. And then all the corking." This was way more work than a healthy person could accomplish in two days, much less a broken one.

"We'll have a gallon of coffee for dinner," he answered. "Still a lot to do here too." He nudged his chin toward the massive diesel engine.

Van appeared in the engine room. "Found it," he said, holding up a tool that Pete nodded at.

"Yell at me when you're ready to measure the planks, El," Pete said as I headed out, glancing at Van, trying to figure out if he felt some flicker of what I did. His face was a blank. Clearly not.

I spent the afternoon categorizing pain, naming each new sensation as I lifted the saw, balanced on the ladder, so that it wasn't so all-consuming, plunging the saw deep into the hull, making neat lines out of the jagged ones. Pete joined me on the beach, twitchy with the lack of hours left, talking fast.

I was to measure every inch of what was gone, and then all those numbers would be transferred to angles carved into a piece of wood that would somehow fill the negative space to an eighth of an inch.

Van moved deep in the interior of the boat while Pete droned on below me, flat on his back on the beach, his foot propped up on the five-gallon bucket. Sharp-edged instructions to mark this, measure this, move the ladder closer so I can reach that. We finished as the sun was setting at nine thirty p.m. and loaded up on the ATVs for more instructions on how to transfer the measurements to the actual planks in the workshop. The rain had pruned my fingers and hunger dug into me. I imagined a shelf in my mind where I could place each feeling in my way. A shelf of complaints, labeled and acknowledged so that I could Do It Anyway. I whipped my hood up as I started the ATV, Pete already roaring off ahead of me, and took one last look at the boat, tried to settle the kicked-up feeling in my chest that had lingered all day after seeing Van earlier.

The wet wind felt good against my face, the vague motion of the bay stretching forever, the huge dark trees rising on the other side of me.

In the workshop, Pete rushed through a description of transferring all the measurements to the two-by-eights I was to shape into the planks to fill each hole to an eighth of an inch. An explanation of all the different hand planes and when exactly to use which one and when never to use others, because the plank would be too small and would leak or the plank would be too big and would snap when bent into place, and I would have to start over, and we would not make the tide, and then he was gone. I stared at the rough-cut planks I'd bought in town, all of Pete's instructions swirling together into an indecipherable clutter in my head. I was not a shipwright. I was going to do everything wrong.

I had to keep my head down and not think about anything other than eighths of inches, exact angles, the smooth, long glide of the hand plane, and the curled shavings that landed at my feet. The pain in my ribs exploded into my head in wild, swirling colors. I packed each color away, swallowed against the bile that rose up my throat.

At some point, Charlotte appeared with a sandwich that I inhaled in four bites. At some point, Pete was looking over my shoulder, double-checking my work, filling up the boiler with buckets of fresh water hauled from the catchment tank. The rain was steady through the night against the workshop, a constant force that I could relax into. The background noise necessary on the stage of my life.

By three a.m., my back and neck ached. I tried to straighten up, but it seemed every single tight muscle was connected directly to my rib cage. Pete was back, his face etched with worry. "You're moving too slow, Ellie. Being too careful. Pick up the pace. Trust yourself. You need this one done and boiling five minutes from now."

Trust yourself. Trust yourself. I kept repeating it in my head. What if I trusted myself with Drew? Would it open up more space between us? If I could judge myself less, would I worry over him less? Did everyone feel as lost as I did? Jesus, I needed a friend. Isolation isn't a place you set out to go, it's a place you look up one day to find yourself in, and only then do you realize how far you'd have to backtrack to get out.

At six a.m., Pete was back, checking on the plank I'd dropped in the boiler two hours earlier. "Let's call it done. Go get Van."

"Doesn't the plank need another couple hours?" I asked.

"Yeah, well, fuck. It'll have to do." He ran his good hand over his whole face in what looked to be an effort to slough off the sleep that remained.

"Where's Van?"

"At his house. There's a trail, apparently." He pointed in the general direction of the woods behind the house and workshop.

As I snaked my way along the path in a soft rain, I couldn't get out of my head the image of my knock at the door waking Van up. Him all disheveled and warm and sleepy. I focused on not tripping over roots as the path cut through a thin arm of land that jutted out between Marbled Inlet and North Bay. Dense blueberry shrub on either side, taller than my head, until it opened up to ferns and shiny green skunk cabbage leaves bigger than Drew. The canopy wove together high overhead in a comforting way that eased the bunching muscles of my back, the pull of sleep on my whole body.

Van's house stood in a clearing. A simple square affair with straight lines and a cedar shake roof. Next to it was a greenhouse just as big. Or what was to become a greenhouse. It was half framed in and not yet enclosed, a woodstove covered in clear plastic in one corner. I continued up to the house and knocked. The front door was paneled and had an intricate design of ivy carved into it.

Movement inside, and then there he was, leaning an elbow against the opened door, looking exactly as I had imagined. "No one's ever knocked on my door before," he said, voice throaty with sleep. "Charlotte sings the whole way over, and Danny starts screaming my name halfway here so he doesn't have to walk the whole way."

"Sorry to disturb you." I stood, awkwardly aware of my arms, trying to not give anything away in my face this time. "Can you help me with the first plank? Bending it in. I know you haven't slept much. I'm not even sure why you're helping, actually."

"I'm going to brush my teeth," he said, and I felt all of the ways I was imposing on him at once. "For your sake." Which made me imagine him close, which made it all worse.

I didn't want to take my boots off, and I didn't want to track the outside muck in, so I stayed just outside the front door, letting all the heat out. The kitchen ran the full length of one wall. Glass jars containing canned fruit, vegetables, and salmon were lined up along two long shelves. The whole house was open and airy. In the center of the room sat a couch and two chairs made of canvas fabric stretched over wood that were draped with deer- and bearskins. Van climbed the wooden ladder to what I assumed was a sleeping loft and came back down wearing a gray hoodie and Carhartts. He dampered down the woodstove in the middle of the room and stepped into his boots, which were next to the door. "Not still raining out, is it?" he asked.

"Ah—"

He smiled a sad smile. "That was a joke. It's always raining out." He shoved his arms into a thick rubber rain jacket and pulled the door closed behind him.

"So . . ." he said as we fell in, single file, back to Danny's, which was all the path would allow. Him a few feet behind me. "You been fishing with Pete your whole life?" No ending *g*'s to his words and a sideways slant to the *i*'s. Like honey on a hot day.

"We've got until September 20 to make fifty grand to buy the boat and permit back from the bookie Pete lost them to."

Van whistled low and soft. "That's not what I was expecting."

"Me neither." We walked the rest of the way in an easy silence until the path widened in front of Danny's house. I turned toward the workshop, suddenly not liking the picture I had painted of Pete. "He wasn't always like that. The gambling got out of control after my mom died."

Van walked along beside me, his hands in his pockets. Just before we got to the workshop, he said, "Must've been hard for him." He opened the door and held it for me, his green eyes tracking mine as I stepped in close to pass through this time. He added in a low, worn-out tone, "That's enough to make a person into something he isn't."

We pulled the plank from the boiler and tied it down to the back rack on the ATV. I hopped on, revved the engine to life. There was no time to lose. If it cooled too much, we wouldn't be able to bend it. "Let's go." I nodded my head for Van to climb on.

"Oh. Yeah, okay." He swung a long leg over and sat down behind me, the heat of him against my back making me feel like I might never need sleep again. He held on to the rack behind him rather than to me and avoided my eyes as we climbed off in front of the *Sarah Louise*.

Pete was waiting for us on the beach and had two ladders set up on either side of the hole in the hull. I immediately set to untying the plank as Van set up both ladders.

Van held one end of the plank in place against the hull as I worked to bolt in the aft end.

"Okay," Pete called. "It's going to take all the C-clamps we have and then pure muscle from there."

"Ohhhh," Van said from the top of his ladder four feet from mine. "Now I see why you needed me."

I rolled my eyes at him. "You're my only option."

One side of his mouth twitched up. "Which is sad for you."

With all the clamps pulling the plank into the approximate curve to match the hull, Van and I began hammering with wedges to get it close enough that I could bolt the rest of it into place. I got in a second set of bolts and then a third set. The fourth was about halfway down the board. This was the point where the bend was the sharpest.

"Looks tight from here, Ellie," Pete called from below. "Probably should've soaked it longer."

"It'll work." I turned to Van. "I'm going to grab us more wedges."

It took another half hour of clamping and whacking the board into the bend we needed. "Alright, I think that's close enough that I can get the next set of bolts in," I said to Van.

As I drilled the hole, a sound like a gunshot went off so close to my head that I dropped the drill and scrambled down the ladder, landing in a heap on the sand and rocks. Above me, the plank had snapped in two, one half bolted in place and the other half in Van's hands.

I dropped my head into the crook of my elbow.

"Get up," Pete said. "Start over."

The rain was cold against my face. Above was a thousand feet of gray. My legs were too heavy to move, and my mind told me to give up, go to sleep.

Van's boots entered my peripheral vision, and then I heard him climb up the ladder I'd just been on and begin removing the broken plank.

~

The rest of Friday was spent flying through the measuring and planing. A loose approximation of things I never allowed myself. A gap in careful consideration through which anything could fall. Charlotte kept Drew occupied, and I scarfed bars and almonds and a whole thermos of coffee and then a second thermos. Van was still working in the engine room with Pete when I showed up with what would be the second attempt at the first plank, and the second plank. I practiced trusting myself in what I would've otherwise called half-assing on the measuring but not the boiling, and we got both planks placed across the hole in the hull.

It was close to midnight when the third plank reached its full cooking time.

"Pete!" I called out as I cut the engine on the ATV and set to untying the plank. He'd have to help me set this one. No way was I going to wake up Van in the middle of the night after he'd been in the engine room helping us all day, since I'd woken him up that morning. "Pete!" I yelled again. He banged on the hull from inside the boat to let me know he'd heard me. I set the ladders and was gathering up the tools we'd need. "Hurry—" I was yelling when Van came around the stern of the boat on the beach. He looked worn down, sleepy, and it froze up my lungs to remember all the times Oliver had looked just like that and I'd wrapped him up in my arms, whispered, "C'mon, let's go to bed," as if the proximity of my body alone could heal his.

"What?" Van asked. I was staring at him. He lifted his ball cap, ran a hand through his unruly curls, and settled it back on his head.

"You're still here?" I spun for the plank and started moving toward the boat. Every minute that passed was a minute of it cooling to the point of snapping.

"Pete's not looking too good," Van said as he set both ladders in place.

Pete came around the corner of the stern. "Let's go!" He swung a hand, indicating *up the ladder, right now* to both of us. Pain bunched up at the corners of his eyes.

Van and I got three sets of bolts in, hammered and wedged and clamped our way through the fourth set of bolts, and then the final three sets, until the plank was securely in place. One plank to go, six hours of corking to fill what looked to be gaping caverns in between the three planks already bolted in, seventeen hours to the tide. I had not bought an extra plank at the shipyard. I'd have to find something in Danny's workshop that might possibly work. I imagined making some janky-ass plank out of something plastic because I couldn't find any wood. I imagined Pete shaking his head, not allowing us to even try to float the boat with a plastic plank.

He interrupted my spooling-out thoughts. "Night, kids. I'm blown out, El. Need to close my eyes for a bit." His hair was wild and his bruised face was deeply etched with exhaustion. He swung his casted leg over the ATV and roared off up the beach. I needed to get back to the workshop, where I would somehow locate a piece of wood to turn into the final plank. Every inch of my body ached. The sand and pebbles at my feet looked like a down feather bed. I gave myself five minutes and splayed out flat on my back on the beach at the base of the ladder I'd been on.

Van eased himself onto the beach at the base of his ladder, propped up on his elbows, staring out at the darkening sea. "You and Pete are a couple of hardcore individuals." The rain had stopped, and a slow even breeze rustled through the alder at the tree line. The mountains across the bay were a blue black. The tide lapped at the aft end of the *Sarah Louise*. A big tide, before the bigger tide.

I rolled my head to the side in the sand to look over at him. "Not really. Just desperate times and all that."

"Still. Brutal to be doing all this with two casts and at least four broken ribs between the two of you."

"Bruised."

"Right." He grinned out at the water.

I rolled my head back so that I was looking up at the *Sarah Louise* looming over me. "I wish I had a drink," I said. Pete's flask was undoubtedly on its way back to Charlotte's with him.

"Me too," Van breathed out. "Exactly why I don't keep any around." Van's proximity, how alone we were, was lightening up my nerves. Since when did I act like this? Since I had allowed myself to six years ago. Since I had chosen so wrong. Except this was different. Oliver was life on a cliff edge, the possibility of the fall thrilling. Van was a slow, easy drive, everything we needed already in the car.

"Why do you live out here?" I asked. It seemed so unlikely. If someone from down south wanted an Alaskan experience, they moved to a town, got a job, went to the bar in the evenings to hang out with other people. They didn't take up in a remote bay unless there was a reason for it. I lifted my head from the sand to peer at him.

He closed his eyes, breathed in slowly, to steady himself, it seemed, confirming he was on the run from something, like so many other men who materialized in Alaska, rarely mentioning a life prior. "What I can't believe is that I followed the rain."

I breathed out slowly, connected myself to the way night pulsed, to the way the ocean was always itself, all I'd ever need. "What's wrong with the rain?"

"Everything is wrong with the rain."

We fell into a silence that was more like a high-pitched ringing in the ears. I watched a patch of night sky get swallowed up by a dark cloud, and that's when I remembered Pete's secret stash. "Wait," I said, forcing my body to sit up because a swig of whiskey to ease everything sounded so good. "Let's go." I pushed up to my feet, ducked under the hulking hull, and climbed the ladder in the one-foot, two-foot manner that was all my body allowed. Van waited until I'd heaved myself over the rail before he followed me up. In the wheelhouse, Van stood as far away as possible against the door as I dug around behind the canned beans and found the pint of Jack Pete had hidden.

Van's eyes widened when I pulled out the full bottle. "Things are getting better and better," he said through a lopsided grin, sliding back to the easier version of himself.

I cracked the seal and tipped the bottle for a slug. It warmed all of me at once. Why was I so hard on Pete? Whiskey was just what you needed sometimes. I held the bottle out to Van. He moved over to lean against the edge of the table that was near vertical. There was no way to sit down given the tilt of the *Sarah Louise*. As he took the bottle, his fingers grazed mine, which felt like a second shot of whiskey. He watched me as he tilted the bottle and took a long pull. He wiped the back of a hand across his mouth and held it out, eyebrows raised. "You going again?"

I took another long drink, and he laughed, shook his head. "Alright, then." His smile like a rope encircling us, nudging us closer.

"What?" I imagined perfectly put-together Southern girls wherever he was from sipping white wine with an impressive poise that I could never pull off with my too-tall body, over-washed sweatshirts, and hair that never saw a day without a ponytail.

"I just never met anyone like you before." He reached for the bottle again, held it up to inspect the level. It was almost half gone. He narrowed his eyes. "What's happening here? We getting ripped?" He took another swallow, eyes sparked up, and back on mine in the dim light.

He was so steady in the face of whatever was pulling at him. Swinging up out of it into playfulness instead of down farther into the dark depths like I did. In his presence, it seemed something even I could practice, could possibly master.

I'd been watching him too long. With too serious an expression, probably. He swiped a hand over his face. "I should let you get back to work." He handed the bottle over. "Thanks for the whiskey."

I took the bottle from him, screwed the top back on, and knelt to put it back in the cabinet. When I stood up, he was stepping through the door. His feet sounded on the ladder, and then it was silent. I ran both hands over my face. "Fuck's sake," I breathed out.

~

I gave myself one minute to stand on the big, silent beach before I fired up the ATV. The wind blew off the water, gentle now, like an apology. The rain was still at bay, the cloud cover high and thin, the mountains towering over the bay, glaciers like sparkling shawls in the moonlight.

Back in the woodshop, I located a piece of scrap wood that wasn't a good choice to make into the plank I'd broken, but it was the only choice. I worked by headlamp to transfer the measurements. My eyes stung with the effort of keeping them open. Coffee felt like a burning necessity, but I didn't want to wake anyone in the house by making it in the middle of the night.

~

At five a.m., Pete found me in the workshop, transferring angles. "Right, good. Did you not sleep? There's coffee on in the house. I'd get you some, but . . ." He plopped down on the stool behind the workbench as I bolted for the door. I peeked in on Drew, who was sleeping sideways across the bed. I had to force myself to turn away after kissing his forehead, running a hand along his tiny, relaxed shoulder. I missed him more than seemed possible.

No one was in the kitchen. I poured myself a cup of coffee, added some cold water to cool it off, drank the whole thing down, then poured myself a second cup.

Pete was checking all my measurements when I got back. "This is the most sorry-ass option for a plank I've ever seen."

I started to defend myself, but he kept on going. "You need it to be cooking by ten a.m. to place it and still have time to cork the seams. Tide's at six p.m. tonight." As if I'd forgotten. The edges of my vision shook with exhaustion as I watched him spin on his one good foot, crutch through the door, rev the ATV, and then, after a flash across the window, he was gone.

The hours rolled by. I didn't look up or give in to the way my back muscles had cemented or the way my ribs now hurt with every breath. I focused on the strength of straight lines, the power of angles, the way the random unlikely scrap of wood took shape into a necessary component of a boat as I shaved away one small layer after another.

I dropped the plank in the cooker, closed my eyes, slouched against a stack of plastic tubs, and squinted at my watch: 1:10 p.m. The reality of our situation was tunneling into me, weedy and thick. The hours between now and the tide felt like a brick wall I was going to have to run through. I steadied myself, shuffled out to the ATV as fast as I could make my body go. The ocean at low tide hovered out in the bay, plotting its return. The power of it a certainty.

Pete met me on the beach when I pulled up. He had all the corking supplies set out. He banged hard against the hull where the engine room was, and just as I slid off the ATV, Van was on the ladder and then ducking under the boat, catching my eye. I felt stupid at the way my heart kicked up. I had to bend over my busted ribs to protect them from it. "Alright," Pete was saying. "We've got four and a half hours before this thing floats. Any chance you've got experience corking seams, Van?"

"I know a lot about pigs and corn." He ducked under the tarp, flipped his ball cap, and resettled it.

"Okay, then," Pete was saying. "Can't fault a man for knowing a lot about bacon. We'll need you to roll the oakum, then you can putty the seams behind Ellie. Depending on how fast she moves, that ought to be a full-time job. And you're going to have to move fast, Ellie, top speed. That's six hours of work."

I turned to Van. "You're not going to have any vegetables this winter because of me."

"Ellie." Pete looked over his shoulder, annoyance splayed across his face. "You won't make it on your own. I can't cork one-handed, and there's still engine work left to finish."

"I didn't have any vegetables last winter, and look how good I turned out." Van grinned across the uncrossable distance between us, the steadiness of him radiating like a heat wave. I wanted to stay right where I was to absorb as much of it as possible.

Pete dropped a canvas bag full of corking supplies at our feet. "Ellie, show him what he needs to know." He moved awkwardly across the sand on his crutches and heaved himself back up the ladder in a harried way that made me understand he was as far behind in the engine work as I was with the planking.

I sat down on the five-gallon bucket on the beach as Van watched. I unpacked the long strand of wispy oakum and rolled it on my thigh, back and forth, until it stuck to itself and compacted. "Roll until it's about this thick," I said. "Important that it's uniform. If it's too thin, water gets through; if it's too thick, I won't be able to pack it into the crease."

Van nodded. "Got it. Roll the nasty dreadlock to that exact thickness."

I huffed out a laugh. "I can't believe you are still helping." I broke off the length of oakum that was ready to go and handed him the huge mass left to roll.

He sat on the bucket in my place as I gathered what I needed from the bag. "Are you kidding? I always wanted to roll—what's this called?"

"Oakum."

"Right, oakum," he said and pressed two fingers hard against his right temple. He ignored my questioning look. He was so self-contained. As you'd need to be, to live out here alone. A fortress of self.

"How's this for thickness?" He held up what he'd been rolling.

"Just right."

I moved the ladder to line it up with the top aft crease between the first plank I'd replaced and the plank above it, time and the tide pressing in. I snapped my ear protection in place and laid the oakum flush with a roll of cotton the same thickness. In one hand, I balanced the long, flat corking iron at an angle my wrist had memorized long ago. I swung the mallet, and the corking iron packed the oakum and cotton into the seam between planks at the perfect depth and tightness to keep us dry belowdecks. I swung again and again, falling into the rhythm of it, one inch at a time.

I pushed past exhaustion into a sort of trance. For hours, all I heard was the staccato *tink, tink, tink, tink* of my mallet hitting the corking iron. I ignored the way each hit vibrated through my wrist and up into my arm. The sharp stab of pain in my side each time the mallet connected with the iron as the hours ticked away and the water begin to flood back toward us.

Chapter 16

As I worked, Pete never emerged from the engine room. Van kept up rolling the oakum and puttying the seams I'd corked. There were so many ways the *Sarah Louise* could sink. If all the seams weren't corked, water would fill the bilge. If the seams were corked, but the planks weren't snug enough against each other, off by one too many passes of the hand plane, water would fill the bilge. How much water was the question. Some, and the bilge pump would handle it, too much, and we'd be on the bottom. If the engine didn't run, we'd be tossed onto whatever beach the tide carried us to. I pushed those thoughts out of my head, concentrated on one swing after the next, one inch of cotton and oakum packed into the seam at a time. One quick twist of the wrist to keep the sea out of this inch and then the next inch.

I wiped away the sweat and rain gathered on my forehead and glanced over at Van, who was six feet away on his own ladder, laying in putty behind me. His eyes slid to me and then out to the dark, moving mass of sea behind us.

Every inch of my body felt as if it might pool if I stopped moving, and so I didn't. I begged my arms to go faster. I ignored everything else, turned my brain off, shaved seconds off every minute, and prayed it would be enough.

At four p.m., I raced to pull the plank out of the cooker. It bent into place much easier than the other three for reasons I didn't want to contemplate. Once Van and I had it secured, we went back to corking, rolling, puttying.

At some point, the rain picked up. At some point, the wind did too. At some point, I started shivering, and at some point, Pete joined Van at the base of the ladder below me. They were moving what was left of our supplies off the beach, preparing for the tide. Van cut the tarp free above me. Six feet of seam left. Seventy-two inches. I could hear the water now, close. When I climbed down to move the ladder forward, the water lapped a few feet away. I scrambled back up the ladder and picked up where I'd left off. Water pushed at the base of the ladder. I readjusted my stance to try to accommodate the motion and kept going. I was on the final plank. Four feet of seam to go.

The water was now working its way under the hull. The *Sarah Louise* shifted against it. Van roared the skiff to life at the back of the bay. Pete's voice from above startled me. He had climbed up the other ladder and stowed it on deck without me noticing. He was getting ready to start watching the bilge once the water reached the heinous gouge in the stem and then the planks. If the boat floated, Van would use the skiff to drag the *Sarah Louise* out deeper and Pete would start the engine. I glanced up, still moving as fast as I could. Pete was hanging over the railing, the look on his face reflecting the same realization I was having. I wasn't going to make it.

Waves slapped up the ladder. There was nothing to hold on to. Water would knock the ladder over soon. My hands flew. *Tink, tink, tink.* One inch and then the next. The *Sarah Louise* shuddered as the water lifted her off the ground and then settled her back on her keel. I needed to be out of the way once she was at the will of the water. The ladder swayed beneath me as the water gained a stronger hold. *Tink, tink, tink.* My mind focused to a pinpoint. *Tink, tink, tink, tink.* One foot of seam left. Van and Pete called to each other over the noise of the outboard as they tied the *Sarah Louise* to the skiff. The sea was crawling up the ladder, a solid, moving mass, and the moon somewhere behind the mass of clouds was pulling me along with it.

My hands were numb, my arms were on fire. Six inches. The *Sarah Louise* lifted again, rolled toward me, and the ladder tipped back, making me weightless for a second, then settled against the boat again. I reached far to my right, off-balance for those last few inches. *Tink, tink, tink.*

The boat lifted and pitched with more force, and the icy water closed over my legs. Three inches of seam left, and then a wave slapped up against the hull, bounced off, and took me with it backward. I toppled into the ocean, and the tide immediately began pushing me toward shore. I swam, my arms grateful for a different movement, the rocks of the beach were under my feet, and then I was crawling up the beach, collapsing into a heap. The sound of the skiff straining against the weight of the *Sarah Louise* filled up the bay.

The *Sarah Louise* groaned as the water pushed her up the beach and the skiff pulled her in the opposite direction. The stern of the skiff dug in dangerously deep as Van juiced everything out of the throttle. The *Sarah Louise* resisted. It wasn't enough. "C'mon, please," I whispered. Another wave picked her up, and she gave in. Pete whooped from inside the wheelhouse, and Van kept the skiff at full throttle, aimed at the opposite shore. The *Sarah Louise* inched away from the beach, floating once again.

My eyes locked on the starboard planks, at the waterline. Was it rising? And then the sound of the engine missing, of Pete trying again, the sharp staccato of it trying to catch, and then the roar of it as it came alive. Our eyes locked through the wheelhouse windows. And then I was sprinting for the inflatable at the tree line. I kept one eye on the *Sarah Louise* as I untied and dragged the inflatable down the beach.

The waterline stayed in the approximate right place, which meant she wasn't sinking fast, anyway. I jumped into the inflatable and covered the distance to the *Sarah Louise,* no longer feeling my ribs or any other part of my body. I climbed aboard. My sister, upright, and solid once again. Standing on the deck, the sea righted itself. No longer dangerous, just a rising tide on a beautiful, overcast evening. Pete came out of the wheelhouse at a fast hobble. "It's coming in those last few inches, but the bilge pump is keeping up just fine. The wood will swell up and take care of most of the rest of it." He wrapped his good arm around my shoulder. "We're good! We did it!" Helping me understand that good enough was good enough and worth celebrating.

"Good job on the engine." It rattled beneath our feet in its familiar hum.

Pete settled into something more rational. "We need to go, but I vote we anchor up for the night to be sure she's seaworthy."

I leaned my head against Pete's chest. "That sounds good to me. I need to sleep."

"Me too, Mo, more than anything."

I found myself some dry clothes, then kept an eye on the bilge as Pete drove us to the protected anchorage at the back of the bay where we'd been headed a week ago.

"So far, so good," I reported as I climbed the stairs up into the wheelhouse. "Who's that?" A troller I didn't recognize was anchored up. "Did they go by earlier today?" How had I not noticed?

"I don't know." Pete shrugged. "I was belowdecks all day."

We dropped anchor and rowed in, Pete on one oar with his good arm, and me on the other with my good arm, in a slightly off, good-enough kind of way that kept us aimed at the break in the trees that was the path to Charlotte's. Just behind the relief of the *Sarah Louise* floating again sat the dread of the next impossibility. I willed myself not to go there, yet. To gift my mind this one small window of rest.

"Wish you'd seen it." Van's voice seeped in under the door as Pete and I pulled off our boots in the mudroom. "The ladder got swept out from under her by the tide, and she leapt like an upside-down flying squirrel, back-flopping into the water. That girl is wild."

Charlotte joined in his laughter, and so did Pete and I, as well as two other men.

"It wasn't that dramatic, was it?" I asked Pete, working my second boot off.

"Nah. Sounds good when he tells it that way, though."

We walked through the mudroom door into the living room, and Drew ran for me. It felt like a lifetime since I'd seen him last. I bent down and wrapped my arms around him, smelling his Drew smell, feeling his unbelievably soft cheek against my wind-hardened face. Charlotte spun in our direction from the counter, her whole being lit up. "Ellie! Pete! This is my son, Brent." Her love stitched like a border around every word. "He and Danny were fishing close by, so they came over for dinner. Come join us. A full house," she said to herself, as pleased as a card player with such a hand would be, as she pulled a stack of bowls from the cabinet.

Drew wriggled out of my arms. "I'm in charge of the spoons. No one can eat soup without a spoon."

"Most important job of the whole shebang," Danny offered up from the table, where he sat with a beer next to Van and Brent, who both also had one. "You made yourself famous around here," he said to me.

I smiled at him and reached out a hand to Brent, who was a younger carbon copy of Danny. "Nice to meet you."

Van got up and grabbed two more cold beers from the fridge as Pete and Brent shook hands and we settled into chairs around the table. Van popped the tops and set one down in front of me and Pete, my eyes sliding out to check on the *Sarah Louise* every few minutes until the warm light of the kitchen, the men's conversation, Drew running back and forth from the table to the kitchen chattering at Charlotte wrapped me up in the way nights like this with Pete and Mom used to. In a way I knew I missed but had been afraid to ever admit how much.

Danny watched Charlotte with Drew, her happiness visibly filling him up. Van, Brent, and Pete talked trash in the way of men enjoying each other's company, Pete's hand rested on the back of my chair. Charlotte filled the bowls a quarter full so that Drew could carry them over to each of us without spilling. "Enough for seconds and thirds and fourths," she called out as she handed Drew the next bowl to deliver, his tongue pinned in the corner of his mouth for maximum concentration. "Good job, Werd," she cooed at him.

This was so clearly what Drew needed. So clearly what we all needed. Community, family, each experience, each night spent in a warm kitchen threading together over and over until the fabric was strong enough to catch any who slipped.

~

I fell into a stupor after a second beer and a full stomach, barely remembering excusing myself, climbing into bed with Drew, falling asleep to the conversation and laughter that continued into the night.

The next morning, well before dawn, I crept outside. The light was on in the wheelhouse of the *Sarah Louise*, and Pete was moving around inside. He'd spent the night on the boat to check the bilge every couple of hours. The *Sarah Louise* pulled at her anchor line as if she were ready to go. I wrapped my arms around myself and smiled out at my sister. "Mom, look," I whispered. "She's alright."

I turned back to get Drew and me ready to join Pete. At the tree line, in the blue-black of predawn light, Van stood with his hands in his pockets, watching me cross the beach.

When I got close enough to hear, he said, "Ellie, I, ah—"

I waited, my breath stalling out. His face etched into sad lines.

"Thanks for all the help. Me and Pete alone wouldn't have made it," I barged into the silence.

"No." He shook his head. "It was a nice diversion." He looked away. "Pete's quite a character."

"He does liven a place up," I agreed.

"You'll make the money," he said, his face cracking into his signature slow grin. "Don't worry so much." Calm washed through me, as it often did when I was around Van. An even keel. As if he'd found just the right angle to cut through the pounding waves to cancel out the damage they could do. The comfort and ease of the night before was still in me. All of us with a place at the table.

"Should be four or five days of the king opener left." I couldn't believe what I was saying, but I kept going. "Kings are bank, cohos not as much. Would be great to have an extra set of hands on board. Just until the opener closed, I mean."

"Hands?"

"You," I stuttered. "Would be great to have you on board with us." My face burned hot despite the cool, misty rain. And because he wasn't saying anything, I let myself babble. "We'll need fuel and supplies in town first, and Pete needs to see Dr. Stone about whatever funk is growing inside his cast. Should be able to get everything done today and head out onto the grounds this evening."

"This evening," Van repeated. He looked scared. His face crowded again with whatever it was he kept not saying.

I started to shake my head. I'd never been so embarrassed. Real life had been shaded by this time out of place in Charlotte's orbit. "Never mind, I don't know what I'm thinking. You've already helped plenty. We'll be fine. Thanks, again." I stepped past him and did everything I could to keep from sprinting toward the trail back to Charlotte's.

"I'd love to," he said gravely.

I froze. Turned, peered at him from under my hood. "You would?"

"I can be in town by four." His eyes had the look of the tide gathering itself to change direction. The rest of his face was a mask. Unreadable.

"Alright."

He nodded once, turned, and walked up the beach.

~

Brent and Danny were clattering around in the workshop as I walked back to the house. When I stepped inside, Charlotte stood up, housecoat pulled tight over a nightgown and slippers. She put one hand on either of my arms, eyes glistening, and said, "Please bring that boy back to see me."

"I will. I promise."

"Soon?" She dropped her arms and turned away.

"Soon."

In the bedroom, I gathered our meager belongings and then lay down next to Drew. I smoothed his hair and kissed his ear. He snuggled in closer to me. "Time to get up, little man."

"No, Mama," he eked out before pulling the covers tighter around his chin.

"The boat's fixed, buddy," I whispered.

His eyes flew open. He rolled onto his back and looked me square in the face. "I don't want to go back on the boat."

I pulled him to me, his shoulder to my chest. "It won't happen again, Drew."

"How do you know?" His voice was so small. The wind so loud at the window. The pull of the sea so strong against the ladder less than twelve hours ago.

I whispered into his ear, "I don't know, actually. All sorts of things are going to happen to us, but you know what? As long as I've got you, and you've got me, we'll get through it."

"What about Grandpa?"

I wanted to trust him, more than anything else in the world, but the old fear was sneaking back in as I faced leaving this bubble of safety. "I don't know."

"There's a lot of things you don't know about," he said to the ceiling.

"I wish it wasn't that way."

"Me too."

~

I got Drew dressed but had to carry him out of the room after he refused to walk. Charlotte had packed us a breakfast, wrapped up in brown paper. Pete was hugging Charlotte, talking too quietly for me to hear.

Charlotte reached for Drew. He looped his arms around her neck, and then his legs around her middle. "Such a good boy," she said, patting his back with great tenderness, tears now streaming down her face. She gave him one long hug, then handed him back.

"I want to go home," Drew said against my neck. The defeat in his small voice sent a crack through my heart. I hated the idea that the carefully reconstructed strands between us were starting to fray already. He needed my undivided attention to help him deal with what had happened. I needed to be on deck every single daylight hour for the next seven weeks. And there it was, the all too familiar juggle of my needs versus his needs, one seemingly always sacrificed for the other.

Charlotte followed us to the door, but didn't move to put her boots on. She was trying to stop crying in front of Drew. Instead, she ran her hand over his hair and cupped his chin one last time and disappeared back into the house.

Danny and Brent appeared at the doorway of the workshop to shake hands and say good luck, and then Pete and I and Drew walked the beach back to where the *Sarah Louise* bobbed at anchor. Pete dropped our few belongings and his crutches into the inflatable, climbed in, and reached for Drew. When Drew saw the inflatable, he screamed, "No, no, no!" His face erupted into a chaos of tight scrunches and rapid blinking as he started to cry.

"Drew, it's okay. We're alright. We're just rowing out to the boat. Look at the water." I turned him so that he could see the flat, calm surface. But it didn't matter. Drew clawed at me. I peeled him off me and got him to Pete, who wrapped him tight in his good arm. I pushed the skiff off the beach quickly and climbed in. Drew fought the whole way. The frantic pitch of his fear carried across the water and echoed up into the icy valleys above us.

Chapter 17

Drew and I slept the whole way to town. Once tied up at the docks, I raced to the grocery with a whiny Drew in tow, and Pete caught a ride up the hill to see Dr. Stone.

The *Sarah Louise* pulled at her lines on the dock in Kings Creek in the offshore breeze, the unpainted new planks an ugly scar at her side. I wanted more than anything to cover them up with paint, at least what I could reach above the waterline. While we waited for the groceries to be delivered, I sat with Drew at the table in the wheelhouse, trying to play Uno but thinking instead about all the chores that still needed to be done before we started fishing in the morning and wondering nonstop if Van would actually show up.

"Mom," Drew kept saying. "Mom, it's your turn."

Pete flung open the wheelhouse door and thumped inside in two startlingly white new casts. "Why are you just sitting there? You didn't get stuck with Steve for delivery, did you? He takes for fucking ever. You have to ask for Marc."

The bruises across his face were still an eerie yellow, and the lines around his eyes and mouth had gotten deeper with the lack of sleep across the past week.

"Mooommmm," Drew whined next to me for the hundredth time, and I broke.

"There's no way, Pete. We've got two months to make $49,000. Impossible." My eyes landed on the drying line Mom had rigged up above the stove for socks and gloves. All of it would be someone else's come fall, which made me feel like I was going to puke. The inroads I'd made toward Drew were gone, the levity in his mood, the peace I'd felt at Charlotte's, all of it evaporated in one day. It was one thing to find it, it was wholly another to hang on to it.

Pete's hair was whipped up all crazy, and his eyes flared. "Knock it off, Ellie." He propped his crutches in the head and swung himself to stand over me. "We resurrected the boat. We've already accomplished the impossible. Now we've just got to fish. Sure, twenty hours a day, but whatever, we know how to do that."

"Hello," a voice called out from the docks, and then footsteps on board, and then Van coming through the wheelhouse door.

"Well." Pete's face lit up like a hundred-watt bulb. "Look what the sweet baby Jesus delivered us. Even better than Steve with his cans of beans." Pete gave me a conspiratorial grin as if he wasn't actually all that surprised at this turn of events.

Van's eyes locked on Drew, and his face fell. I stood up, stepped in between them, unease caging my heart. Now that I thought about it, he'd rarely been in such close proximity to Drew out at Charlotte's.

Van's eyes moved to mine. "Which bunk is mine?" he asked, a small duffel slung over his shoulder.

"Top bunk. Starboard side." I pointed toward the focsle as Pete headed out to do the million things left to do before we could untie. *Just a couple days,* I told myself. *Just until kings close.* It was one thing to invite a stranger into your house, it was quite another to head out into open water with him on your boat. Men walked off the ferry all the time with nothing but a wallet and a bunch of secrets. The misty rain had a way of helping keep those secrets. Something cold and hot ran over my skin at the same time.

Van tossed his bag on the bunk and came back up, this time avoiding looking over at Drew, which was almost worse. "Engine run smooth on the way over?" he asked.

"Yeah." My voice tiptoeing around whatever the fuck was going on. I watched him close, but his face was set like stone, unreadable again. Dread poured into my veins. I never should've asked him to join us. I should've just trusted that Pete and I would pull it off. Except a third pair of hands for kings might make all the difference. It would certainly equal an extra hour of sleep here and there, which I desperately needed.

"I'll go see if Pete needs any help on deck."

Through the window, I watched Pete show Van the row of hooks that needed sharpening and then leave him to it as he rolled himself out of the pit.

Pete stopped to jab a few fingers into the top of his new cast and rub hard. I imagined he had some sort of awful skin disease based on how many times seawater got in, not to mention some boat grime and fish guts.

Steve rolled up with a dolly full of boxes of food. He handed them over the rail, and I carried it all into the wheelhouse.

Drew settled on the floor next to me as I packed food into the higher cabinets, and he worked on the lower one. He wailed when the soup cans he was stacking tumbled out and rolled away. "It's alright." I pulled my way back to the calm, patient version of myself that had built a playdough lookout tower only a few days ago. "It's always hard to get everything from town packed into this little space." I channeled Charlotte's pleasure at being elbow to elbow with Drew, heads bent together as they washed dishes. I kissed him on the temple, pulled him onto my lap as I sat down with him. "Let's do it together. I'll show you my tricks. This used to be my job."

He nodded against my chest, still weepy. Drew wiped his nose with his forearm, and together we made everything fit.

Later that night after town had fallen away behind us and we were anchored up on the grounds, I cornered Pete by the galley sink. "Do you think Van acts weird around Drew?" I whispered. Van was reading in his bunk in the focsle.

Pete raised his eyebrows at me. "What?"

"He seems uneasy around him."

Pete shrugged one shoulder.

"You've noticed?"

"Kids are tough. They are terrible roommates who leave their shit out everywhere and throw a lot of fits." He gave me a *get over it* look. "I'm sure it's nothing."

~

The next morning, Van stirred in the top bunk as soon as I began to extricate myself from Drew's limbs in the bottom bunk at 3:45 a.m. Sunrise was at 4:30, and we needed all the hooks in the water by then.

Van had been helpful the day before. He and Pete had spent all the evening getting things organized and ready out on deck, allowing me to spend that time in the wheelhouse with Drew. It took a lot of urging, but Drew slowly got chatty, as we kept the boat on course for Blair Cliffs, our best guess as to where the kings would be the next morning. As Drew steered the boat from my lap, I worked hard to recreate the bubble of time outside of time I'd felt in the day and a half of convalescence at Charlotte's.

In the chilly black of pre-morning, Pete was already up, starting coffee.

Van rolled over as I located my hoody sweatshirt. "I'm up," he said. He pushed up onto an elbow, his hair curling over on itself in every direction, and squinted at me. "I'm ready," he added.

I laughed despite myself. He was the embodiment of how much fishing could hurt before he'd even fished a single day. "You sure?"

"Yeah." He started kicking out of his sleeping bag. I slept in long underwear and assumed he did too, but just in case he was about to climb out of the bunk in nothing but boxers in the two feet of available space where I was currently standing, I turned and headed up the stairs. I kept one eye on him, though, given his close proximity to Drew, who was still sleeping in the bottom bunk, his arms and legs flung about. I poured myself a cup of coffee.

"You buy him a crew license?" Pete asked from the skipper's chair.

"No."

"Ha!" Pete's bruised face wrinkled up into a grin. "Fuck the Man!"

I rolled my eyes. "It's just for a few days." It was big trouble if the Coast Guard caught us fishing with unregistered crew, but we needed every dollar we had, which wasn't many after the repairs, fuel, and food.

When Van stepped into the wheelhouse, I headed out on deck. A few minutes later, I was in the pit setting gear, when he showed up again, coffee cup in hand, looking no more awake than he had in the focsle. The clouds were hazy and low on the water, just beginning to go from black to gray. Rain blew in thin, gauzy curtains all around us.

"Pretty out here," he said. "I guess." He took a sip of his coffee and squinted at the dark water and darker mountains, readjusting his ball cap.

In the pit, I moved at my usual pace, which suddenly seemed breakneck now that there was someone enjoying a cup of coffee and the weather. I kept my hands moving, getting ready to set the lines. He stood watching for a minute or so and then said, "Is there a cupholder around here?"

"Just the sink."

"Ah." He turned, stepped into the wheelhouse, and then came back out and walked over to the pit. "You know, even tractors nowadays have cupholders."

"You are definitely going to want your bibs." I pointed at where he'd hung them outside the wheelhouse along with Pete's and Drew's the day before.

"Ah," he said again and set to pulling them on.

While the gurdy fed out, I peered over at Van as he yanked the overalls over his boot heel. "You ever fished before? Shooting them doesn't count."

He got one boot through and fed the other leg in, his face smooth and clear of whatever was bothering him the night before, despite the early hour. "Buckshot spreads out real nice. Get a bunch at once, and you don't even have to untangle them from a net." He waved his hand toward the water behind the boat.

I stopped. "There's no net on a troller." Holy shit. I reminded myself he was free labor, that he was helping us out because he was nice. I would find some way for him to inch us closer to the fifty grand, even if he had no idea what he was doing.

"Well, that's good news." Van smiled as he pulled the straps up onto his shoulders and dropped into the pit next to me. "What?" he said while I continued to stare at him. "I'm a fast learner."

"I hope so."

He nodded as I said pull this, don't touch this, do this, don't do that, until the sky lightened and the bell rang, and he did this and didn't do that and got a bright king over the side without bruising it. "Shoo-dawg!" he hollered as he lifted it up onto the cleaning table, smiling full and unhindered. "That's a big one!"

"Not bad. Pretty average."

His eyes widened in disbelief. "If you were from anywhere but Alaska, you'd think that was a big fish."

I cracked up as I spun the fish on the table and delivered the killing blow. He held up his hands. "Okay, alright, if that's how it's gonna be, I'll just catch us a bigger one." With that one word, *us*, the feeling I'd had crowded around Charlotte's kitchen table ballooned around the deck. He turned back, let the line out, and began reattaching gear.

"That's the spirit." I picked up the knife and slit the throat latch with a quick flick of the wrist. Van began to whistle. The sound ran down my spine like ice.

"I could put some music on," I offered. "Speakers are pretty good." It had been so long since I'd played music on deck, I'd almost forgotten it was an option. I peered through the window into the wheelhouse and caught a glimpse of Pete moving around in the galley, likely getting

Drew breakfast. The fact that Drew had not yet poked his head out to whine for me was a good sign.

"I'll have you know I've been complimented on my whistling skills in the past." He glanced over and grinned as he continued to work the line on his side. A little clumsy, but he was getting it.

"Bad luck to whistle on a boat." I clambered out of the pit.

"What? Why?"

"Challenges the wind, brings storms. It was also the signal to mutiny on the *Bounty*."

"Now that's a good book," Van said. "Very instructive."

I set up the music, and soon we were listening to 90s on 9. The clouds burned off, and suddenly, it was a blue-sky day, one of the precious few we got each summer. The sun sparked off the snow at the tops of the sharp peaks and faded the gray out of the water until it turned a deep blue. I raised my face to the sun to let it pool around my eyes.

Pete kept us in the fish, and Van and I settled into a rhythm of him pulling fish, me cleaning and packing. By eleven a.m., when Pete hopped out on deck with ham and cheese sandwiches and Drew on his heels, we had nineteen kings in the hold. If we could somehow catch eighty a day across the rest of the opener, and then have a better-than-good coho season, we'd make the money we needed. Except, in my whole life, we'd never caught that many kings in one day. I peeled my gloves off.

"What's my duty?" Drew asked, peeking out from behind Pete's legs.

"Survey the scene," Pete said and handed me my sandwich. Van glanced at Drew, a look I couldn't read passing over his face before it turned almost cruel.

Drew stood up straight and peered at Pete, oblivious to both me and Van. "A ring-tailed lemur doesn't know how to do that."

"You're Agent X right now," Pete countered, "who does know how to do that." He reached the other sandwich to Van, who climbed out of the pit to grab it. Another sidelong glance at Drew. What the hell?

"I want to be a ring-tailed lemur," Drew wailed.

"Are you hungry?" I interrupted. "Pete, did you give him breakfast?"

"I've done this before, you know."

My rising unease with Van, the enormity of the task ahead of us, Drew back to a mess, me unable to hold on to any semblance of the calm mom I wanted to be, all of it swirled up into a pointy, sharp arrow I slung at Pete. "Poorly."

Pete shot me a wounded look, and I felt 100 percent horrible. He turned to Drew. "Don't you want to be something cool from around here? An eagle?" Drew screwed up his mouth. Pete went on. "A bear? A whale? I don't even know where ring-tailed lemurs live."

"Madagascar," Drew answered, irritation like a buzz saw in his tone, an exact replica of my tone.

Van kept his eyes on Drew. Was I overreacting? Or was it weird?

"It's an island," Drew said to the blank look Pete was giving him. "In Africa. Chris and Martin have explained it a hundred times."

Great. He was back to his TV friends. I turned the music off, suddenly needing wind and gulls and the chink of rigging, not Pearl Jam.

Pete blew out a breath as if this wasn't the first time he'd been offered up wisdom from the Kratt Brothers. "Okay, ring-tailed lemur, let's go back in, and I'll teach you how to survey the scene and check the perimeter. I guess you can be some sort of security cat." He held open the door. Van hadn't taken a bite of sandwich yet. It sagged in his hand.

"No, Grandpa." Drew's voice fell off the cliff into exasperation. "A lemur isn't a cat. They don't have retractable claws."

The door shut behind them, and I swung around on Van. "What is it?"

Van closed his eyes at the question. The bell rang, signaling another fish. He moved back to the pit, tossed his sandwich over the side, and hauled the fish in.

~

In the early evening, both Van and I stripped off our bibs, standing within a foot of each other but miles apart. It had been a full afternoon of working side by side in the grip of a tight silence. Pete was moving us to a different bay around a rocky corner since we'd caught nothing in the past half hour. A seiner bobbed in the distance. We'd pulled the gear for the forty-minute run and were taking advantage of the downtime to eat.

Pete was serving up mac and cheese for early dinner with a side of half-warm, half-cold canned corn. Van looked as turned inside out as I felt. Pete, on the other hand, was riled up. He clapped his hands together and rubbed them against each other after he set the food on the table. "Van, you are a lifesaver! Forty-six kings! Elvin Cove is going to be good. You've got at least a dozen more to clean, Ellie?"

"Yeah. I need to get back to it. Going to take a while."

"Van can keep working the lines while you get caught up, if you're not caught up by the time we get there." Pete turned to Van. "Think you can run both sides?"

Van squinted one eye and rubbed at his jawline. "Imagine so."

Pete clapped his open palms together again. "Thanks for helping, man. This is going to turn it all around. I can feel it." Pete's eyes lit up in the way they used to when he was losing big and some small chance came out of nowhere.

I gritted my teeth at the way Pete controlled reality by just describing it differently. Drew was half buried in his bowl of mac and cheese. The white kind was his favorite. "He's only with us for three days, Pete." Being sour with Pete blew some steam off the pressure cooker of the afternoon with Van, even though I hated myself for not being able to resist it.

"Y'all mind if I ask you something?" Van asked.

"Sure," Pete said, sliding in next to him on the bench seat.

"Is it a common thing to make fifty grand in two months of fishing?"

Pete said yes at the same time as I said no.

Van looked from one of us to the other. "So, what you're saying is, maybe."

I shook my head. "Some boats can clear that much, we typically don't."

"We'll find the fish," Pete said as he scooped the rest of his mac and cheese into Drew's bowl. "This kid can eat."

Drew smiled so wide, at what he obviously took as a compliment, several pieces of macaroni fell out.

"It doesn't matter how good we are at finding them if they're not there to find."

"Ellie, goddamn it." Pete groaned. "The attitude." I knew he was right, but it was the deeply grooved track of my life since becoming a single mom. Despite having found a way to climb out for that brief respite at Charlotte's, now that we were back out, the days pressing in, the money feeling impossible to make, the likelihood of having to go back to town in September, find a job, put Drew back in day care. All of it was a force stronger than my own will shoving me back into the familiar groove of overwhelm and irritation.

I shook my head. "It's not an attitude, Pete. It's reality." I stood up, dropped my plate in the sink, and went back out on deck to keep cleaning fish. The weather was changing, the light air filling in with the heavy promise of rain.

Van came out and leaned into a corner of the pit, watching the water, waiting until I had a few ready for him to pack into the hold. It seemed the silence would continue, which made me want to scream. When Pete lined up in Elvin Cove, I scrambled to clean the final fish. When he dropped into trolling speed, I fed two lines out. Van packed the last fish and took over his line.

I hauled in the first fish, and while I was cleaning it, Van pulled in a second. He laid it up on the table and worked the gaff out.

"You should go in," I said as I sliced open the belly of the fish. "You've already been out here for fifteen hours. And even I don't want to be out here with me." I kept my eyes on the sharp edge of knife against the deep pink of the salmon.

"In my experience, life generally blows," he said as he fed his line back out, clearly getting a feel for the gurdy. "But fishing's pretty cool."

He didn't go in. We fished side by side, both of us tolerating me but mostly both of us relaxing into the forever gray of water and sky, the thin cotton clouds caught in the long arms of hemlock and spruce. We pulled the gear when night closed in at nine thirty, finished cleaning and packing the seventy kings we'd caught, anchored for the night, and dropped into bunks by eleven thirty. Then hauled ourselves up four hours later and started over.

~

The next day, there were no fish anywhere we tried. I got quieter, Drew got whinier, Pete got more annoying. I reorganized everything on deck four times. Van watched and got out of my way. At noon, Pete fell asleep in the skipper's chair. "Go lie down," I said as a lame form of apology. "I got it." I stared at the chart, trying to remember where we'd caught fish in the past anywhere close to where we were, trying to discern currents and tides, likely places for fish to hole up, to wait, to gather.

"What is there to do?" Drew wailed behind me. "I'm bored. I hate this boat."

"Stop it, Drew," I said, too sharp.

"I just want to go home," he said in a smaller voice.

"This is home. Until I figure something else out. Go find something to do and stop complaining at me." I was fully back in my old skin.

I kept my eyes on the chart, my mind focused on the task at hand, which was more important, I told myself, than entertaining Drew. He needed to know how to entertain himself. He needed to not be coddled. Life would not coddle him. Where was the middle line, and why did I always miss it? I watched him climb into our bunk, pull out Dog, and begin to reprimand him. I closed my eyes, trying to shut it all out. All the ways I was messing up Drew, all the money we'd lost by not being where the fish were for the past eight hours, the way a helium balloon of hope rose in my chest over those days at Charlotte's that I could be a better parent had lifted me up and then popped, dropping me face-first onto concrete from some incredible height.

~

At two p.m., I was still in the skipper's chair when the fish finder displayed a single boomerang image. I jumped up. Van looked up from the table, where he was reading, and Pete opened an eye from the focsle bunk, where he was sprawled out with a sleeping Drew on his chest. "Where you going?" Pete called out.

"To set the gear."

Pete untangled himself from Drew, came up the stairs, and squinted at the fish finder. "For one fish?"

"Yes, Pete, for one fucking fish," I said, pushing through the door, grateful when it closed between us. One fish was fifty more dollars.

Van came outside as I was dropping into the pit. There was no reason for him to be out here for one fish, which I was about to say, tired of his silence, tired of all of them, all of it, everything. He sat down on the edge of the hold, stretched his long legs out in front of him.

"What?" I said, the blood in my veins running fast, the word sharp enough to cut bone.

"Why do you hate Pete so much?" he asked, face closed and locked, voice hard. "Seems there's a lot more to it than him betting the boat."

"Why are you so weird around Drew?" I shot back.

He swept his eyes across the building waves, the muscle at his jawbone pulsing. "I'm just saying that's a big ball of hate to carry around all the time. Looks heavy." He stood up and walked away.

Chapter 18

After the single first king, Pete found several more sporadically, but then nothing for an hour. I ducked in to grab a bar.

Drew sat next to Van on the same side of the table, coloring. Van was holding his book, but not reading. His eyes moved from Drew's arm moving in wide arcs to color the sky to his thin neck to the rest of his body hunched over the picture. I picked Drew up, which broke Van's trance. His eyes shot to mine.

"Mama!" Drew wrapped his body around mine. The way he always forgave my terrible moods so easily made me feel like the worst human in the world. I moved Drew over to my hip and steadied myself against the counter as the boat went up and over the next wave. Drew was too big to be carried like that, but he felt younger suddenly. Like when he was just learning to walk and the world was more dangerous.

"Pull the gear," Pete said from the skipper's chair. "We're headed to Stewart Straight. Guys on the radio are saying it sucks, which means they're killin' it and don't want anyone else to know."

"That's a long run," I countered. "Eight hours?"

"Worth the time," he said, distracted with charting his new course. "Always kings in there."

"You're going to waste eight of the twenty-nine hours left of the opener with no hooks in the water?"

"No other choice, Ellie. No fish over here." He looked over his shoulder at me. "I'll keep the fish finder on. We'll drop the gear if we find a pocket on the way."

Drew squirmed out of my arms and perched himself next to Van again. He worked at any white patches left in the sky with the blue crayon.

I chewed my lip, loath to leave him there. Van's body was rigid even though he went back to reading. The intensity of our interaction had not dissipated. The inside of my veins itched as I watched the two of them for a minute longer. Eventually, I convinced myself that, while Pete was clearly distracted by his latest and greatest idea, he was only a few feet from Drew and would round on Van like a bear at the first sign of distress. And Drew didn't looked stressed. He looked content, tongue pinning the corner of his mouth as he dropped one crayon for another and started in on making individual blades of grass.

Out on deck, alone, I tried to suss out if I was overreacting. As a single woman in the world, I'd developed that other sense that recognized a certain dissonance in a man's look or behavior that meant I should cross the street or leave the bar. It didn't always make sense, and it wasn't always right, but there was no doubt that it had saved me more than once. After Drew was born, that sense went into overdrive. It was never a good idea to ignore it.

I made a quick stir-fry for dinner, set a bowl down in front of Van and Drew, still at the table, and handed a bowl to Pete, who was still in the chair. "No boats," I commented on the wide-open water in all directions while keeping one eye on Drew.

"Because there's no fish," Pete said between forkfuls. "Everyone's over by Stewart Straight. You and Van need to get some sleep," he added. "Tomorrow's going to be a long day."

"I don't like stir-fry." Drew pushed the bowl away. He was stomping a long row of tiny dinosaurs with the big dinosaur in his hand.

Van set his book down and took up his bowl. He muttered a thanks, but aside from that hadn't said a word since our interaction on deck.

"Drew, why don't you move your dinosaurs to the bunk, and I'll make you a peanut butter sandwich instead."

He looked up, wary. I almost never gave in to his picky tendencies. Not one to miss an opportunity, he scooped up the dinosaurs, made a mountain out of the sleeping bag in our bunk, and got to work helping each one individually climb it.

Pete's silence as he ate had to do with him figuring tides and shelves and moon angles and whatever else he used to cook up exactly where to drop the hooks. The silence between me and Van seemed in direct proportion to my big ball of hate throwing everything off-kilter. As forks began to scrape the bottom of bowls, Van said, "I'll clean up," without meeting my eyes.

I curled into the bottom bunk with Drew and helped the last couple of dinosaurs up the mountain, for which I received a huge peanut butter grin. Without even forcing toothbrushing, Drew and I and Dog fell asleep in a heap, and I didn't wake up until Pete shook my arm. "Ellie," he whispered. "I found them. Get up!"

I untangled myself. It was dark out, and Pete's face was half in shadow. "What time is it?"

"Three."

"We're in Stewart Straight?" I asked as I pulled on a sweatshirt.

"No," Pete said. "Stewart Straight was a bust; I've been driving around all night. We're out in front of Cabot Cove."

"Cabot Cove?" I shoved my legs into fleece pants. We'd never fished this far west before.

"I know," Pete said as he turned for the stairs. "We'll figure it out."

I shoved my feet into boots, reached back, and whipped my hair into a ponytail with the rubber band I'd slept with on my wrist. "Pete, we don't know this area." There were charts and there was knowledge. We knew where Sam Clem's boat lay on the ocean floor outside Rocky Bay, waiting to snag lines. We knew where the huge icebergs caught up at the end of Smith Channel and patiently waited to crush hulls. Van shifted in his bunk.

"It'll be fine, Ellie," Pete said as he thumped over to the coffee maker. "I'll keep my eyes open. You need to get the gear in now, we're in the fish. Might even bite before the sun comes up, and it'll help run off any other jackasses that get the idea to fish over here. I'll bring coffee out."

I located my winter hat and pulled it down over my ears. Van dropped out of the bunk as I ran up the stairs.

I huddled in my rain gear in the pit as I got flashers, spoons, and hoochies ready and started to feed the line out. It was raining sideways, a clear sign of fall starting to close out summer. It was never a good idea to drop the gear in the water before daybreak, but if we could just log some huge days, we might have enough come September 20. But then what? Was a down south crime syndicate mob boss going to be true to his word? I felt again the beady stare of the man who had handed me the envelope of cash in Kings Creek. How far in was I? I shivered at the idea that I'd already put Drew in danger. And who was to say they wouldn't disappear Pete when he showed up with a bag full of cash on the twentieth? This was 100 percent different than meeting Hank to hand over the $150 you lost on the Mariners. This was no good. This was real trouble. By the way Pete's eyes creased whenever the end of the season came up, he knew it too.

The bell rang, pulling me out of the building dread. At least momentarily. A big metallic king. I had it on the table and had the second line spooling out by the time Van stepped out on deck. He ducked against the rain, pulled on rain gear, and dropped into the pit next to me.

"Mornin'," he said and took over the second line, which produced three more kings in quick succession.

The rain beat on the side of my hood, found its way inside. Cold rivulets chilled the skin of my neck, dampened the collar of my sweatshirt. The knife sliced, thin and precise, despite the way the fish slid on the table with the roll of the boat, despite how numb my fingers were inside my gloves. I finished cleaning the four fish, climbed into the hold, and packed them all in ice.

When I got back to the cleaning table, there were three more kings, and Van was half in, half out of the boat, leaning over the rail and working on getting the next one in. He looked to be struggling against the heavy slowness that had consumed him yesterday.

Pete never brought out coffee, and Van didn't say anything else. We worked side by side as the morning light took hold and the top layer of ocean turned to fog. Van's heavy mood combined with mine and pulled us under.

My arms ached and my head pounded, but the fish were piling up. Pete appeared with four ham sandwiches a couple of hours later. Based on how quickly Van peeled off his gloves, I guessed his stomach was as empty as mine was.

"There's a tender two miles north. We'll sell there. But let's hang out here longer, don't you think?"

I nodded, mouth full of sandwich. The food was clearing my head. Pete had added mayo and banana peppers, a combination he knew I loved.

"Mom." Drew came out, still pulling his second boot on. Pete dropped a hand to Drew's upper arm to steady him as the boat rolled over the next wave. Drew didn't have a life vest on. "Grandpa says my grandma was afraid of ravens. No one's afraid of ravens. He's lying."

Van turned away, watched the surface of the sloppy water, his back to Drew, who continued, "You said Grandpa was a liar, and you're right."

Pete's face creased with hurt. Why had I said that to Drew? If I had friends, someone else to talk to, maybe I wouldn't say shit like that to him. I couldn't look at Pete. I focused on Drew instead. "She actually did get nervous around ravens. She thought they were powerful. Smarter than us. She thought most animals were smarter than us."

Drew squinted at me. The driving rain was soaking his right side. He didn't seem to care, which for some reason soothed me. "So he's not lying?"

"No. He's not lying."

Pete pulled Drew into his good leg as the *Sarah Louise* rocked over the next roller.

"C'mon, Drew. Let's go back in," Pete said quietly.

I wiped the rain off my face with my forearm. When I was four, Pete was one constant thing. Drew seemed too little to manage the kaleidoscope Pete had become, not to mention the kaleidoscope I'd been for the entirety of Drew's life. Unless Pete had only seemed to be one constant thing. Unless he'd figured out how to be a constant thing for me, despite the kaleidoscope of adulting. I stared at the door he'd disappeared behind. I needed to stop letting my anger drive. All it did was run shit over.

The bell rang on Van's side, and he handed over his second sandwich for me to hold while he pulled his gloves back on and turned to the line. He worked the fish, lifting it over the side, moving steady and slow. I didn't know how to bridge the mawing gap between us, I only knew that I wanted to feel again the steady calm of him I'd felt in Marbled Inlet. The steady calm of myself I'd felt there. I wanted to somehow trigger it in him for both of us. But when was I ever good at people? I peered out at the sideways rain and constant rollers. I was only ever good at this.

The *Sarah Louise* kept us moving together, and the rain had us working close at the center of the pit as it blew all around us. Once he had the fish in the cleaning tray, he pulled his gloves off again. Our raw red hands grazed as I handed him his sandwich. Van dropped his eyes to mine, and for just a second, I saw it. The way he'd been completely hollowed out by something, the same as me.

Or maybe he let me see it. And it was clear he wasn't going to let either of us run from ourselves any longer. My stomach dropped. He took a step back, leaned up against the side of the pit, and asked, "So what is it with Pete?" He had reclaimed the steady version of himself, his lack of quick movements uncomplicating the complicated.

"You first?" I said, trying to match his tone. "What is it with Drew?" The rigging clanked and slapped as the *Sarah Louise* angled through the waves. The rain misted everything, the trees black and foggy on the edge of the island we were closest to.

Van watched the water move as the rain and haze filled in all the space above it. "It was raining. The kind of rain that dumps out of the sky. Not like this." The words came out measured, as if he could only stand a certain number at a time. "The truck never saw them. My wife, she was pulling out. Probably distracted by the baby."

"Oh god," I muttered, reaching out for the side of the pit.

His eyes found mine, hung on with what appeared to be the last of his strength. "Megan. My daughter. She would be just a bit older than Drew."

I covered my mouth with a hand and let the motion of the *Sarah Louise* envelop me. Three-foot swells, the slow horizontal movement that was part of the forward momentum. "I'm so sorry," I whispered, taking a step closer, wanting to reach out but afraid to.

He stared at the sandwich in his hand. "Drew is the first kid I've been around since." The rhythmic slap of wave against hull filled all the space around us.

"Your wife?" I ventured.

He shook his head and peered out again at the swell. "Neither made it." He looked shattered. I didn't think, I stepped into him and wrapped my arms around his back.

"I'm so sorry," I said against the skin at the base of his neck. "I can't imagine . . ."

He pulled me in tight, and it felt like our strength did more than double. "I'm so sorry," I said again. The boat rolled, pulling us apart, and we both adjusted our feet to keep upright. His eyes were wet, red-rimmed. I leaned up against the pit where he had propped himself, and we both watched the water spool out behind us. "I've been awful. To you." I meant in general, to everyone, but this was all I could get out.

He shook his head. "You were just protective of your boy. Because you're a good mom."

I huffed out a sigh. "Not really."

"I should've told you earlier so you didn't worry. It's just— I've never said it out loud before." He pressed his lips together. "Kind of brings it all back." The next time the boat rolled, it slid us a little closer so that we were touching shoulder to hip as we watched the whitewash churn out behind the boat. Neither of us moved back. He took a deep breath. "Your turn."

I told him all of it, from the cancer diagnosis to the morning I found Pete behind the bar in Kings Creek. "I just needed him to be a parent a little bit longer after I lost Mom."

"But his own demons overtook him." He braced his feet as the boat gave way to a roller bigger than the previous set. "As they do."

A cold wind tore up everything around us, but I felt everything go still. What had happened to me as a parent when push came to shove? The exact same thing. Van took a deep breath. "So much to regret," he said. "I'd like to stop racking up things to regret." The bell rang on his side, and he turned for the lines. I watched him go through the motions of getting the fish on board, one newly learned motion after the next, performed without error.

~

Van matched me hour for hour throughout the day. In the small confines of the pit, we were careful with each other in a new way. We were in the fish, which precluded much talking, and I, for one, spent a long time going back through our conversation, felt something solid between us taking shape.

Pete brought us food periodically. My feet fell asleep, my hands went numb and stayed that way. My hair plastered itself to my neck and face as the rain blew in under the hayrack for hours on end. As evening gathered around us, I kept cleaning and packing, and Van ran both lines, hauling in king after king after king. When we fished out Cabot Cove, we pulled in the lines and took a short break while Pete moved us one bay north. The grounds were busy on this final day of kings: seiners off capes, longliners traveling past, more trollers working their drags.

When Pete thumped out on deck to holler at us to pull the gear, night was minutes away from closing in for good, and the rain was a loud hiss on the surface of the water.

Van leaned his head on his elbow on the edge of the pit once his line was stowed, eighteen hours after he'd dropped it in the water. "Is this normal?" A mountain of fish slid around in front of him.

"No. Not in any sense of the word. None of it."

Pete came flying out the door. "Look at all those fucking fish!" he yelled. "We did it! You guys did it," he corrected himself.

"You're the one who kept us in the fish all day," I said.

"That's a lot left to clean," he said, beaming. "Wish I could help." He flexed the fingers at the end of the casted right hand, which were still swollen, although they'd lost their purple tint. "I'll do a shit job, though. I'll just stay in here where it's dry and warm and find us somewhere to anchor up. We'll sell in the morning, and then hit the cohos." He slammed the door behind him.

His final sentence hung in between us, whipped and tossed in the wind as we turned to look at each other. The silence stretched.

"Cohos," Van said as if he were turning the word over. He flipped his ball cap and resettled it, his wet hair curling up around its edges. He peered over at me. "I'm guessing you need to catch a lot of them."

"More than a lot," I agreed.

He nodded as he slid the first fish over to me to start cleaning and hauled himself out of the pit. As he disappeared into the hold to shovel ice around, to make some room for all the fish that needed to be added, I was unsure if he'd catch a ride home on the tender tomorrow or if he'd be in the pit with me for another long day, but I knew clearly which one I preferred.

~

The next morning, Will was standing on deck ready for the lines I was set to toss, cooler at his feet. As always, his smile seemed to erupt out of every single part of him. I tossed him the line just as Van appeared around the corner of the wheelhouse with another bumper and tied it off. Will was so stunned, the bowline hit him across the chest, making me crack up. He scrambled for the line as the *Sarah Louise* nudged up against the tender.

"How . . ." He looked from one to the other of us and back, bowline slack in his hand.

Pete shot Will a *what the fuck* look through the wheelhouse window as the bow swung out, and he tried to figure out why we weren't tied off, straining at our lines, settling against the tender. I could feel the way Pete's hand hovered over the throttle, trying to anticipate. Will whipped the line around the cleat and then scrambled across the deck to where Van tossed him the stern line and whipped that one tight too.

Will held up his gloved, meaty hands, shaking his head. "No beers 'til you explain what's going on here. Wait—" His face cracked into a smile. "This is because of me! I'm a matchmaker! Everyone gets two beers!"

Van shook his head. "I'm just helping out." And all the fun drained away. Of course, that's what was happening. I'd been a fool to think anything other.

"I'll still take two beers," I called out, funneling all my energy into seeming to have known this all along.

"But how—" Will's face crumpled in confusion as he pointed from me to Van and back a couple of times.

"I sunk the boat in Marbled Inlet and rebuilt it on the beach."

Will's thick tangled eyebrows disappeared into his wool cap. "Oh shit," he breathed out.

"Van helped us and is still helping because we have to make fifty grand before the season ends to buy the boat and permit back from the bookie up in Juneau Pete lost both to." I suddenly didn't care who knew. It was all the truth. We were in the shit and needed help, and Van was altruistic and that was that. And now that Will knew, everyone in the fleet would know. The dread of everyone finding out unhitched itself from me. Let them judge us.

Will's eyebrows had not reappeared. "I changed my mind. You can have as many beers as you want."

We off-loaded the entire contents of the hold, and Will handed us a check for $7,700, which Pete disappeared quickly into the wheelhouse with, Drew on his heels, leaving Van and I standing out on deck, Will moving aft to untie us from the tender.

"I'm sure you can catch a ride with Will back to town." I couldn't look at him. Instead, I guzzled my third beer, which was helping me get the words out or possibly just making me babble. "I appreciate all you've done. Big help at a crucial time." A slow smile was spreading across Van's face. I swallowed the rest of the stupid words, took another sip as Will tossed our stern line and it thumped on the deck of the *Sarah Louise*. Immediately, the stern began to swing out.

"Now's the time to jump," I said, cutting my eyes over to Van, who laughed.

"It's a valuable skill I'm learning here," he said with a slight tilt of his head. "Could be useful to make some extra cash fishing now and again. Maybe for Charlotte and Danny's son."

I stared at him, tried to read his face, but it was impossible. He was right. It was good to be proficient in commercial fishing if you were going to live in Southeast Alaska, but was that it? Was that all of it? "You want to stay?"

Will threw us a look as he moved past us toward the bowline. "You idiots going to haul in your lines or what?" Neither of us moved.

Van's gaze landed on mine. I felt the strength of him then, the way his brokenness and mine added up to less brokenness somehow. "I want to stay."

"Oh" was all I could manage.

The bowline thumped onto the deck, and Pete hit the throttle, bumpers banging around. "Ellie!!" Pete hollered, which finally threw me into action, pulling in bumpers and stowing the bowline. Van moved to the stern line, we peeled off from the tender, and Will stood grinning and shaking his head.

In the wheelhouse, Drew sat in Pete's lap, helping him steer. Pete spun around and nodded once at Van as he came in behind me, as if he wasn't surprised he was still on board.

"Okay, so," I said. "Hand me the legal pad." I pointed at the drawer to Pete's left. He handed it over along with a pen. I sat down at the table and began calculating, partly because it needed to happen and partly because I needed something to do, like math. "We need to catch $42,300 of coho in two months minus a couple days. At an average of five pounds and a dollar fifty a pound, that's approximately . . ." I scribbled numbers. "Five thousand six hundred forty fish. Plus another three grand to cover fuel, ice, and food. That's a total of somewhere around six thousand cohos. About a hundred a day. Fuck."

"Maybe he'll take less," Pete said, an uncharacteristic unease settling on his face.

"Has he ever settled for less?"

"Never," Pete said without looking over. He pulled his flask out of the drawer. "Ellie," he said, and my lungs froze up at the tone. "You know how I said this new bookie had never threatened me?"

I looked down. "Oh, Pete."

He held his hand out, palm up. "He hasn't." Pete took a swig out of his flask. "Not me, anyway." His face broke into uneven lines. "But there's rumors. I just took it for that, but I've been on the radio a bit, asking some direct questions now that we'll be meeting him with a bunch of cash in a duffel here in a matter of weeks."

I could feel Van watching Pete as closely as I was.

"And?"

"Well." Pete took another long swallow from the flask. "One of Jensen's boys got mixed up pretty good last winter. Claims this new bookie is money laundering for a drug cartel family down south. That's where the thugs come from. Jensen says the family has taken control of the bookie's operation at this point. That they topped off the fuel tank of a Cessna with water because the pilot wasn't paying up."

"Jesus," I breathed out. "Hydrolock?"

"Yeah. Mid-flight." Pete paused. "I want to be as honest as I can with you, Ellie. I didn't know any of this, mostly because my head was in the sand, where I like it, where it serves no one but me, but now, there's so much more to it. What I'm saying is, we need to have the fifty grand by the twentieth, to keep things as smooth as they've always been between me and him." He turned back to the wheel, tucked the flask away. "Get the gear ready, we'll be fishing in an hour. The fleet's been catching sixty per day average. We're better than average."

Chapter 19

In the pit, I was able to keep my mind off the looming interaction with the bookie. I would take Drew elsewhere and leave Pete to it. But at night, in my bunk, my mind circled and circled. Leave Pete in his two casts to it? Find him dead this time out in the alley behind the bar?

In the days that followed, I focused on staying as present as possible with Drew. Worked hard to settle my mind back into the routine daily tasks from the minute I woke up each day. Pete seemed to be doing the same. He'd left his flask in the cabinet since his admission, kept himself and Drew occupied in the wheelhouse with one invented game and activity after another.

"Hey, Drew, want to come out on deck with me?" I asked on the third morning of fishing coho when I came in for a fifth cup of coffee.

He looked up from a box of spare parts usually kept in the engine room, now on the kitchen table. "Pete says I can take any of these apart I want to, as long as I put them back together. But I have to do it over this." He pointed to a baking sheet settled on top of a hand towel, to catch any rolling-away pieces. There were also several wrenches and a couple of screwdrivers.

Pete looked over at the mention of his name, nodded once at Drew, and turned back to correct our course and to fiddle with the fish finder. He, Van, and I had settled into a routine over the first few days of coho. Pete was up first and got the coffee going. Van and I had the lines in the water by daybreak, and then Van ran the port side lines and I ran the starboard side. Van took over all four lines once we pulled in enough that I needed to switch to cleaning. We were out on deck late into the night, finishing packing and cleaning the fish from the day. I had worked at packing away whatever Van had stirred up in me along with the residual way my ribs still ached through the days. I focused instead on how nice it was to have a friend. Drew had been spending more and more time with us on deck working the hose for me as I cleaned. Van watched Drew from a distance, and Drew accepted his silences without much notice.

Bent over his oil-stained box of spare parts, Drew said, "If I take something apart, I can see what the insides look like. Pete says it's good to know what the insides look like."

I ran a hand along his back. "That is a good thing to know. How about when you're ready for a break, you can come help me on deck? I've got a new job for you." Anything to keep my mind off the fact that rather than the one hundred fish per day we needed, we'd caught eighty-seven the first day of cohos, ninety-one the second, and only thirty-five so far today. In any quiet moment, my mind raced toward any other possible way to fifty grand, any other possible way to not lose everything.

"Okay," he agreed.

Forty minutes later, he stepped out on deck in bib-overall rain pants and a life jacket. The rain had let up for the time being at least, and there was a cool breeze blowing out of the north. The solid gray ceiling of cloud had lifted to somewhere around a thousand feet, and the ocean slopped lazily against the hull as we moved through it at trolling speed. I watched with satisfaction how easily Drew moved across the deck, no longer stiff-legged.

He sat down in his usual perch outside the pit, with me and Van at either end keeping an eye on our lines.

"You've mastered your job keeping the cleaning tray clean. I thought maybe you'd like to bag roe when we catch a humpie, like this one here." I shuffled the pink salmon out of the stack of fish. "See how she looks different? You can keep the money from any roe you bag and clean." The canneries bought roe, but not for much, so we usually didn't bother with it.

"Can I buy the fire truck at the hardware store?" Drew asked. "The one with all the lights and the loud siren?" His voice so full of thrill and wonder, it made me laugh.

A quick smile flickered on Van's face.

"Yep." I turned around and found the extra-small dishwashing gloves I'd picked up in town. "I even got you your own pair of gloves."

"Just like you and Van!" Drew squealed.

I showed him how to remove and rinse the eggs and bag them up.

He slowly and carefully followed every direction until he had one bag done.

"Great job, buddy. If you keep at it, you'll make enough for the fire truck. Maybe even enough for the police car also."

Drew gasped and dove into his work with new vigor. I held the next pink open for him, and he gently separated the salmon eggs from the rest of the innards, his chest solid and heavy against my arm.

"Pretty cool, huh?" I asked as we peered inside the depths of the salmon.

"What? The guts?"

"Yeah." I smiled over at him, never happier than in that exact moment in my damp sweatshirt in the cool haze of late summer, splattered in fish guts, with Drew by my side. I knew with a sudden clarity that even if there were no more days like this one, the fact that we got this one was a gift.

Still bent over the task at hand, Drew asked, "Do birds have guts?"

I laughed. "They do, but we don't catch birds."

"What if we did? What if we were birdermen instead of fishermen?"

The laugh that burst out of Van was without any of the weight that usually saddled him around Drew.

Drew, Van, and I worked on deck for hours, Drew chattering, Van methodically pulling in fish after fish, me not thinking about numbers, for once, but instead about the long arm of history reaching from my mom, through me, to Drew. All of us connected by the repeated daily actions of spooling out lines, pulling in fish, and breathing in salt air, in the small space of a wooden deck.

~

That afternoon, I relished a rare slow moment in the pit alone. Pete was moving us south, and I'd just finished pulling the lines in. He'd picked out a cove in the vicinity of the Stikine River, where he was certain we'd find the biggest bunch of cohos yet. Drew had given up the day's long wait for the next humpie and wandered back inside. After we'd cleaned and stored all the fish from the morning, Van had gone in to rest up in the hour we had before we'd be fishing again.

Pete wound us through the channel markers in the narrow arm of sea to the west of the island that Kings Creek held on to. As we left the channel, the mudflats at the mouth of the river spread out before us. The Stikine had always been mine. A short boat ride from Kings Creek, it was a series of ever-changing braids and attitudes, speckled with hot springs, churned-up water, massive log jams, and terminal glaciers. Props were easily ripped off by hidden rocks and trees that had tumbled into the river, which meant jetboats only. Even still, every year, boats were crushed by an unseen obstacle under the water, people tangled and pinned in the log jams. The Stikine wasn't for the faint of heart, so, of course, Pete had decided he would teach me to navigate all its pitfalls, to read its braids, to anticipate its constantly changing moods. He'd turned over the helm of our small, always-breaking-down jetboat to me at age eight and insisted, from that point forward, I be afraid but not scared.

The mudflats looked innocent enough now at the height of the flood tide. Four to six feet of water covering all of it, easily passible. At low tide, all the water drained out, and the mudflats turned into a quicksand that sucked men in up to their hip bones or chests and held them there until the tide flooded back in.

The water in the flats was brown but looked as if someone had poured a layer of milk on top. A strange reluctance to mix between fresh and salt water. I hadn't been up the Stikine in years, but I closed my eyes and saw the exact arc of the first curve, could almost feel the speed of a jetboat underneath me skimming the surface of the water like a blade on ice. The Stikine cut a path into the heart of Canada. One hundred and sixty miles of rushing water and forested mountains before you reached the first settlement of people in a small village of Telegraph. I loved being up the Stikine, in the palm of so much land left alone, the power of it a tangible pulse.

The *Sarah Louise* moved at a snail's pace compared to a jetboat. I watched the gray world slowly slide by, listened to the pull of the wind in the rigging, the call of the seabirds. With a sinking clarity, I felt the exact measure of what I would lose if we couldn't catch enough fish. Pete had forced me to name what I wanted just before we lost it forever. The number of days left, the number of dollars necessary, all of it felt sharp-edged and mean.

On the rocky shore in front of me, a black bear and her cub were scraping mussels off rocks. I watched the power in the shoulders, the slow, methodical scraping and chewing. The way she was fully engaged in the task at hand. I thought of the way we all rushed around in town, of how I'd be a part of that instead of this next summer. Everything ached as I hauled out of the pit, stripped off my bibs, and pushed through the door to the wheelhouse.

I stopped short. Van and Drew were bent over an extra gurdy we kept in case one broke. Drew's small hand ran over the pieces as Van spoke softly, explaining how each worked in concert with the rest. Neither looked up at my entrance. Pete came out of the head, hopping on one foot, steadying himself against the wall with his one good arm as if two limbs instead of four were no big deal. "You gonna lay down?" he asked. "We're probably forty minutes out. We'll need the gear in the water at the mouth of the bay, so not much of a nap." Before he settled back in the skipper's chair, he followed my eyes, which had not left the two heads bent toward each other. Van with his ratty cap and curls, Drew with his stick-straight hair and tongue pressed to the corner of his lip in concentration as he worked a bolt loose while Van held the gurdy still. When the bolt pinged against the baking sheet, Van smiled and said, "There you go, good job," with such a carefully calibrated mix of pain and kindness that it broke me in two.

I lay down in the bottom bunk, listening to the smooth arc of Drew's questions weaving through the slow instructions of Van as they put the gurdy back together, all the individual pieces working in tandem once again.

~

Later that evening, Van hoisted himself out of the pit. "Enough already." He pulled his gloves off.

I looked up from the seventy-eighth fish I'd cleaned that day. "What?" I studied his face. Was he done with us? He should be. I didn't want him to be. There was no reason for him to be working twenty-hour days just because Pete and I had to. The fish were erratic, our daily numbers were erratic. He should get back to his own life. My mind raced for how many more hours before we were close to a ferry terminal that could take him back to Kings Creek, to his skiff tied up at the public dock, to his house with the hand-built couches and clean clothes and no fish slime covering everything.

"Can I be in charge of the radio?" Van asked with an exasperated expression.

"Oh," I said, blinking a couple of times. "Yeah, sure."

He crossed the deck. Behind him, water and sky indistinguishable from each other. The world simplifying itself into one color.

Van punched some buttons, and the '90s disappeared into the deep twang of a man singing. Van closed his eyes, tipped his head to the forever gray and sang along, his accent taking over his whole self.

I laughed.

He looked over. "What now? Country music calls in the sharks?"

"You singing along might." I slid the cleaned fish into the holding bin and pulled the next into the cleaning tray, trying to mask the way the adrenaline flush of him departing was now draining out of my body, leaving my legs weak.

Van dropped back into the pit next to me. "This is so much better."

"Why didn't you say anything?" I asked.

"I was trying to be Alaskan."

Van sang along the rest of the evening and into the night, and I got a cultural education in barefoot blue jean nights, muddy riverbanks, and fields full of corn and cotton.

Chapter 20

"Mom, if you are listening . . ." I whispered into the dead calm all around. Pete was tucking us into an unfamiliar bay. Eleven days of cohos, and we had yet to break a hundred any of those days. "We need help." We needed a miracle, and I'd lived long enough to know that those didn't generally show up when you needed them.

It was midmorning, and the surface of the water was calm, not a ripple in sight. The trees were still and dark, the shore's secrets kept. "Not here, Pete," I added as the bay held its breath in a way that suggested there were no fish anywhere.

Drew had dragged Van inside to help him take apart and put back together the spray nozzle on the sink, which had been leaking. Instead of replacing it, we'd been fixing it several times a season for almost two decades. Drew had assigned himself the job and was taking it very seriously. It had become clear over the past week that he preferred Van's easy, patient way of explaining anything in his take-apart and put-back-together box to my way or Pete's way.

I dropped the gear in the water as Pete adjusted to trolling speed, then jumped when the bell rang, and dove for the gurdy as the fish broke the surface.

When the bell rang again, Van came out and dropped into the pit next to me. Another fish hit and then another. Pete hollered from inside at the same time as I whooped outside. Van was bent over the rail, aiming the gaff.

"Don't miss him," I said. "We can't miss a single one."

Van swung the gaff, delivered the stunning blow, flipped it with a quick turn of the wrist, gaffed the fish, and had him on board in just a few seconds. Van and I pulled in three more in a row. "Holy shit!!" I yelled.

Van turned around, his hair dripping with rain, a wide smile on his face. "You better get moving on the cleaning business. I have a feeling I'm going to get a good jump on you."

Pete made a second pass through the bay before another troller showed up. Drew stuck his head out the door. "Any humpies yet?"

"Not yet, bud." He was halfway to the fire truck of his dreams. "I'll holler if we get one."

Two more passes through the bay, and we'd tapped out the coho. We pulled the gear, and Van packed while I cleaned. When we stepped inside for a quick sandwich, Pete was fidgeting in his chair. "Alright," he said as he studied charts on the computer.

Van stood at the sink, spreading peanut butter and jelly on bread. Drew sat at the table, working on the nozzle. He held up a small round piece of plastic and screwed up his face into a question directed at Van. "This one next?"

"Yep, that's the one," Van said, all long limbs and an easy smile, first for Drew, then for me. It had begun to hurt to constantly control the way I wanted to reach for him, to drag my eyes away, to remind myself he was not the fourth corner to our triangle.

"Alright what," I said, crowding up behind Pete, refocusing. We had to be right about where the fish were.

"Two places look good," Pete said. "Something good is about to happen, I can feel it. Shannon Point is two hours from here, we'll hit the tide just right and it should be hot." He pointed to it on the chart. "Or Davis Bay. We've had good luck out front, and it's closer, so we could have the gear in the water longer." He pointed out a separate section of the chart and then waited.

"Pete—" I sighed. "You're better at this than me."

He shook his head back and forth once. "Tell me what you think. We'll decide together." The boat rocked over slow rollers. "Pete—" I was almost begging. I didn't want it this time. The responsibility of a wrong choice.

"Trust yourself. For once. And me." He waited.

I reached for the tide book. "What's the tide?"

"18.6, then a negative 2.2," he answered before I got to the right page.

"In that case, it's going to funnel out of Davis Bay pretty fast. We'll run the risk of twisting lines."

"But if we can keep the lines straight, we'll have more time with gear in the water." He continued to study the chart.

"We could troll this line here." I slid my finger across the shoreline south of Shannon Point, which would make the most of the current and the tide. "It'll be more of a time crunch, though. But it seems worth it?"

"If we tangle up in front of Davis Bay, we're screwed."

"Yeah," I agreed.

"There's the bay north of Shannon Point, that's often good too." He tapped his finger on the chart.

"Maybe. It's going to get shallow quick on a negative 2.2."

"Good point. Might not be able to even get in there if we fish the south shoreline first, which is likely to be better."

"But it gives us another good option if there's time."

He nodded his agreement. "Shannon Point, then?"

"Sounds good."

Pete nodded, clicked back to the chart for where we were currently, and corrected course for Shannon Point. The anxiety began to build in my body immediately. Fishing, like parenting, was all about trusting yourself, and I was no good at it.

~

Two hours and a hard nap later, Van and I waited in the pit as the lines spooled out behind us just south of Shannon Point. *Please, please, please, please* was all my mind could muster. We both watched the surface of the water.

I fixed my eye on the bell, willed it to ring. It remained silent. "Shit!" I peeled my gloves off and hauled out of the pit in one smooth motion. "This isn't working."

I stepped into the wheelhouse to tell Pete we needed to come up with something else fast. I found Drew kneeling in the skipper's chair, steering on his own. "Hold her steady, Drew," Pete was saying as he stood next to him, fiddling with the settings on the fish finder. Without turning around, Pete said, "They're in here somewhere, Ellie, balled up. Drew and I will find them. You just hang out in the pit and practice patience." To Drew, he said, "Turn a little bit that way." Drew turned slowly in the direction Pete pointed. It was a practiced motion, not quick and erratic in the way of four-year-olds, but slow and controlled in the way of fishermen. I stood watching for so long, mesmerized, that Pete turned around to check that I was alright.

Back out on deck, Van was still watching the unsettled gray water. "I'm beginning to hate salmon," he said as I dropped back into the pit. When he saw the look on my face, he said, "You okay?"

"Ah," I said, still stunned at how much Drew had transformed and how clearly I had not. "I don't know how to trust anything." My whole body ached with the admission.

He breathed out a smile. "Me neither." He dropped his head. "How are we this young and this jaded?" The *we* got its hooks in me, yanked at my heart.

I laughed because there was nothing else left to do. "There's no hope for us."

He watched me across the pit, a chaos of wind and water and clouds and fishing gear and lines all around us, but everything stilled when he smiled in a sad way and said, "Maybe there is."

The bell on my side sounded first, and then Van's, and then mine again, wild and erratic with more than one fish.

"Here we go!" Van yelled as we both dove for our gear.

"Here we go," I said under my breath and hoped that was the case.

We caught fish at a steady pace through the afternoon and into the evening hours. Pete had come out to celebrate at least three times and wink at me twice. The sound of the shovel against ice rang out into the night as I cleaned one fish after another in the glare of the spotlight while Pete snaked us between islands. Van climbed out and dropped the cover of the hold back into place. He turned, counted the fish in front of me. "Ninety-seven."

"Ahhhhh," I said to the sky. "That's so many fish. And still not enough." It was more of a statement than any sort of complaint. Ninety-seven fish was unbelievable.

Van sat down in Drew's usual perch above me. "Why not catch a flight to Vegas? Do the two-to-one thing you did before?"

"I was lucky before. That was a really stupid bet." I reached for the next fish.

"Why not negotiate for more time? Even just an extra couple weeks, maybe a month, of fishing might do it."

"The season closes on September 20. Illegal to fish past that."

"Doesn't really sound like this guy would be open to negotiation anyways."

I slid the cleaned fish ready to be packed in the hold toward him. "I'm scared." It came out of nowhere. My head jerked up to see if maybe he hadn't heard.

"I've got no doubt you and Pete will manage this next situation the same way you seem to manage everything, with a shitload of grit and street smarts."

I sighed. "Did you know there's only ten paved miles of streets in Kings Creek?"

He smiled. "I did not."

"Thanks for the vote of confidence, anyway. I suppose ten miles of street smarts is better than eight, like they have over in Kake."

"Exactly," he said, his grin returning. "Meantime, what other wild ideas you got to get us over that fifty grand finish line?" I wanted him to look at me like that forever, to always willingly track into and back out of the dark places right along beside me.

"Nothing yet," I said, his mood infusing mine as I reached for the next salmon to clean. "You?"

"My job out here as I see it is to kill fish and wait for the next outrageous plan one of you two come up with."

I laughed. "You're not even getting paid."

"Yeah, I wanted to talk to you about that." His face fell into seriousness.

The blood drained out of my head. Of course he should have a crew share, but a crew share of zero was zero.

"I'm just kidding." He laughed. "You should see your face right now. This is my community service."

I tried to collect myself. "You owe the community something?"

"I do." He nodded as he moved back to the hold, opened it up, and returned for the fish ready to pack. "I was a real jackass in the years between leaving home and coming up here." He dropped into the hold and left me alone to spend some more time wondering at the secret corners of him.

Chapter 21

I finished the cleaning, handed all the fish down to Van in the hold, and left him to pack them in tight and spread the ice evenly. I peeled off my bibs and stepped into the warmth of the wheelhouse. Pete looked up from the chart he was studying. "Come take a look. What do you think of this area?" I peeked down the stairs at Drew's sleeping form.

"He crashed out a couple hours ago. We have to pick one of these three spots." He pointed at the chart pulled up on the computer, and then clicked between two others. We discussed tides, temperatures, winds, and the peculiarities of coho until we came to a decision.

"I'm sorry, Pete."

"For what?" he asked.

"For all of it."

"Ah, El, it's not your fault I'm a shit parent."

I shrugged. "I think you're a pretty good shit parent, for what it's worth."

He clapped his hands together, grinned. "I'll take it."

~

For three more weeks, we fished every day, bouncing around in the nineties, twice hitting triple digits. We barely slept, the three of us accomplishing the work of five; Drew had bagged enough roe for at least three fire trucks. Exhaustion and the steep edge of hope buzzed through my body like blood.

It was still dark when Pete poked me in the side because I'd overslept the alarm that was buzzing two inches from my ear. "Let's go," he said to me as he shook Van's shoulder to wake him.

I got dressed in a daze.

Out on deck, I was moving slow. Van came out sipping his coffee and handed me a steaming cup.

The rain beat loud and unharmonious on the hayrack above us as we settled into our respective sides of the pit. It hissed against the water and rose up in a feathery mist.

In the cold dark of the early morning, the lines dragged slowly behind us, empty. It would be another half hour before the fish could even see the gear. I closed my eyes and said into the morning that was hinting at winter, "We need to catch a lot of fish today, Van."

Van squinted out into the rain over his coffee. "Looks pretty fishy."

Pete began to zig and zag, a clear sign he was searching. Which meant the fish finder was blank. We were so close. We had $34,000 and twenty days left to fish. I drained my now cold coffee and held out my hand for Van's mug. He followed suit. Inside, I filled up both our mugs and came back out.

"Why the diner coffee cups? Why not the insulated kind? With a top." He mimed snapping a lid onto a bougie coffee mug the way an executive with tippy-tappy shoes might have.

I gave him a look. "That wouldn't be very fisherman-like."

He sighed, reaching up a hand to take his rapidly cooling coffee in the diner cup. "It would be hot-coffee-like."

"The next time you come along to bail us out of a bad deal with a bookie, I'll be sure to pick up a mug with a lid for you."

"That'd be great." He smiled. "So thoughtful."

We'd fallen into an ease of work and banter. Van used his downtime to play Uno with Drew, or puzzle over some taken-apart thing in his take-apart box. It did not seem an easy task for Van, but with every interaction, something around his eyes relaxed a bit more. Pete appeared to understand too that he needed room, and so we both gave it to him. Drew loved the attention and took to digging an elbow into Van's thigh to see exactly what Van was showing him over the baking sheet that caught all the bolts and washers they freed from whatever they were building.

Aside from those small breaks, we worked all day, every day. And now it was the final day of August, and in the next twenty days, we had to catch more than a hundred fish every single day.

Van was watching the lines, still talking. "I don't mind the work, except my back is probably broken. It's the waiting for the fish to bite that's brutal."

"Yeah."

"Like a vise grip to the throat."

I gave him the side-eye.

"Too dramatic?" he asked, one eyebrow cocked.

I laughed.

"I sound like my mother," he said. "Except she would've worked in a cuss word."

I liked to hear of other people's mothers. The Sunday check-in calls, the come-on-over-for-dinners. It was like hearing about a warm, beachy vacation spot. "What's she think of you living up here?"

In the lifting shadows of daybreak, he shifted. "She quit talking to me a few years into the self-destructive phase."

"Sorry, I didn't mean to—"

"Naw, it's alright," he interrupted. "You see, it gets worse. I drank myself into a stupor after the accident. I holed up at our hunting cabin, ran anyone off who came up. Lost everything to the bank. Went back to roping on a borrowed horse, eventually got a job at a dude ranch in Wyoming taking rich people on fake cattle drives. That's where I met Jeff Davis. He tours around Southeast on a yacht every year. He met Danny and Charlotte when he was anchored up in Marbled one year, and ever since then, he hauls a bunch of diesel to the homestead and trades Danny for venison. His girlfriend does hair and brings Charlotte a load of products every year."

"Products?" I looked at him. "Her hair is so . . ." I held my hands over my head to indicate the puffed-out situation.

Van cracked up. "I know!"

"So you caught a ride on a yacht to Marbled Inlet?"

"Naw." He readjusted his legs, propped himself against the edge of the pit. "Jim just told me about some land for sale in North Bay."

"How'd you buy land if you'd lost everything to the bank?"

His face drained of all color, and I wanted to vacuum up the intrusive question.

"I started a college account for Megan on the day she was born." He looked away. "Money was just sitting there."

"A way out," I said, the words like steps on thin ice. There were more words necessary, but I couldn't find them. I wanted to somehow say I knew that feeling of nothing left to lose, that raw state of life where your options whittle down to just the one thing that would never make sense otherwise.

He slowly shifted his gaze back toward me and nodded, the rest of the words not necessary. "Moving to Alaska seemed crazy at first, I'd never even been here. But the more I thought about it, more it sounded about right."

The sky lightened around us, the sun rising somewhere behind the thick clouds and heavy rain. The world went from blue to gray.

"What sounded right about it?" I really did want to know what sounded right about scraping out a home on this cold coast to a farmer from somewhere cars got so hot you couldn't touch them.

He shrugged. "No one to lie to up here."

I winced. I was mostly convinced he wasn't a serial killer, but there was always a chance. "Were you lying about the pigs and corn?"

He huffed out a laugh. "No. I bounced around from one dude ranch to another across Wyoming and Montana. Met a few beautiful women, always making up some mysterious past so I didn't have to talk about the real one. Lies and smoke and mirrors." He pushed himself off the edge of the pit abruptly, wedged his empty coffee cup in with the extra flashers. "Apparently, staying up all hours killing fish has got me feeling the need to tell only the truth and confess all my sins." He leaned over the rail, checking the line, fiddling with the gear unnecessarily.

I waved my arm to encompass the boat, the building waves, the blowing rain. "This can have a strange effect on people."

"Ain't that the truth," he muttered, looking soft at the edges while still solid in the middle. As if vulnerability weren't something to hide, just a part of the mix. Something to stir until it dissolved into everything else.

~

We caught twelve fish across the next hour. I paced. Outside, then inside, then outside, then back inside to study the chart behind Pete, to discuss any other options in the area we were already in, to watch the clock.

At noon, I was slumped over in the pit alone, head down, back aching. We had seven and a half hours left before dark. We'd caught forty-two fish. I'd lost track of where Pete had taken us, the shoreline of branches reaching out over rough rock, mussels, and seaweed. The bell rang, jumping me into action. Van came out and watched me haul in one lone fish. After I cleaned and packed the fish, and stood around for a bit more waiting for another, I pulled the lines in. Van was still outside. "What are you doing?"

"Making a decision."

I stepped in the wheelhouse and pulled up the charts. "Time to change it up, Pete." I studied the charts, focused on what I knew to be true of fish and currents and tides. I shut down the part of my mind that wanted to argue, to rationalize, to give up. I imagined my mom, her confidence, the way she would nod once, and that would be it. Sure and smooth and clear.

I turned the laptop toward Pete. "Here." I pointed to a channel three hours to the west.

He scanned the contours of the area on the chart, double-checked the tide book and the weather. "Looks good, Mo."

Chapter 22

By late afternoon, the rain was coming in sideways and hard. I was tossed around in a three-foot chop as I set the gear, my muscles moving in and out of locked positions in response to the erratic movement of the *Sarah Louise* under me. Van had wedged himself into the corner at the other end of the pit. Rain found its way inside my hood, down my back, and up my sleeves. I shivered as the cold rivers prickled across my skin.

Once the gear was out and Pete hit trolling speed, the waiting started. The minutes crawled through me. The bell rang, and I pulled a fish in. Van pulled one in on his side. The minutes stretched, the rain beat against the deck, and the *Sarah Louise* rocked in the uneven chop. The bell rang again, resulting in only one more fish. Anxiety rose up inside me, threatened to pull me under. I reined my mind in and thought instead about Mom's hands at the cleaning table, on the gurdy, the brake, my shoulder, my back. Her laugh rolling out over the water and through me. The tilt of her head, the angle of her smile, I could see her so clearly, the chaos of wind and water as backdrop. Tears joined the rain on my face as I climbed out to pack the cleaned fish in the hold. How could we be so close and so far all at once?

Pete altered course, headed closer to shore.

"You see something?" Van asked as he placed another fish on the cleaning table and peered in the direction I was looking.

"Wondering what Pete's doing." He was trolling way too close to the beach. "He's going to drag the lines on the bottom." Suddenly the bells on both sides sounded and didn't stop. Van pulled in a fish, and then I did. Then he had another, and I had two more. Pete whooped from inside, and the high pitch of Drew imitating him made me smile as I worked the gear. As the fish piled up and began to slide close enough to the rail that they might be returned to the sea, I yelled over to Van, "You good to run lines on both sides while I clean?"

"Hell yeah," he hollered back. He raced from one side to the other as I cleaned as fast as I dared, the knife sharp and exact, my hands aching and sore and then numb.

When I opened the hold and dropped in, Pete came out on deck. "Did you see how close I got?" he yelled down to me, his eyes running over the piling-up fish. "Unbelievable!" He left as fast as he'd appeared and was soon lining us up for another nerve-racking cut against the beach.

I packed in another layer of fish in the hold. Then I was back to cleaning as fast as I could, while Van kept pulling them in. Pete kept swinging through the door, checking the hold over my shoulder, Drew imitating everything he did, including the look of sheer joy at the way the fish were piling up.

I cleaned and packed and cleaned and packed. Van pulled in fish after fish, keeping his head bent to the task. We hustled around each other, him covering the lines, me jumping in when needed and cleaning in between.

We kept going for hours until somewhere around what felt like way past dinnertime when the bells fell silent. Van leaned back, covered in scales and slime. We worked together to clean and store the fish on deck as the bells remained silent.

Pete appeared out on deck. "Pull the lines. We gotta go. There's weather north of us, moving this way. We've got to find a good anchorage before dark." Seconds after the wheelhouse door closed behind him, Pete began increasing the speed of the boat.

"Hurry!" I yelled at Van as I dove into the pit. "The lines will tangle."

I moved faster than I thought possible, and Van matched my pace. The rain blew in under the hayrack, coming at us sideways. Once the lines were in, and all the fish were cleaned and packed, Van and I slumped in the pit across from each other.

"Did we make it?" Van asked, ducking inside his hood against the blowing rain.

"One hundred seventeen. A boat record."

He wiped at the rain dripping off his nose. "If I weren't worn to the bone, I'd probably feel happy about that."

"Don't get me wrong, I couldn't be more appreciative about you helping us out." My neck was too tired to keep my head up much longer. "But I'm not really sure why you're so willing to half kill yourself."

"One time, I bought a Mustang just to take this drop-dead gorgeous girl out." He laughed. "I had to sell it before the first payment was due." He took a deep breath and blew it out. He studied me for a minute in his slow, contemplative way. "I get these headaches. They started after Kelly and Megan died. Like an ice pick to the temple. Days at a time wishing I didn't exist." He rested his hands on the edge of the pit on either side of his body. "Too much stewing, I think. Spiraling. Thinking in the dark. Then you go and wreck on Danny's beach, and suddenly there's someone else to think about besides my own damn self." He must've been spooked by whatever way I was looking at him. He shifted, pulled his gloves off, and grinned. "That and you're a lot cooler than the girl I bought the Mustang for." He hopped out of the pit just as Pete came barreling through the door, a look of actual fear on his face.

"Is it Drew?" I was up and out of the pit in half a second, with Van on my heels.

"Drew's fine," Pete said. The three of us huddled under the hayrack. "Game's up, Mo. I got four guys calling me on the radio. The bookie is demanding we meet him tomorrow at noon at the bar in Kings Creek with the fifty grand."

"What? He can't do that. He gave us until the end of the season. Why would he do that?"

Pete shook his head. "I have no idea." Pete glanced out at the wind gathering over the water. "Weather's coming up. We can anchor south of town for the night and sell in the morning. Where we at after this haul?"

"Thirty-five, thirty-six thousand. I don't get what's happening."

"I don't either. But, we've got most of the money. I'll just go and talk to him."

"He's not going to take fifteen grand less, and why is the bookie himself showing up?"

"Maybe the details just got lost in translation. He can't call me, so he called a few others in the fleet who relayed the message over the radio. We're probably not meeting him. Probably just the regular gig where he sends a guy." Pete looked anything but convinced of what he was saying.

"This all sounds super fucking sketch. I have to get Drew off the boat."

The door rattled behind us.

"Mama," Drew called out. I opened the door, kicked out of my bibs, and picked him up, truly afraid now of how this all might play out. Drew tucked his head against my chest.

"I'll take him to Charlotte's," Van said. "She would love to see him. We can hang out there until you and Pete get things"—he fumbled—"worked out."

"Charlotte?" Drew asked, pulling his head up off my chest.

I peered at Van. He turned toward me, his face as earnest and clear as I'd ever seen it. "We can catch a flight out of Kings Creek in the morning."

It was awful and necessary. I wanted Drew off this boat, off the island, tucked away somewhere safe, but we had never been apart for a night. I nodded a quick *thank you* to Van.

"What do you say, bud?" Van asked. "Want to go see Charlotte with me? I imagine she's ready to make another pie by now, maybe even some cookies. And I've got a greenhouse that needs building. You're pretty handy with tools, I've noticed."

Drew bit down on a smile. "Can we play Uno at Charlotte's?" he asked.

"Am I going to lose again?" Van asked.

"Yes." Drew's face broke open into a smile. "Probably a lot of times." He put his small hands on either side of my face and turned my head to face him. "Can I go, Mom? Charlotte needs help with her dishes, and I'm the only one who builds the moats right. She said so. And I want to go on a floatplane."

"You do?" I said in disbelief.

"Will I sleep at Charlotte's?" he asked.

"Yep," Van said. "And I'll crash on her couch. We'll have a sleepover."

"A sleepover!" Drew squealed. "I never had a sleepover before!"

"That's fun, huh?" I said, trying to hide how crushing it was that the horrible kids at day care made fun of him instead of inviting him to sleepovers. "Should we pack up? You'll probably want to bring Dog."

"Dog!" he squealed as he wiggled out of my grasp and pulled me by the hand back toward the wheelhouse. Shortly thereafter, Pete started up the engine, and I heard Van finishing up our deck chores.

We all ate cereal for dinner in a heavy, hold-your-breath kind of silence. Drew and I brushed our teeth at the kitchen sink, and then I curled my body to his in our bunk, and the hot, silent tears began. Was this it? The final night on the *Sarah Louise*? The idea of no life out on the water with Drew wrapped its hands around my throat and squeezed. A future in town loomed dark and rainy and depressing.

My mind whirled with what might happen the next day at the bar. At this point, the boat and permit were worth more than the cash we'd have on hand. The bookie would sell the boat and permit. Pete and I would split the money we'd made over the season. I'd have enough for first and last month's rent and the deposit on a new place to live for me and Drew. I'd use the rest to pay down my credit cards. I tried to feel the welcome hand of a fresh start in town, less debt, but I couldn't. The

Sarah Louise would be someone else's. A life out on the grounds would not be Drew's. I'd have to find some random job in town. At the cannery, maybe, for the end of the season. I could work on the fillet line. Fourteen-hour shifts in a cavernous concrete building. The sea there, but out of reach. And, of course, there was always the possibility the bookie would take the cash and permit, and keep the title.

Another wave of fear pounded through me at the thought that Jessica might've filled Drew's spot in the day care in this time we've been gone. Then what? I had no idea. The very thought of Drew at Jessica's twelve inches from the TV screen all day created a pit in my stomach. I tried to remember the last time his shoulder had pulled rhythmically, the last time he'd blinked a hundred times to steam off the anxiety. I couldn't think of it.

I kicked out of my sleeping bag. Pete was driving us north, flask in his hand. He turned when I came up the stairs, not looking all that surprised I was awake.

"How far from the anchorage?" The wind wasn't so bad now that we were in the lee of a long, skinny island and the rain had eased up. "Doesn't look too bad out." I stood next to him, hip balanced so the easy seas didn't toss me. We both peered out at the water ahead.

"'Bout an hour out. Not supposed to get terrible until tomorrow afternoon and then blow through the next day. Lot of boats headed back to town, sounds like. You should fly out with Van and Drew tomorrow. I want you out of here."

I sighed. Pete had gotten himself into this, had gotten all of us into this. I could walk away. The image of him under the trash bags in the alley flooded my mind along with these long days on the boat. His mind at work in the wheelhouse, my body at work in the pit. We had always been a good team. He needed me now as much as I needed him after Mom died, I could see that. I took a deep breath, my ribs finally allowing it. "We'll find our way through together."

~

At eight a.m. we tied up at the cannery dock and waited our turn to off-load in Kings Creek. The weather had settled overnight, but there was something in the air that the entire fleet must've felt. A certain slow gathering at the edges that would boil over by noon if the marine forecasters were right. With only two weeks left in the season, most of the fleet was ready to celebrate, a solid season behind us, everyone a few steps away from the edge of risk, where we'd all been at the beginning of the season.

Once all our salmon were off-loaded, I walked through the steady rain along the thick, splintered wood of the dock to the office to collect the check. My legs felt weak and shaky as my mind ricocheted around whatever the bookie might have in store for us.

~

Five minutes later, I was back outside, check in hand, rain misting everything. I'd not yet looked at it. There was no way it could be enough to get us to $50,000, but some Pete-shaped part of me imagined that maybe it was. Gulls screamed overhead, the cannery a low constant thrum of activity and men's voices punctuating the morning. I pulled the check apart, one fold at a time. The bolded numbers streaked with rain.

"Ahhhh!" the frustration of having given it all I had and that still not being enough rose off me, startling a fisherman who was on his way in to collect his check. We were $14,000 short.

~

"We gotta go," Pete said as soon as I stepped into the wheelhouse. "Their flight's in thirty minutes, and we've got to cash checks at the bank." He was filling a duffel with cash and checks, Drew was chatting as Van packed up his few belongings, my nerves were on fire.

After the bank, the four of us walked down to the floatplane dock.

I knelt in front of Drew. "I'm so proud of how brave you are, buddy," I said, noticing how small he looked under the wide straps of his backpack.

"How many sleeps will you be gone for?" he asked, blinking a few times.

"Just one, or two at the most," I said in the steadiest voice I could muster.

The sound of a Cessna whined overhead, and Drew squirmed away. He bounced on his toes as he watched the pilot touch down in the open water and head our direction.

Drew clung to my leg as the pilot cut the engine and hopped out onto the float to tie up. "Howdy, folks," he called out from behind aviator sunglasses. "Not so bad down here. Already closing up around Juneau." He tied off to the dock and then popped open the baggage compartment in the tail. Van handed over his duffel, and Drew shrugged out of his backpack and held it precariously over the water, imitating Van. The pilot took it, stuffed it into the compartment, and snapped it closed.

"Do you fly this thing all by yourself?" Drew asked, studying every single move the pilot made.

He laughed. "I do! You ever been in a Cessna before?"

"NO!" Drew's eyes were bright, the small sad twitchy version of him instantly evaporated.

The pilot laughed and said, "The charter was for two?" He looked up at the group of us.

"Yep," Van said. "Me and Drew."

"Can I sit in the front?" Drew couldn't hold still.

"Probably better for weight if you both sit in the front. Promise not to touch anything?" The pilot gave Drew an unsure look.

Drew answered gravely, "I promise."

"Let me give you a lift, Drew," Van said, as he was the closest to the plane. Drew raised his arms to Van, as he had to me a million times, as trusting and wide open to the world as I'd ever seen him. Van lifted him carefully and a little away from his body at first, but Drew whipped an arm around Van's neck and smashed their bodies together. Van wrapped both arms all the way around him. My eyes stung.

Van settled Drew in the front seat, and Drew fisted his hands in his lap to keep from being tempted by all the levers as his eyes roamed over every detail of the instrument panel. Drew started asking questions immediately, drawing the pilot's attention. "What's this do? What's down at your feet? How do we get off the water? Do you have sunglasses for me?"

Van stepped back onto the dock and dipped his head to mine. "Well," he said, low enough that only I could hear. "That was the wildest first date I've ever been on."

My pulse pounded as his hand reached for and gently rested on my hip.

"Is that what this was?" I somehow managed to say as he pulled me toward him, his green eyes focused so intently on mine, his hair curling against his forehead under his ball cap.

"Yeah." He nodded easily. "And this is the part where I would walk you home, and up to your front door, except it's all whacked and there's an airplane."

I laughed. "You think there'll be a second date?" His arms looped around my back, pulling my body tight against his, sending me into some new orbit I didn't know existed. "I hope so," he said, his lips still moving as they gently touched mine. He pulled back, and whispered as he stepped away, "Please be careful."

In the plane, he settled Drew in his lap, buckled the two of them together, and wrapped a protective arm across him.

The pilot untied, shoved off the dock, and scrambled in. As the floatplane came alive and taxied out into the gentle waves, I realized I hadn't yet moved.

Pete was staring at me, wide-eyed.

I checked my watch and caught my breath. "Eleven fifty. We gotta go."

"Guess you don't think he's weird anymore?" Pete asked as he limped in a hop-run to keep up. He'd ditched the crutches for this particular outing.

"No weirder than me," I said.

Pete laughed. "Well, that's not saying much."

I felt more than heard the floatplane gathering up speed behind us as we walked toward the road. The space between Drew and I opened up like a crevasse.

~

"Is there some sort of protocol here?" I asked Pete while we waited for an old Ford truck to pass before we crossed Main Street. The entrance to the bar sat in the middle of the low-slung string of buildings that made up downtown.

"We make our way to the far-right barstools, order a Jack Daniel's on the rocks, and when the bartender sets it down, we say, 'Haven't had one of these in a while.' Then she says, 'Sounds like you're due, then.' We drink up while she makes a phone call. When she gives us the nod, we head to the bathroom, where one of the bookie's guys either collects money or hands over what's owed."

"Did you come up with this?" I needed him to talk, to keep my mind off whatever was about to happen. We crossed the wet street.

"No, but it's good, don't you think?" Pete kept his voice light, but I could feel him turning edgy. "Ellie," he said before we stepped through the door. "We're good at thinking on our feet."

My eyes took a minute to adjust to the single dark room of the bar, which was busy. It seemed a lot of the fleet had decided to ride out the storm in town. Caroline spotted us first from a barstool close to the door. "Look who it is!" she called out, her eyes dropping to the duffel gripped in Pete's good hand. "Hey! Listen up!" she yelled to the room. "It's happening! The *Sarah Louise* will be returned to her rightful owners." She winked at me. Will had clearly shared the news. And, of course, everyone had heard the radio chatter last night. Which, come to think of it, was likely why the bar was so packed.

Miles Holcomb took a break from digging grubby hands into the free popcorn in the red-and-white-striped carnival popcorn maker to eye Pete just as the bartender called over, “Use a fucking bowl, Miles.” She was petite and blond and had a look on her face like she might choke him out. Her eyes slid over me and Pete and then back to the beer she was pouring. She slopped it onto a tray with a bunch of others and stepped out from behind the bar. Pete nodded once in Miles’s direction, and I watched him to be sure he was over the herring slight. In the way of community self-policing, it seemed justice had been served and both the defense and prosecution were at rest and life could go on.

We made our way along a row of tables to our right, Pete shoving Deano’s shoulder and Deano putting him into a headlock, Cal from the *Sally J* raising a glass to us, Jensen and his two boys looking up from their pool game to give us a grave nod.

“Hey, hey,” Silas from the *Katie Anne* said as he stepped past us, balancing four full-to-the-brim shots of something amber. “Big day for you two?” Neither of us answered. What was there to say? How many people were aware of the deep, dark underworld the bookie was a part of? My eyes darted from fisherman to fisherman, all faces I’d grown up with, trying to read worry or fear, but most of their faces always had some level of the two. It was a part of the life we’d all chosen or stuck with for this long.

We sat at the barstools on the far right and waited for the bartender to come back. Pete kept the two handles of the duffel in a tight fist in his good hand. I scanned for the bookie’s man I’d met earlier in the summer and tried to keep the bile from inching any farther up my throat.

“Two Jack Daniel’s on the rocks,” Pete said when the bartender returned. My mind was spinning fast, not landing anywhere. The room became all angles, the air thick.

She poured the drinks light and set them in front of us. “Been a while since I had one of these,” Pete remarked as he took his first sip.

"Guess you're due, then," the bartender said through droopy makeup and a thin sweater that had seen too many washings. She wiped her hands on the rag hanging off her belt loop and disappeared into a back room off the bar.

Pete and I knocked our drinks back. The bartender reappeared, gave us a slight nod and a dead stare. We stood up and turned toward the bathroom. "Not in the bathroom this time. Out back," she said, stone-faced. "In the alley." Pete froze. I studied the hard line of her mouth. The smallest hint of a smile grazed her face.

Tension radiated off Pete as we made our way to the back of the barroom, both still in our raincoats.

"This ever happened before?" I asked as we entered the narrow hallway that led out into the alley. We passed a sign on the women's bathroom that read BUSTED and then the dank-smelling men's room.

"No," he said. I picked my way past a mop and a stack of carboard boxes with the Budweiser label. Pete turned around in front of the back door, his face ridged with worry. "Why don't you go back to the boat, Ellie. I got this." The dim hallway reeked of spilled beer and mold.

"We're much better off when we're in the shit together," I said. "Let's go." I stepped past him through the back door to the exact spot I'd found him buried under a pile of trash just three months earlier.

I gasped at the man standing in the dim, rainy haze of the alley. He was ages older than the last time I'd seen him.

"Jesus," Pete breathed out next to me. "Hank, man, what happened to you?"

"Back in ranks with dear old dad, I see," Hank said to me with dead eyes. "You two make up?"

I was too stunned to speak. He was all swagger and height and perfect down-south teeth when Pete and I'd met him. Now, he looked run over.

"What are you doing here?" Pete's words were careful, like he was creeping up on a cornered animal.

"You got the money?" Hank took a step forward. The rain blew up the alley. The low cloud cover hanging just at the top of the building.

"What's going on here?" I asked. "What do you have to do with the bookie Pete placed a bet with?"

Hank pulled a cigarette out of one rain jacket pocket and a lighter out of the other. Cupped his hand in the practiced motion of smokers in rainy places and lit it. "I am the bookie Pete placed a bet with." His hooded eyes fixed on mine. "Ellie." The space between us pulled taut. I felt again deep in my chest the ringing echo of his feet on the gangplank of the ferry that night. "And the bookie you placed a bet with a couple months ago."

Pete stilled next to me. "It's been you this whole time?" He cocked his head. "I mean, on the one hand, way to build a business, but Jesus fuck, looks like it's taken a toll on you."

Hank's angry gaze had not moved from me. "How've you been?"

My mouth was dry. It was Hank, I kept telling myself. It was just Hank. He wasn't going to murder anyone. At least, the old Hank was not going to murder anyone, but it was clear there wasn't much left of the old Hank; even his voice was unrecognizable. "Why'd you call us in early?" My voice sounded too thin. "What do you want?" I clarified.

He took a drag on his cigarette. "The money." He lifted his chin toward the duffel still gripped in Pete's good hand. "Obviously."

"We don't have the full $50,000." I shifted my weight evenly between both legs. Readying myself for whatever was coming.

"I know," he said. "I'm going to take whatever you've got." There was too much emphasis on the word *take*. "How much is it?"

"You have the title on you?" Pete asked.

Hank smirked. "You have the permit on you?" he asked as he pulled from his pant pocket the title still in the thin waterproof bag it had always lived in and held it out for us to see. "How much money is it?"

Pete narrowed his eyes as he pulled the permit from his sweatshirt pocket. "There's thirty-six thousand in the duffel. Chances are good we would've made the fifty if you'd left us to it for another couple weeks."

My heart slammed into my rib cage as Pete continued. "Given that the original deal seems to be off, how about you take the cash, we keep the title and permit, and we call it good."

Hank squinted one eye as he blew out a stream of smoke.

Pete slid the permit back into his pocket. It was worth about the same as the money in the bag.

"Yeah, alright," Hank said, title still held up between the two of them, but the words were laced with something dark. I checked Pete's face to be sure he'd registered it. He had. The men moved toward each other, eyes locked. In the dim shadows of the alleyway, Hank shoved the title back in his pocket, fisted the burning cigarette into Pete's neck, yanked the duffel from his hands and the permit from his pocket, and took off running. Pete hit the pavement with a dull thud, knocked off-balance on his one good leg.

Without thinking, I dove for Hank. My shoulder connected to his rib cage, and we bounced off the back door of the bar with a deafening clang. Years of frustration and anger and exhaustion came out of me in one long shriek. Hank and I hit the ground and rolled. Will came flying through the back door of the bar, still zipping up his pants, and roared, "What the hell is—"

I got a handful of raincoat, caught an elbow in the head, and then Hank was back on his feet, duffel and permit clutched to his chest, hurling himself down the narrow alley toward the street. "Catch him," I yelled up at Will as Deano, Jensen and his boys, Caroline, Silas, and some other lookie-loos barreled into the alley from the bar. "He's got all of it," I screamed. "The title, permit, and cash."

Just short of where the alley dumped back out onto Main Street, Hank was tackled by one of Jensen's boys. Caroline yanked the duffel and permit out of his grip as Deano landed one punch and then another. "Where's the title, you fucking loser." Silas pulled at Hank's pockets until he found it.

Will steadied me as I stood while Jensen was getting Pete back to his feet. "Are you okay?" Will asked as Deano launched into Hank, who was curled up on his side, his face a mess of blood and gore, and landed another kick to his ribs.

"Stop," I yelled, but no one did. "Stop," I yelled louder, sprinting toward where Hank lay. "He's Drew's dad!" I screamed.

A blanket of silence. Only heavy breathing clouding up into the cold midday air. After a long, slow moment, Caroline moved first. She dropped the duffel at my feet and handed me the permit. She put a hand to my shoulder. "We'll leave you to it, then." She caught the eyes of a few, and they all began filing back into the bar. Silas handed me the title with a nod as he passed. Pete let out a long breath, somewhere close by, as I bent down to the crumbled form on the concrete. No one would place bets with a guy named Oliver, he'd explained to me years ago, obviously proud of how the made-up name offered cover and a tougher persona.

"Ollie?" I said, reaching out a hand to his shoulder. He flinched at my touch.

He pushed himself slowly up to sitting, his head hung low as I knelt next to him. He spit blood and then turned to me with a shattered look. "Drew?" he asked with an echo of the boy I once loved fiercely. "Why didn't you tell me?" His voice was just above a whisper. I tried to swallow, but my throat was closed. He brought a hand to his lip, checked it for blood before squinting over at me. "We were so happy." His voice disappeared into the last word, the dark, endless sadness in his eyes plowing through me.

"I'd already lost Pete to gambling and drinking. I couldn't bear to lose you to meth."

He blinked against the swelling of one eye, the rest of his face rimmed in sorrow. "How could you keep something like that from me?"

It hit me then, the way I cut people out so completely. A chainsaw to a branch, a whole reaching direction forever removed. The pattern of it. The imagined security of it that never arrived.

He wiped his face with his shirt, smearing rain and blood. "He's, what, five?"

I nodded. "Why are you trying to take everything?"

He huffed out something that sounded like a laugh. "If you needed proof you made the right choice, I guess you've got it now." He raised his gaze to mine, his words slow and gravelly. "I owe a really bad dude a lot of money. I've got a buyer flying in from Juneau this afternoon to buy the boat and permit. The money from all three won't pay what I owe, but it'll buy me a few days to figure out I don't know what else." He looked from me up to Pete, who was standing directly behind me, the duffel back in his hand. "Was Drew out there with you these past few months?"

"He was," Pete said in a way that let me know he was in neutral but ready to switch into whatever gear the situation demanded.

"He likes fishing?" Hank asked, grimacing as he tried taking a deep breath. "In his blood, I guess."

"Getting passed down a boat makes all the difference in how you make a living around here," I said.

"He'll find something else."

"Or you could leave him the boat and permit." The rain hissed against the broken concrete of the alley around us. The heavy, dark cloud cover made it feel more like dusk than noon.

He turned his head and spit out another glob of blood. "It'll be my life this time, Ellie, if I don't pay up. The guy's probably already on his way down here. I was supposed to meet him out the road with this money ten minutes ago. I've got until tonight to get him the rest." He looked so old, and yet it was so easy to imagine the other version of him playful in our kitchen, reaching for me, whole days in bed, an entire world all our own.

"I can get you out of here."

Both Pete and Hank looked at me.

"Up the Stikine to Telegraph. You can walk off into Canada with that duffel. No one will ever find you. You keep the $36,000, we keep the title and permit, Drew grows up fishing. A gift from his parents."

The uncut corner of his lip hinted toward a smile. "His parents." He huffed. "You and me." But then his face fell. "I shouldn't be anyone's parent." His gaze flicked to the duffel in Pete's good hand. His face hardened, and he morphed back into a stranger, a dangerous man.

I grabbed both his arms, held fast and tight to the boy I knew was still in there somewhere. "This isn't who you are. Let's both start over. You give me and Drew a boat, I give you a road out."

None of us moved as everything else moved in ever closer—the tide, the guy after him, the storm. Oliver watched me with dead eyes long enough for our entire history to play out in the narrow space between us. As the rain hissed and the wind funneled up the alleyway, he dropped his head. "Okay," he said along with a slightest nod of agreement.

I moved quick, slipped my arm around his back, and helped him to his feet, my body notching into its place against his. "My Lady Luck," he said, soft and low.

"My Ace of Spades," I whispered back in the way I always had, which released all the feelings I'd ever had for Oliver at once. A fire hose to the chest. Perhaps making room for all the feelings was the path to steadiness, like a narrow canyon that finally opened its arms, allowing the river to spread out wide and slow down. Perhaps part of loving someone was remaining in that arms-wide-open way, allowing the river to change and shift over time without trying to make it fit into any one particular shape.

"We need to hurry," I said. "Cutting it close on the tide."

"Helluva plan, Ellie," Pete said, a white blister forming on his neck in the shape of a cigarette. "Except Telegraph is a hundred and sixty miles from here, and there's a storm big enough to beach the whole fleet at the bar."

I ignored him. "Can you walk?" I asked Oliver, still holding on to him while he tried out the first couple of steps.

"And in what boat?" Pete did not look ready to hand over the money.

"In the jetboat you're going to steal," I said.

"Ah," Pete said. "You mean borrow."

I nodded toward the bar. "Any one of those guys would give me their boat, but once one of them knows what we're doing, all of them will. Chances are good one of them will crumble when your guy shows up looking for you."

"All valid points," Pete said, his bottom lip pressed into his top lip. We moved as quickly as Oliver could through the gusting wind and rain down to the docks. I kept an eye out the whole time, my blood on fire in my veins at the thought of some hooded man with a silencer around every corner.

Pete dropped into one of the tied-up jetboats and snapped the cover off the outboard. He buried his hands in wires, snapped something free, and raised his voice to be heard over the wind. "At the controls, Ellie."

"You picked the worst one," I said as Oliver and I climbed in. It was basically a bathtub that looked to be welded by a preteen.

"New ones are hot-wire proof," he said just before the engine roared to life. I shoved off the dock, buried the throttle, and cranked the wheel. The stern dug in, the boat swung around, and we were off down the channel, wind and rain pounding in sideways, town and all its complexities falling away behind us.

Pete joined me behind the three-sided plexiglass rain and wind barrier around the stand-up console, the duffel now strapped across his chest. Oliver huddled into his raincoat, tucked up against the curve of the gunwale.

"Just like old times!" Pete said in reference to the jetboat we'd owned long ago, also the shittiest of the lot. "What's the tide?" he asked.

"Negative 2.8 at one p.m."

I tapped at the throttle to see if there was anything more. "Come on, come on," I whispered to the boat. "Hurry up!" The flats would be emptying of water quickly. A jetboat could run in a few inches of water if you didn't slow down and fall off step. You could stay off the bottom so long as you read the water right. Any hidden rock, any tree limb, any small patch of pebbles sucked up into the engine, and you'd beach.

If you were lucky, you'd get tossed around in the boat. If you were not lucky, you'd get tossed out into the quicksand mud.

We rounded the south end of the island, and the mudflats came into view, patches of mud already showing with the outgoing tide. I blasted out across the mudflats at full speed, no hesitation, the stern drifting, a light touch at the wheel to bring it back in line. Pete grinned. We hadn't been up the Stikine together since before Mom died. "That's my girl!" Pete said and let out a whoop as we crossed over from the deeper water of the channel into the shallower edges of the mudflats. I glanced down at Oliver, who smiled back a little more freely as town fell behind us and the Stikine welcomed us into its own separate world.

I leaned on the throttle, asking it for more as we flew out across the open expanse on inches of water. As the water whipped underneath us, I scanned just ahead for signs of thinning water over raised mud, a rock rolled out onto the flats by the river and tumbled along with the outgoing tide. Anything that hinted at something underneath, something that had to be avoided.

"Go! Go! Go!" Pete hollered next to me. The shared adrenaline of it felt good. The way he trusted me completely felt even better. I cut right, knowing the river was deepest there where it joined the sea, reading the water ahead, weaving around anything suspicious, but only with the slightest pull of the wrist to keep us from losing the forward momentum.

The closer we got, the more the river water slapped and rolled as it mixed with seawater, and the harder it was to guess at what might be underneath. Pete sat down, back rounded into the inside curve of the hull, huddled down in his rain jacket, and Oliver joined me behind the plexiglass. The sky was dark with the storm. Rain power washed us from the side, running down my neck and up the sleeves of my raincoat. I let it all soak me to the bone. How much I loved him, how trusting I'd been, how I'd found the courage to make the right choice for Drew, forged a path for us on our own, as messy and not perfect as it had been, I'd been giving it my all the whole time, and I still was, I could see it now.

As we turned into the brown mouth of the river, the current squirreled the boat under us. The trees disappeared into the clouds on either side. Spruce and hemlock branches woven tight in a hundred-year embrace. The current was fast and full-bodied. My mind came alive with long-ago memories of how to read it, how to stay safe, how to live in the messy chaos of things much more powerful than myself.

I cut in tight to the shore on the next curve, knowing it was wide enough that there would be no logjam on the other side. Exposed roots whipped by on our left. I watched the top few inches of water, kept my mind on this one thing, this only thing, right now.

The river pushed underneath us with more force as it narrowed and deepened and rolled between steep forested mountains on either side.

Directly after the next curve, the main channel split in two, a small, flat, grassy island in the middle. I pulled left first, the gentlest tug, before I noticed an odd swirl on the surface of the water just ahead. I corrected right, and we fishtailed through the better of two bad options. The island whipped past us and dumped us back out into the main channel.

We threaded our way into Canada through country so wild it seemed no one had been there since the last time I had. There was room to spread out, time to let it seep in deep. I drank it all in, let it fill in all the empty spaces that life, so far, had carved out of me.

~

Hours later, we pulled up to a small wooden floating dock in front of the village of Telegraph. Oliver and Pete were both on their feet. Pete turned to me with one last long look before he ducked out of the strap and handed the duffel over to Oliver. I thought about how hard we'd worked for every dollar in that bag, how focused I'd been on it adding up to enough. I wanted to tell Pete it was all enough, the whole summer had been exactly the right amount of everything, even though all our hard-earned money was about to walk off into Canada.

Oliver reached out a hand, and Pete shook it. Oliver looked over to me. I stepped into him, and he pulled me into a hug. "You always were sort of pushy."

I smiled into his shoulder. "Good luck," I said as Oliver stepped out of the boat. He stood on the edge of the mainland, looking up at the small collection of buildings, at the road out, and then turned back. "Is he anything like me?"

"He's quite a drummer," I said. "Not so sure about the vocals."

Oliver's broken and angular face moved toward a smile. "It'll come. Don't rush it." And then he turned, and I let the love that had once felt like flying, then like an albatross around my neck, then like a forever bruise, shift and change into the unexpected shape of hope for him.

~

The mudflats were at flood tide when we crossed them again, racing the oncoming darkness. I backed off the throttle for the first time in hours, just short of town. "You think this guy is looking for his boat?"

"I think this guy is drunk at the bar. I think his life is a wreck. I mean, look at his boat," Pete said. "Even so, let's wait until it's all the way dark to tie it back up at the dock."

I found us a cove to tuck up into to wait, and Pete tossed the anchor, which was just a thin rope wrapped around a hunk of concrete. I killed the engine, collapsed against the gunwale, and listened to my ears ring in that particular pitch a jetboat ride creates.

Pete eased himself down next to me. "We did it, Mo," he said, joy filling up his face. "This has been the best summer of my life." Pete wrapped me up in his one good arm on the stolen jetboat as the rain blew out the rest of the day and evening moved in.

~

We boated back into the harbor without running lights as the narrow channel whipped up into a froth with the storm. We tied up silently and snuck back to the *Sarah Louise*. I found an entire roll of quarters and dry clothes and took the longest, hottest harbor shower of my life.

~

The next morning over coffee in the wheelhouse, we waited for the DMV to open, the title sitting on the table between us. I thought about finding something in the cupboards to eat, but I was too nervous. The sea was calm and placid, the cloud layer high and unimposing as if making amends for the day before.

"So, we need to forge his signature like he signed it over to us?" I asked.

Pete looked refreshed after sleep and a shower and some strong coffee. "Yeah. We'll just make it slanty and scribbly. Easy. Not that it matters. Does the DMV lady know you or anything about our situation?"

"I don't think so."

"Just don't act shifty when you're in there, and you'll be fine."

I swallowed down the wave of nausea finally breaking over me. "Pete, I—"

"A deal's a deal, Ellie."

"But I—"

He held his hand up to make me stop. "Let me be an upstanding guy here, Ellie. I need the practice. The boat was always meant to be yours. Let's get the title taken care of first, and when the library opens later, we can fill out the permit paperwork online to transfer ownership of that too."

I watched him limp down the stairs, root around in the focsle, pull a sweatshirt over his head, and fill a to-go mug with coffee, and then it was eight a.m. and I was walking into the DMV with a forged title, Pete saying he'd wait outside.

I sat in the mostly empty row of folding chairs in the brown-carpeted waiting room. When my name was called, I walked up to the counter and said, as normally as I could, that I'd just bought a boat and needed the title reissued. The gray-haired no-nonsense woman typed things, scanned things, stapled things, swiped my credit card, and I walked out the dazed new owner of the *Sarah Louise*.

Pete pushed off the wall where he'd been waiting when I stepped outside. I walked right into his arms. "Thank you," I whispered. "For coming back."

~

An hour later, we stood on the floatplane dock. I had just maxed out a fourth credit card to pay for a flight out to Marbled to pick up Drew. It would take us days and more money in fuel to run the *Sarah Louise* out to get him than the price of the floatplane.

"We're broke again," I said.

"Yeah," Pete agreed.

"I owe a lot of credit card companies a lot of dollars. Drew and I will need help fishing the last few weeks of coho. And a little while after that, winter kings." I chewed on my lip and kept my eyes on the approaching Cessna.

Pete followed my gaze out to the glint of wing as the Cessna curved into its final approach. "Sounds like you're in a pinch."

"Pretty much."

The Cessna came in low and lined up to set down on the water. We both watched the pilot's final leveling adjustments until it touched down smoothly in front of us. Pete turned as it taxied for the dock. "I mean." He shrugged, smiling. "I guess I could help you out."

Acknowledgments

First and foremost, thanks to my family—Nate, Wes, and Mike—who are endlessly supportive.

Thanks to Diane Reed Veach, who helped me dream up Ellie's adventures as we planted seedlings so long ago in a greenhouse out the road.

Thanks to writing friends Erika Krouse, Paula Younger, Jenny Shank, Jennifer Sullivan, Buzzy Jackson, and Michelle Theall, who have read and advised me through many versions of this book.

And to my literary agent, Andrea Somberg, who is the best agent a girl could ask for.

Thanks to Nancy Holmes and Celia Johnson, my editors at Lake Union, for their hard work and clear vision.

And finally, thanks to Mike Stainbrook and Paul Converse, who read early drafts and let me ask them endless questions about commercial fishing.

About the Author

Photo © 2014 Ben Klaus

Rachel Weaver is the author of the novel *Point of Direction*, which was named a Top Ten Book to Pick Up Now by *O, The Oprah Magazine* and was the winner of the 2015 WILLA Literary Award for contemporary fiction. It was also chosen by the American Booksellers Association as a Top Ten Debut for Spring 2014 and by IndieBound as an Indie Next List pick. Prior to earning her MFA in writing and poetics from Naropa University, Rachel worked for the US Forest Service in Alaska studying bears, raptors, and songbirds. She is on faculty at Wilkes University's low-residency MFA program and at Lighthouse Writers Workshop. For more information, visit www.rachelweaver.net.